PENGUIN BOOKS

FAVOURITE WINTER STORIES FROM FIRESIDE AL

Veteran CBC announcer and award-winning broad-caster Alan Maitland, popularly known as Fireside Al and Front Porch Al, has delighted listeners across the country with his storytelling. He was co-host of CBC Radio's flagship current affairs program, "As It Happens," from 1974 until 1993. In 1980 he and then co-host Barbara Frum shared an ACTRA Award for Best Public Affairs Broadcasters. Before he retired to Mahone Bay, Nova Scotia, in 1993, Maitland spent forty-six years at the CBC, contributing to a variety of programs including "The Gordie Tapp Show," "Action Set," "Read to Me," and his own music series, "Maitland Manor." He continues to read stories on the air for the CBC in his incarnations as Fireside Al and Front Porch Al.

"The story is like the wind," the Bushman prisoner said. "It comes from a far off place, and we feel it."

Laurens Van der Post, *A Story Like the Wind*

Favourite Winter Stories from

Fireside Al

SELECTED
AND
INTRODUCED
BY

ALAN MAITLAND

Penguin Books

PENGUIN BOOKS
Published by the Penguin Group
Penguin Books Canada Ltd, 10 Alcorn Avenue, Toronto, Ontario M4V 3B2
Penguin Books Ltd, 27 Wrights Lane, London W8 5TZ, England
Penguin Books USA Inc., 375 Hudson Street, New York, New York 10014,
U.S.A.
Penguin Books Australia Ltd, Ringwood, Victoria, Australia
Penguin Books (NZ) Ltd, 182-190 Wairau Road, Auckland 10, New Zealand

Penguin Books Ltd, Registered Offices: Harmondsworth, Middlesex, England

First published in Viking by Penguin Books Canada Limited, 1994
Published in Penguin Books, 1995

10 9 8 7 6 5 4 3 2 1

Introductions, Notes and Selection Copyright © Alan Maitland, 1994

Manufactured in Canada.

Canadian Cataloguing in Publication Data

Main entry under title:
Favourite winter stories from Fireside Al

ISBN   0-14-023844-1

1. Short stories, English.   2. Short stories, Canadian (English).*   3. Short
stories, American.   4. English fiction - 19th century.   5. English fiction -
20th century.   6. Canadian fiction (English) - 20th century.*   7. American
fiction - 19th century.   8. American fiction - 20th century.
I. Maitland, Alan.

PR1285.F3 1995   823'.010836   C94-931464-1

Permissions appear on pages 273–74.

*This book is dedicated
to all the short story enthusiasts
who have found joy in listening
and brought joy to the reader*

ACKNOWLEDGMENTS

I am in debt to CBC's Mark Starowicz for starting the stories on "As It Happens," and of course to those who continued them. To Barbara Frum who dubbed me Fireside Al. To Jackie Kaiser of Penguin for transferring them from tape to the written page. It's exciting to see them collected in print. To George Jamieson and Don Mason for doing much of the early work. And to the many who have enjoyed the stories over the years on CBC radio. Now you can read them for yourselves. Enjoy!

Fireside Al

INTRODUCTION

The love of a good story is something I first acquired from my father. As a minister, he was used to speaking in public, and as a minister's family we were used to hearing him speak. But it was still something special when he told his stories. "Once upon a time when I was a little boy and lived in Renfrew…" he would begin, and we'd settle in for a tale from his childhood. We didn't think of him as making these stories up. They just rolled out of him, filled with details and adventure and warm memories of his past. It became something of a joke—this "Renfrew" place. We lived in the Ottawa valley then, not really very far from the Renfrew of father's stories, but the village he described seemed as if it was from another continent. Our only means to visit this place was through my father's stories, and we greedily looked forward to each new instalment.

He didn't make up all the stories. Sometimes he told us his version of stories he had read as a child. His favourites soon became our favourites, and we'd sometimes look up the "official" versions in the books at school or in the local library. It didn't really matter where the stories came from. What mattered was that father had made them his own. They were "his" stories, and later, as I read them to myself, I would often hear my father's voice.

That love of a good story has stayed with me all my life. Sometimes I've been lucky enough to tell stories and call it "work." This has been the most rewarding part of my career—doing what comes naturally and what I enjoy, and what brings enjoyment to others.

My first experience reading stories on the radio came about thirty years ago. I was a CBC announcer, looking for a new program idea. My good friend and former neighbour Ruthie Faux was visiting, and I told her I was having trouble coming up with this new show. "Forget the music," Ruthie said, "Why don't you just read to me? I've got a radio in every room, and I could happily wander through the house listening to your stories." And that was the beginning of a regular program on CBC radio, "Read to Me." I chose the stories, mostly from my own collection, even some that my father had read to me long ago, and recorded them simply—no sound effects, just reading from the book. The show was a success—it always amazes me how much simple things somehow manage to reach people. I still hear from listeners who say they remember that program from thirty years ago.

My other great experience reading stories on the radio came after I started working on "As it Happens." At Christmas time in 1977 we decided to record a few holiday stories. Something from Dickens, a version of "Yes, Virginia, there is a Santa Claus," and a little poetry. Every year after that we added a couple of stories, and every year our listeners asked for more, until we had created our own Christmas tradition.

We didn't use the nickname at first. It was a couple of years later that Barbara Frum ad-libbed some lines about lighting a fire, putting her feet up, and sipping some hot chocolate while Fireside Al was reading. From then on I was officially "Fireside Al"—and we would often chat in the studio as if we were somewhere cozy and warm and comforting, instead of in a rather austere studio behind glass with a panel and a microphone. Of the many wonderful things that Barbara did for me, I will always remember how she gave me the name of Fireside Al.

And now I have the enjoyment of collecting some of those stories together. It's been great fun for me to go through the old books and files, gathering together the stories that I like best. It's been a challenge too: to choose my old favourites and to try to include some new stories as well.

The one thing that I have looked for in every story is that it should be a good winter story. I don't know exactly how to describe a "winter" story, but I think we all recognize it when we find one. It's different from the stories or books that you take to the beach or read on the back lawn in the summer time. It's the kind of story that you just *know* should be read indoors, by the fire if possible, perhaps with your feet tucked up under a blanket on the sofa while the cold wind blows outside the door. It could be happy or sad or festive or frightening. It's the type of story that snuggles up around you the way a warm fire wraps you in its glow.

The stories here are from many different places, from times old and new, some comic, some thoughtful, some like little fables and others that simply strike me as ones that I would like to have read to me. Most of these stories, whether old or new, are in the tradition of what I would call "good old stories." Stories that are easily recognized, simple stories—stories that have a sort of warmth about them. Stories to enjoy.

TABLE OF CONTENTS

Buggam Grange:
A Good Old Ghost Story

by
STEPHEN LEACOCK
(1869–1944)

"Buggam Grange" is Leacock's version of the scary ghost story. All the elements are in their place: a ghost in the closet, a ride along a gloomy lane. But Leacock can never pass up the chance for a little mischief, and the story of "Buggam Grange" takes a few unexpected twists and turns along the way. I think mischief is what Leacock is really all about, and in "Buggam Grange" he turns the conventional ghost story just slightly on its head. It seems strange to think that Stephen Leacock has now been dead for fifty years. "Buggam Grange" makes him seem so suddenly alive.

T he evening was already falling as the vehicle in which I was contained entered upon the long and gloomy avenue that leads to Buggam Grange.

A resounding shriek echoed through the wood as I entered the avenue. I paid no attention to it at the moment, judging it to be merely one of those resounding shrieks which one might expect to hear in such a place at such a time. As my drive continued, however, I found myself wondering in spite of myself why such a shriek should have been uttered at the very moment of my approach.

I am not by temperament in any degree a nervous man, and yet there was much in my surroundings to justify a certain feeling of apprehension. The Grange is situated in the loneliest part of England, the marsh country of the fens to which civilization has still hardly penetrated. The inhabitants, of whom there are only one and a half to the square mile, live here and there among the fens and eke out a miserable existence by frog fishing and catching flies. They speak a dialect so broken as to be practically unintelligible, while the perpetual rain which falls upon them renders speech itself almost superfluous.

Here and there where the ground rises slightly above the

level of the fens there are dense woods tangled with parasitic creepers and filled with owls. Bats fly from wood to wood. The air on the lower ground is charged with the poisonous gases which exude from the marsh, while in the woods it is heavy with the dank odors of deadly nightshade and poison ivy.

It had been raining in the afternoon, and as I drove up the avenue the mournful dripping of the rain from the dark trees accentuated the cheerlessness of the gloom. The vehicle in which I rode was a fly on three wheels, the fourth having apparently been broken and taken off, causing the fly to sag on one side and drag on its axle over the muddy ground, the fly thus moving only at a foot's pace in a way calculated to enhance the dreariness of the occasion. The driver on the box in front of me was so thickly muffled up as to be indistinguishable, while the horse which drew us was so thickly coated with mist as to be practically invisible. Seldom, I may say, have I had a drive of so mournful a character.

The avenue presently opened out upon a lawn with overgrown shrubberies and in the half darkness I could see the outline of the Grange itself, a rambling, dilapidated building. A dim light struggled through the casement of a window in a tower room. Save for the melancholy cry of a row of owls sitting on the roof, and croaking of the frogs in the moat which ran around the grounds, the place was soundless. My driver halted his horse at the hither side of the moat. I tried in vain to urge him, by signs, to go further. I could see by the fellow's face that he was in a paroxysm of fear and indeed nothing but the extra sixpence which I had added to his fare would have made him undertake the drive up the avenue. I had no sooner alighted than he wheeled his cab about and made off.

Laughing heartily at the fellow's trepidation (I have a way of laughing heartily in the dark), I made my way to the door and pulled the bell-handle. I could hear the muffled reverberations of the bell far within the building. Then all was silent. I bent my ear to listen, but could hear nothing except perhaps the sound of a low moaning as of a person in pain or in great mental distress. Convinced, however, from what my friend Sir Jeremy Buggam had told me, that the Grange was not empty, I raised the ponderous knocker and beat with it loudly against the door.

But perhaps at this point I may do well to explain to my readers (before they are too frightened to listen to me) how I came to be beating on the door of Buggam Grange at nightfall on a gloomy November evening.

A year before I had been sitting with Sir Jeremy Buggam, the present baronet, on the verandah of his ranch in California.

"So you don't believe in the supernatural?" he was saying.

"Not in the slightest," I answered, lighting a cigar as I spoke. When I want to speak very positively, I generally light a cigar as I speak.

"Well, at any rate, Digby," said Sir Jeremy, "Buggam Grange is haunted. If you want to be assured of it go down there any time and spend the night and you'll see for yourself."

"My dear fellow," I replied, "nothing will give me greater pleasure. I shall be back in England in six weeks, and I shall be delighted to put your ideas to the test. Now tell me," I added somewhat cynically, "is there any particular season or day when your Grange is supposed to be specially terrible?"

Sir Jeremy looked at me strangely. "Why do you ask that?" he said. "Have you heard the story of the Grange?"

"Never heard of the place in my life," I answered cheerily, "till you mentioned it to-night, my dear fellow, I hadn't the remotest idea that you still owned property in England."

"The Grange is shut up," said Sir Jeremy, "and has been for twenty years. But I keep a man there—Horrod—he was butler in my father's time and before. If you care to go, I'll write to him that you're coming. And since you are taking your own fate in your hands, the fifteenth of November is the day."

At that moment Lady Buggam and Clara and the other girls came trooping out on the verandah, and the whole thing passed clean out of my mind. Nor did I think of it again until I was back in London. Then by one of those strange coincidences or premonitions—call it what you will—it suddenly occurred to me one morning that it was the fifteenth of November. Whether Sir Jeremy had written to Horrod or not, I did not know. But none the less nightfall found me, as I have described, knocking at the door of Buggam Grange.

The sound of the knocker had scarcely ceased to echo when I heard the shuffling of feet within, and the sound of chains and bolts being withdrawn. The door opened. A man stood before me holding a lighted candle which he shaded with his hand. His faded black clothes, once apparently a butler's dress, his white hair and advanced age left me in no doubt that he was Horrod of whom Sir Jeremy had spoken.

Without a word he motioned me to come in, and, still without speech, he helped me to remove my wet outer garments, and then beckoned me into a great room, evidently the dining room of the Grange.

I am not in any degree a nervous man by temperament, as I think I remarked before, and yet there was something in the vastness of the wainscotted room, lighted only by a single candle, and in the silence of the empty house, and still more in the appearance of my speechless attendant which gave me a feeling of distinct uneasiness. As Horrod moved to and fro I took occasion to scrutinize his face more narrowly. I have seldom seen features more calculated to inspire a nervous dread. The pallor of his face and the whiteness of his hair (the man was at least seventy), and still more the peculiar furtiveness of his eyes, seemed to mark him as one who lived under a great terror. He moved with a noiseless step and at times he turned his head to glance in the dark corners of the room.

"Sir Jeremy told me," I said, speaking as loudly and as heartily as I could, "that he would apprise you of my coming."

I was looking into his face as I spoke.

In answer Horrod laid his finger across his lips and I knew that he was deaf and dumb. I am not nervous (I think I said that), but the realization that my sole companion in the empty house was a deaf mute struck a cold chill to my heart.

Horrod laid in front of me a cold meat pie, a cold goose, a cheese, and a tall flagon of cider. But my appetite was gone. I ate the goose, but found that after I had finished the pie I had but little zest for the cheese, which I finished without enjoyment. The cider had a sour taste, and after having permitted Horrod to refill the flagon twice, I found that it induced a sense of melancholy and decided to drink no more.

My meal finished, the butler picked up the candle and beckoned to me to follow him. We passed through the empty corridors of the house, a long line of pictured Buggams looking upon us as we passed, their portraits in the flickering light of the taper assuming a strange and life-like appearance as if leaning forward from their frames to gaze upon the intruder.

Horrod led me upstairs and I realized that he was taking me to the tower in the east wing in which I had observed a light.

The rooms to which the butler conducted me consisted of a sitting room with an adjoining bedroom, both of them fitted with antique wainscotting against which a faded tapestry fluttered. There was a candle burning on the table in the sitting room but its insufficient light only rendered the surroundings the more dismal. Horrod bent down in front of the fireplace and endeavoured to light a fire there. But the wood was evidently damp, and the fire flickered feebly on the hearth.

The butler left me, and in the stillness of the house I could hear his shuffling step echo down the corridor. It may have been fancy, but it seemed to me that his departure was the signal for a low moan that came from somewhere behind the wainscot. There was a narrow cupboard door at one side of the room, and for the moment I wondered whether the moaning came from within. I am not as a rule lacking in courage (I am sure my reader will be decent enough to believe this), yet I found myself entirely unwilling to open the cupboard door and look within. In place of doing so I seated myself in a great chair in front of the feeble fire. I must have been seated there for some time when I happened to lift my eyes to the mantel above and saw, standing upon it, a letter addressed to myself. I knew the handwriting at once to be that of Sir Jeremy Buggam.

I opening it, and spreading it out within reach of the feeble candle light, I read as follows:

My dear Digby,

In our talk that you will remember I had no time to finish telling you about the mystery of Buggam Grange. I take for granted, however, that you will go there and that Horrod will put you in the tower rooms, which are the only ones that make any pretense of being habitable. I have, therefore, sent him this letter to deliver at the Grange itself. The story is this:

On the night of the fifteenth of November, fifty years ago, my grandfather was murdered in the room in which you are sitting, by his cousin Sir Duggam Buggam. He was stabbed from behind while seated at the little table at which you are probably reading this letter. The two had been playing cards at the table and my grandfather's body was found lying in a litter of cards and gold sovereigns on the floor. Sir Duggam Buggam, insensible from drink, lay beside him, the fatal knife at his hand, his fingers smeared with blood. My grandfather, though of the younger branch, possessed a part of the estates which were to revert to Sir Duggam on his death. Sir Duggam Buggam was tried at the Assizes and was hanged. On the day of his execution he was permitted by the authorities, out of respect for his rank, to wear a mask to the scaffold. The clothes in which he was executed are hanging at full length in the little cupboard to your right, and the mask is above them. It is said that on every fifteenth of November at midnight the cupboard door opens and Sir Duggam Buggam walks out into the room. It has been found impossible to get servants to remain at the Grange, and the place—except for the presence of Horrod—has been unoccupied for a generation. At the time of the murder Horrod was a young man of twenty-two, newly entered into the service of the family. It was he who entered the room and discovered the crime. On the day of the execution he was stricken with paralysis and has never spoken since. From that time to this he has never consented to leave the Grange where he lives in isolation.

Wishing you a pleasant night after your tiring journey,

I remain,
Very faithfully,
Jeremy Buggam.

I leave my reader to imagine my state of mind when I completed the perusal of the letter.

I have as little belief in the supernatural as anyone, yet I must confess that there was something in the surroundings in which I now found myself which rendered me at least uncomfortable. My reader may smile if he will, but I assure him that it was with a very distinct feeling of uneasiness that I at length managed to rise to my feet, and, grasping my candle in my hand, to move backward into the bedroom. As I backed into it something so like a moan seemed to proceed from the closed cupboard that I accelerated my backward movement to a considerable degree. I hastily blew out the candle, threw myself upon the bed and drew the bed clothes over my head, keeping, however, one eye and one ear still out and available.

How long I lay thus listening to every sound, I cannot tell. The stillness had become absolute. From time to time I could dimly hear the distant cry of an owl and once far away in the building below a sound as of someone dragging a chain along a floor. More than once I was certain that I heard the sound of moaning behind the wainscot. Meantime I realized that the hour must now be drawing close upon the fatal moment of midnight. My watch I could not see in the darkness, but by reckoning the time that must have elapsed I knew that midnight could not be far away. Then presently my ear, alert to every sound, could just distinguish far away across the fens the striking of a church bell, in the clock tower of Buggam village church, no doubt, tolling the hour of twelve.

On the last stroke of twelve, the cupboard door in the next room opened. There is no need to ask me how I knew it. I couldn't, of course, see it, but I could hear, or sense in some way, the sound of it. I could feel my hair, all of it, rising upon my head. I was aware that there was a presence in the adjoining room, I will not say a person, a living soul, but a presence. Anyone who has been in the next room to a presence will know just how I felt. I could hear a sound as of someone groping on the floor and the faint rattle as of coins.

My hair was now perpendicular. My reader can blame it or not, but it was.

Then at this very moment from somewhere below in the building there came the sound of a prolonged and piercing cry, a cry as of a soul passing in agony. My reader may censure me or not, but right at this moment I decided to beat it. Whether I should have remained to see what was happening is a question that I will not discuss. My one idea was to get out and to get out quickly. The window of the tower room was some twenty-five feet above the ground. I sprang out through the casement in one leap and landed on the grass below. I jumped over the shrubbery in one bound and cleared the moat in one jump. I went down the avenue in about six strides and ran five miles along the road through the fens in three minutes. This at least is an accurate transcription of my sensations. It may have taken longer. I never stopped till I found myself on the threshold of the Buggam Arms in Little Buggam, beating on the door for the landlord.

I returned to Buggam Grange on the next day in the bright sunlight of a frosty November morning, in a seven cylinder motor car with six local constables and a physician. It makes all the difference. We carried revolvers, spades, pickaxes, shotguns and an ouija board.

What we found cleared up forever the mystery of the Grange. We discovered Horrod the butler lying on the dining room floor quite dead. The physician said that he had died from heart failure. There was evidence from the marks of his shoes in the dust that he had come in the night to the tower room. On the table he had placed a paper which contained a full confession of his having murdered Jeremy Buggam fifty years before. The circumstances of the murder had rendered it easy for him to fasten the crime upon Sir Duggam, already insensible from drink. A few minutes with the ouija board enabled us to get a full corroboration from Sir Duggam. He promised moreover, now that his name was cleared, to go away from the premises forever.

My friend, the present Sir Jeremy, has rehabilitated Buggam Grange. The place is rebuilt. The moat is drained. The whole house is lit with electricity. There are beautiful motor drives in all directions in the woods. He has had the bats shot and the owls stuffed. His daughter, Clara Buggam, became my wife. She is looking over my shoulder as I write. What more do you want?

The Story of the Goblins Who Stole a Sexton

by
CHARLES DICKENS
(1812–1870)

"The Story of the Goblins Who Stole a Sexton" is in part an early version of A Christmas Carol, and the reader will easily recognize in Gabriel Grub a forerunner of the more famous Scrooge. The listener response to my early reading from A Christmas Carol was so overwhelming that we thought it would be nice to find some more material in a similar vein. Pickwick Papers, from which "The Story of the Goblins" has been taken, proved to be just the thing, and over the years I have read a number of pieces from Pickwick. This, to me, is Dickens at his early best—revelling in the darkness of a goblin underworld.

I n an old abbey town, down in this part of the country, a long, long while ago—so long, that the story
must be a true one, because our great grandfathers
implicitly believed it—there officiated as sexton and
grave-digger in the churchyard, one Gabriel Grub. It by no
means follows that because a man is a sexton, and constantly
surrounded by emblems of mortality, therefore he should be a
morose and melancholy man; your undertakers are the merri-
est fellows in the world; and I once had the honour of being
on intimate terms, with a mute, who in private life, and off
duty, was as comical and jocose a little fellow as ever chirped
out a devil-may-care song, without a hitch in his memory, or
drained off the contents of a good stiff glass without stopping
for breath. But, notwithstanding these precedents to the con-
trary, Gabriel Grub was an ill-conditioned, cross-grained, surly
fellow—a morose and lonely man, who consorted with
nobody but himself, and an old wicker bottle which fitted into
his large deep waistcoat pocket—and who eyed each merry
face, as it passed him by, with such a deep scowl of malice and
ill-humour, as it was difficult to meet, without feeling something the worse for.

A little before twilight, one Christmas Eve, Gabriel shouldered his spade, lighted his lantern, and betook himself towards the old churchyard; for he had got a grave to finish by next morning, and, feeling very low, he thought it might raise his spirits, perhaps, if he went on with his work at once. As he went his way, up the ancient street, he saw the cheerful light of the blazing fires gleam through the old casements, and heard the loud laugh and the cheerful shouts of those who assembled around them; he marked the bustling preparations for next day's cheer, and smelt the numerous savoury odours consequent thereupon, as they steamed up from the kitchen windows in clouds. All this was gall and wormwood to the heart of Gabriel Grub; and when groups of children, bounded out of the houses, tripped across the road, and were met, before they could knock at the opposite door, by half a dozen curly-headed little rascals who crowded round them as they flocked upstairs to spend the evening in their Christmas games, Gabriel smiled grimly, and clutched the handle of his spade with a firmer grasp, as he thought of measles, scarlet-fever, thrush, hooping-cough, and a good many other sources of consolation besides.

In this happy frame of mind, Gabriel strode along: returning a short, sullen growl to the good-humoured greetings of such of his neighbours as now and then passed him: until he turned into the dark lane which led to the churchyard. Now, Gabriel had been looking forward to reaching the dark lane, because it was, generally speaking, a nice, gloomy, mournful place, into which the townspeople did not much care to go, except in broad day-light, and when the sun was shining; consequently, he was not a little indignant to hear a young urchin roaring out some jolly song about a merry Christmas, in this very sanctuary, which had been called Coffin Lane ever since the days of the old abbey, and the time of the shaven-headed monks. As Gabriel walked on, and the voice drew nearer, he found it proceeded from a small boy, who was hurrying along, to join one of the little parties in the old street, and who, partly to keep himself company, and partly to prepare himself for the occasion, was shouting out the song at the highest pitch of his lungs. So Gabriel waited until the boy came up, and then dodged him into a corner, and rapped him over the head with his lantern five or six times, to teach him to modulate his voice. And as the boy hurried away with his hand to his head, singing quite a different sort of tune, Gabriel Grub chuckled very heartily to himself, and entered the churchyard: locking the gate behind him.

He took off his coat, put down his lantern, and getting into the unfinished grave, worked at it for an hour or so, with right good will. But the earth was hardened with the frost, and it was no very easy matter to break it up, and shovel it out; and although there was a moon, it was a very young one, and shed little light upon the grave, which was in the shadow of the church. At any other time, these obstacles would have made Gabriel Grub very moody and miserable, but he was so well pleased with having stopped the small boy's singing, that he took little heed of the scanty progress he had made, and looking down into the grave, when he had finished work for the night, with grim satisfaction: murmuring as he gathered up his things:

> Brave lodgings for one, brave lodgings for one,
> A few feet of cold earth, when life is done;
> A stone at the head, a stone at the feet,
> A rich, juicy meal for the worms to eat;
> Rank grass over head, and damp clay around,
> Brave lodgings for one, these, in holy ground!

"Ho! ho!" laughed Gabriel Grub, as he sat himself down on a flat tombstone which was a favourite resting-place of his; and drew forth his wicker bottle. "A coffin at Christmas! A Christmas Box. Ho! ho! ho!"

"Ho! ho! ho!" repeated a voice which sounded close behind him.

Gabriel paused, in some alarm, in the act of raising the wicker bottle to his lips: and looked round. The bottom of the oldest grave about him, was not more still and quiet, than the churchyard in the pale moonlight. The cold hoarfrost glistened on the tombstones, and sparkled like rows of gems, among the stone carvings of the old church. The snow lay hard and crisp upon the ground; and spread over the thickly-strewn mounds of earth, so white and smooth a cover, that it seemed as if corpses lay there, hidden only by their winding sheets. Not the faintest rustle broke the profound tranquillity of the solemn scene. Sound itself appeared to be frozen up, all was so cold and still.

"It was the echoes," said Gabriel Grub, raising the bottle to his lips again.

"It was *not*," said a deep voice.

Gabriel started up, and stood rooted to the spot with astonishment and terror; for his eyes rested on a form that made his blood run cold.

Seated on an upright tombstone, close to him, was a strange unearthly figure, whom Gabriel felt at once, was no being of this world. His long fantastic legs which might have reached the ground, were cocked up, and crossed after a quaint, fantastic fashion; his sinewy arms were bare; and his hands rested on his knees. On his short round body, he wore a close covering, ornamented with small slashes; a short cloak dangled at his back; the collar was cut into curious peaks, which served the goblin in lieu of ruff or neckerchief; and his shoes curled up at his toes into long points. On his head, he wore a broad-brimmed sugar-loaf hat, garnished with a single feather. The hat was covered with the white frost; and the goblin looked as if he had sat on the same tombstone very comfortably, for two or three hundred years. He was sitting perfectly still; his tongue was put out, as if in derision; and he was grinning at Gabriel Grub with such a grin as only a goblin could call up.

"'It was *not* the echoes," said the goblin.

Gabriel Grub was paralysed, and could make no reply.

"What do you do here on Christmas Eve?" said the goblin sternly.

"I came to dig a grave, sir," stammered Gabriel Grub.

"What man wanders among graves and churchyards on such a night as this?" cried the goblin.

"Gabriel Grub! Gabriel Grub!" screamed a wild chorus of voices that seemed to fill the churchyard. Gabriel looked fearfully round—nothing was to be seen.

"What have you got in that bottle?" said the goblin.

"Hollands, sir," replied the sexton, trembling more than ever; for he had bought it of the smugglers, and he thought that perhaps his questioner might be in the excise department of the goblins.

"Who drinks Hollands alone, and in a churchyard, on such a night as this?" said the goblin.

"Gabriel Grub! Gabriel Grub!" exclaimed the wild voices again.

The goblin leered maliciously at the terrified sexton, and then raising his voice, exclaimed:

"And who, then, is our fair and lawful prize?"

To this inquiry the invisible chorus replied, in a strain that sounded like the voices of many choristers singing to the mighty swell of the old church organ—a strain that seemed borne to the sexton's ears upon a wild wind, and to die away as it passed onward; but the burden of the reply was still the same, "Gabriel Grub! Gabriel Grub!"

The goblin grinned a broader grin than before, as he said, "Well, Gabriel, what do you say to this?"

The sexton gasped for breath.

"What do you think of this, Gabriel?" said the goblin, kicking up his feet in the air on either side of the tombstone, and looking at the turned-up points with as much complacency as if he had been contemplating the most fashionable pair of Wellington's in all Bond Street.

"It's—it's—very curious, sir," replied the sexton, half dead with fright: "very curious, and very pretty, but I think I'll go back and finish my work, sir, if you please."

"Work!" said the goblin, "what work?"

"The grave, sir; making the grave," stammered the sexton.

"Oh, the grave, eh?" said the goblin; "who makes graves at a time when all other men are merry, and takes a pleasure in it?"

Again the mysterious voices replied, "Gabriel Grub! Gabriel Grub!"

"I'm afraid my friends want you, Gabriel," said the goblin, thrusting his tongue further into his cheek than ever—and a most astonishing tongue it was—"I'm afraid my friends want you, Gabriel," said the goblin.

"Under favour, sir," replied the horror-stricken sexton, "I don't think they can, sir; they don't know me, sir; I don't think the gentlemen have ever seen me, sir."

"Oh yes they have," replied the goblin; "we know the man with the sulky face and grim scowl, that came down the street to-night, throwing his evil looks at the children, and grasping his burying spade the tighter. We know the man who struck the boy in the envious malice of his heart, because the boy could be merry, and he could not. We know him, we know him."

Here the goblin gave a loud shrill laugh, which the echoes returned twenty-fold: and throwing his legs up in the air, stood upon his head, or rather upon the very point of his sugar-loaf hat, on the narrow edge of the tombstone: whence he threw a somerset with extraordinary agility, right to the sexton's feet, at which he planted himself in the attitude in which tailors generally sit upon the shopboard.

"I—I—am afraid I must leave you, sir," said the sexton, making an effort to move.

"Leave us!" said the goblin, "Gabriel Grub going to leave us. Ho! ho! ho!"

As the goblin laughed, the sexton observed, for one instant, a brilliant illumination within the windows of the church, as if the whole building were lighted up; it disappeared, the organ pealed forth a lively air, and whole troops of goblins, the very counterpart of the first one, poured into the churchyard, and began playing at leap-frog with the tombstones: never stopping for an instant to take breath, but "overing" the highest among them, one after the other, with the utmost marvellous dexterity. The first goblin was a most astonishing leaper, and none of the others could come near him; even in the extremity of his terror the sexton could not help observing, that while his friends were content to leap over the common-sized gravestones, the first one took the family vaults, iron railings and all, with as much ease as if they had been so many street posts.

At last the game reached to a most exciting pitch; the organ played quicker and quicker; and the goblins leaped faster and faster: coiling themselves up, rolling head over heels upon the ground, and bounding over the tombstones like foot-balls. The sexton's brain whirled round with the rapidity of the motion he beheld, and his legs reeled beneath him, as the spirits flew before his eyes: when the goblin king, suddenly darting towards him, laid his hand upon his collar, and sank with him through the earth.

When Gabriel Grub had had time to fetch his breath, which the rapidity of his descent had for the moment taken away, he found himself in what appeared to be a large cavern, surrounded on all sides by crowds of goblins, ugly and grim; in the centre of the room, on an elevated seat, was stationed his friend of the churchyard; and close beside him stood Gabriel Grub himself, without power of motion.

"Cold to-night," said the king of the goblins, "very cold. A glass of something warm, here!"

At this command, half a dozen officious goblins, with a perpetual smile upon their faces, whom Gabriel Grub imagined to be courtiers, on that account, hastily disappeared, and presently returned with a goblet of liquid fire, which they presented to the king.

"Ah!" cried the goblin, whose cheeks and throat were transparent, as he tossed down the flame, "This warms one, indeed! Bring a bumper of the same, for Mr. Grub."

It was in vain for the unfortunate sexton to protest that he was not in the habit of taking anything warm at night; one of the goblins held him while another poured the blazing liquid down his throat; the whole assembly screeched with laughter as he coughed and choked, and wiped away the tears which gushed plentifully from his eyes, after swallowing the burning draught.

"And now," said the king, fantastically poking the taper corner of his sugar-loaf hat into the sexton's eye, and thereby occasioning him the most exquisite pain: "And now, show the man of misery and gloom, a few of the pictures from our own great storehouse!"

As the goblin said this, a thick cloud which obscured the remoter end of the cavern, rolled gradually away, and disclosed, apparently at a great distance, a small and scantily furnished, but neat and clean apartment. A crowd of little children were gathered around a bright fire, clinging to their mother's gown, and gambolling around her chair. The mother occasionally rose, and drew aside the window-curtain, as if to look for some expected object; a frugal meal was ready spread upon the table; and an elbow chair was placed near the fire. A knock was heard at the door: the mother opened it, and the children crowded round her, and clapped their hands for joy, as their father entered. He was wet and weary, and shook the snow from his garments, as the children crowded round him, and seizing his cloak, hat, stick, and gloves, with busy zeal, ran with them from the room. Then, as he sat down to his meal before the fire, the children climbed about his knee, and the mother sat by his side, and all seemed happiness and comfort.

But a change came upon the view, almost imperceptibly. The scene was altered to a small bed-room, where the fairest and youngest child lay dying; the roses had fled from his cheek, and the light from his eye; and even as the sexton looked upon him with an interest he had never felt or known before, he died. His young brothers and sisters crowded round his little bed, and seized his tiny hand, so cold and heavy; but they shrunk back from its touch, and looked with awe on his infant face; for calm and tranquil as it was, and sleeping in rest and peace as the beautiful child seemed to be, they saw that he was dead, and they knew that he was an Angel looking down upon, and blessing them, from a bright and happy Heaven.

Again the light cloud passed across the picture, and again the subject changed. The father and mother were old and helpless now, and the number of those about them was diminished more than half; but content and cheerfulness sat on every face, and beamed in every eye, as they crowded round the fireside, and told and listened to old stories of earlier and bygone days. Slowly and peacefully, the father sank into the grave, and, soon after, the sharer of all his cares and troubles followed him to a place of rest. The few, who yet survived them, knelt by their tomb, and watered the green turf which covered it, with their tears; then rose, and turned away: sadly and mournfully, but not with bitter cries, or despairing lamentations, for they knew that they should one day meet again; and once more they mixed with the busy world, and their content and cheerfulness were restored. The cloud settled upon the picture, and concealed it from the sexton's view.

"What do you think of *that*?" said the goblin, turning his large face towards Gabriel Grub.

Gabriel murmured out something about its being very pretty, and looked somewhat ashamed, as the goblin bent his fiery eyes upon him.

"*You* a miserable man!" said the goblin, in a tone of excessive contempt. "You!" He appeared disposed to add more, but indignation choked his utterance, so he lifted up one of his very pliable legs, and flourishing it above his head a little, to insure his aim, administered a good sound kick to Gabriel Grub; immediately after which, all the goblins in waiting, crowded round the wretched sexton, and kicked him without mercy: according to the established and invariable custom of courtiers upon earth, who kick whom royalty kicks, and hug whom royalty hugs.

"Show him some more!" said the king of the goblins.

At these words, the cloud was dispelled, and a rich and beautiful landscape was disclosed to view—there is just such another, to this day, within half a mile of the old abbey town. The sun shone out from the clear blue sky, the water sparkled beneath his rays, and the trees looked greener, and the flowers more gay, beneath his cheering influence. The water rippled on, with a pleasant sound; the trees rustled in the light wind that murmured among their leaves; the birds sang upon the boughs; and the lark carolled on high, her welcome to the morning. Yes, it was morning: the bright, balmy morning of summer; the minutest leaf, the smallest blade of grass, was instinct with life. The ant crept forth to her daily toil, the butterfly fluttered and basked in the warm rays of the sun; myriads of insects spread their transparent wings, and revelled in their brief but happy existence. Man walked forth, elated with the scene; and all was brightness and splendour.

"*You* a miserable man!" said the king of the goblins, in a more contemptuous tone than before. And again the king of the goblins gave his leg a flourish; again it descended on the shoulders of the sexton; and again the attendant goblins imitated the example of their chief.

Many a time the cloud went and came, and many a lesson it taught to Gabriel Grub, who, although his shoulders smarted with pain from the frequent applications of the goblin's feet, looked on with an interest that nothing could diminish. He saw that men who worked hard, and earned their scanty bread with lives of labour, were cheerful and happy; and that to the most ignorant, the sweet face of nature was a never-failing source of cheerfulness and joy. He saw those who had been delicately nurtured, and tenderly brought up, cheerful under privations, and superior to suffering, that would have crushed many of a rougher grain, because they bore within their own bosoms the materials of happiness, contentment, and peace. He saw that women, the tenderest and most fragile of all God's creatures, were the oftenest superior to sorrow, adversity, and distress; and he saw that it was because they bore, in their own hearts, an inexhaustible well-spring of affection and devotion. Above all, he saw that men like himself, who snarled at the mirth and cheerfulness of others, were the foulest weeds on the fair surface of the earth; and setting all the good of the world against the evil, he came to the conclusion that it was a very decent and respectable sort of world after all. No sooner had he formed it, than the cloud which closed over the last picture, seemed to settle on his senses, and lull him to repose. One by one, the goblins faded from his sight; and as the last one disappeared, he sunk to sleep.

The day had broken when Gabriel Grub awoke, and found himself lying, at full length on the flat gravestone in the churchyard, with the wicker bottle lying empty by his side, and his coat, spade, and lantern, all well whitened by the last night's frost, scattered on the ground. The stone on which he had first seen the goblin seated, stood bolt upright before him, and the grave at which he had worked, the night before, was not far off. At first, he began to doubt the reality of his adventures, but the acute pain in his shoulders when he attempted to rise, assured him that the kicking of the goblins was certainly not ideal. He was staggered again, by observing no traces of footsteps in the snow on which the goblins had played at leap-frog with the gravestones, but he speedily accounted for this circumstance when he remembered that, being spirits, they would leave no visible impression behind them. So, Gabriel Grub got on his feet as well as he could, for the pain in his back; and brushing the frost off his coat, put it on and turned his face towards the town.

But he was an altered man, and he could not bear the thought of returning to a place where his repentance would be scoffed at, and his reformation disbelieved. He hesitated for a few moments; and then turned away to wander where he might, and seek his bread elsewhere.

The lantern, the spade, and the wicker bottle, were found, that day, in the churchyard. There were a great many speculations about the sexton's fate, at first, but it was speedily determined that he had been carried away by the goblins; and there were not wanting some very credible witnesses who had distinctly seen him whisked through the air on the back of a chestnut horse blind of one eye, with the hind-quarters of a lion, and the tail of a bear. At length all this was devoutly believed; and the new sexton used to exhibit to the curious, for a trifling emolument, a good-sized piece of the church weathercock which had been accidentally kicked off by the aforesaid horse in his aerial flight, and picked up by himself in the churchyard, a year of two afterwards.

Unfortunately, these stories were somewhat disturbed by the unlooked for reappearance of Gabriel Grub himself, some ten years afterwards, a ragged, contented, rheumatic old man. He told his story to the clergyman, and also to the mayor; and in course of time it began to be received, as a matter of history, in which form it has continued down to this very day. The believers in the weather-cock tale, having misplaced their confidence once, were not easily prevailed upon to part with it again, so they looked as wise as they could, shrugged their shoulders, touched their foreheads, and murmured something about Gabriel Grub having drunk all the Hollands, and then fallen asleep on the flat tombstone; and they affected to explain what he supposed he had witnessed in the goblin's cavern, by saying that he had seen the world, and grown wiser. But this opinion, which was by no means a popular one at any time, gradually died off; and be the matter how it may, as Gabriel Grub was afflicted with rheumatism to the end of his days, this story has at least one moral, if it teach no better one—and that is, that if a man turn sulky and drink by himself at Christmas time, he may make up his mind to be not a bit the better for it: let the spirits be never so good, or let them be even as many degrees beyond proof, as those which Gabriel Grub saw in the goblin's cavern.

The Loons

by
MARGARET LAURENCE
(1926–1987)

There are some stories that are shaped around a single image—or sometimes even a sound—which remains with the reader long after the story is finished. In "The Loons" it is the "ululating" sound, the crying of the loons, that continues to echo in the reader's mind even after the book is back on its shelf. In going over these stories to make this collection I was impressed to find how fresh and how powerful Laurence's story remains. I think it is the crying of the loons that makes the story so memorable—still fresh and still vivid even long years after I first read it.

Just below Manawaka, where the Wachakwa River ran brown and noisy over the pebbles, the scrub oak and grey-green willow and chokecherry bushes grew in a dense thicket. In a clearing at the centre of the thicket stood the Tonnerre family's shack. The basis of this dwelling was a small square cabin made of poplar poles and chinked with mud, which had been built by Jules Tonnerre some fifty years before, when he came back from Batoche with a bullet in his thigh, the year that Riel was hung and the voices of the Metis entered their long silence. Jules had only intended to stay the winter in the Wachakwa Valley, but the family was still there in the thirties, when I was a child. As the Tonnerres had increased, their settlement had been added to, until the clearing at the foot of the town hill was a chaos of lean-tos, wooden packing cases, warped lumber, discarded car tires, ramshackle chicken coops, tangled strands of barbed wire and rusty tin cans.

The Tonnerres were French halfbreeds, and among themselves they spoke a *patois* that was neither Cree nor French. Their English was broken and full of obscenities. They did not belong among the Cree of the Galloping Mountain reservation, further north, and they did not belong among the Scots-Irish and Ukrainians of Manawaka, either. They were, as my Grandmother MacLeod would have put it, neither flesh, fowl, nor good salt herring. When their men were not working at odd jobs or as section hands on the C.P.R., they lived on relief. In the summers, one of the Tonnerre youngsters, with a face that seemed totally unfamiliar with laughter, would knock at the doors of the town's brick houses and offer for sale a lard-pail full of bruised wild strawberries, and if he got as much as a quarter he would grab the coin and run before the customer had time to change her mind. Sometimes old Jules, or his son Lazarus, would get mixed up in a Saturday-night brawl, and would hit out at whoever was nearest, or howl drunkenly among the offended shoppers on Main Street, and then the Mountie would put them for the night in the barred cell underneath the Court House, and the next morning they would be quiet again.

Piquette Tonnerre, the daughter of Lazarus, was in my class at school. She was older than I, but she had failed several grades, perhaps because her attendance had always been sporadic and her interest in schoolwork negligible. Part of the reason she had missed a lot of school was that she had had tuberculosis of the bone, and had once spent many months in hospital. I knew this because my father was the doctor who had looked after her. Her sickness was almost the only thing I knew about her, however. Otherwise, she existed for me only as a vaguely embarrassing presence, with her hoarse voice and her clumsy limping walk and her grimy cotton dresses that were always miles too long. I was neither friendly nor unfriendly towards her. She dwelt and moved somewhere within my scope of vision, but I did not actually notice her very much until that peculiar summer when I was eleven.

"I don't know what to do about that kid," my father said at dinner one evening. "Piquette Tonnerre, I mean. The damn bone's flared up again. I've had her in hospital for quite a while now, and it's under control all right, but I hate like the dickens to send her home again."

"Couldn't you explain to her mother that she has to rest a lot?" my mother said.

"The mother's not there," my father replied. "She took off a few years back. Can't say I blame her. Piquette cooks for them, and she says Lazarus would never do anything for himself as long as she's there. Anyway, I don't think she'd take much care of herself, once she got back. She's only thirteen, after all. Beth, I was thinking—what about taking her up to Diamond Lake with us this summer? A couple of months rest would give that bone a much better chance."

My mother looked stunned.

"But Ewen—what about Roddie and Vanessa?"

"She's not contagious," my father said. "And it would be company for Vanessa."

"Oh dear," my mother said in distress, "I'll bet anything she has nits in her hair."

"For Pete's sake," my father said crossly, "do you think Matron would let her stay in the hospital for all this time like that? Don't be silly, Beth."

Grandmother MacLeod, her delicately featured face as rigid as a cameo, now brought her mauve-veined hands together as though she were about to begin a prayer.

"Ewen, if that half-breed youngster comes along to Diamond Lake, I'm not going," she announced. "I'll go to Morag's for the summer."

I had trouble in stifling my urge to laugh, for my mother brightened visibly and quickly tried to hide it. If it came to a choice between Grandmother MacLeod and Piquette, Piquette would win hands down, nits or not.

"It might be quite nice for you, at that," she mused. "You haven't seen Morag for over a year, and you might enjoy being in the city for a while. Well, Ewen dear, you do what you think best. If you think it would do Piquette some good, then we'll be glad to have her, as long as she behaves herself."

So it happened that several weeks later, when we all piled into my father's old Nash, surrounded by suitcases and boxes of provisions and toys for my ten-month-old brother, Piquette was with us and Grandmother MacLeod, miraculously, was not. My father would only be staying at the cottage for a couple of weeks, for he had to get back to his practice, but the rest of us would stay at Diamond Lake until the end of August.

Our cottage was not named, as many were, "Dew Drop Inn" or "Bide-a-Wee," or "Bonnie Doon." The sign on the roadway bore in austere letters only our name, MacLeod. It was not a large cottage, but it was on the lakefront. You could look out the windows and see, through the filigree of the spruce trees, the water glistening greenly as the sun caught it. All around the cottage were ferns, and sharp-branched raspberry bushes, and moss that had grown over fallen tree trunks. If you looked carefully among the weeds and grass, you could find wild strawberry plants which were in white flower now and in another month would bear fruit, the fragrant globes hanging like miniature scarlet lanterns on the thin hairy stems. The two grey squirrels were still there, gossiping at us from the tall spruce beside the cottage, and by the end of the summer they would again be tame enough to take pieces of crust from my hands. The broad moose antlers that hung above the back door were a little more bleached and fissured after the winter, but otherwise everything was the same. I raced joyfully around my kingdom, greeting all the places I had not seen for a year. My brother, Roderick, who had not been born when we were here last summer, sat on the car rug in the sunshine and examined a brown spruce cone, meticulously turning it round and round in his small and curious hands. My mother and father toted the luggage from car to cottage, exclaiming over how well the place had wintered, no broken windows, thank goodness, no apparent damage from storm-felled branches or snow.

Only after I had finished looking around did I notice Piquette. She was sitting on the swing, her lame leg held stiffly out, and her other foot scuffing the ground as she swung slowly back and forth. Her long hair hung black and straight around her shoulders, and her broad coarse-featured face bore no expression—it was blank, as though she no longer dwelt within her own skull, as though she had gone elsewhere. I approached her very hesitantly.

"Want to come and play?"

Piquette looked at me with a sudden flash of scorn.

"I ain't a kid," she said.

Wounded, I stamped angrily away, swearing I would not speak to her for the rest of the summer. In the days that followed, however, Piquette began to interest me, and I began to want to interest her. My reasons did not appear bizarre to me. Unlikely as it may seem, I had only just realised that the Tonnerre family, whom I had always heard called half-breeds, were actually Indians, or as near as made no difference. My acquaintance with Indians was not extensive. I did not remember ever having seen a real Indian, and my new awareness that Piquette sprang from the people of Big Bear and Poundmaker, of Tecumseh, of the Iroquois who had eaten Father Brebeuf's heart—all this gave her an instant attraction in my eyes. I was a devoted reader of Pauline Johnson at this age, and sometimes would orate aloud and in an exalted voice, *West Wind, blow from your prairie nest; Blow from the mountains, blow from the west*—and so on. It seemed to me that Piquette must be in some way a daughter of the forest, a kind of junior prophetess of the wilds, who might impart to me, if I took the right approach, some of the secrets which she undoubtedly knew—where the whippoorwill made her nest, how the coyote reared her young, or whatever it was that it said in Hiawatha.

I set about gaining Piquette's trust. She was not allowed to go swimming, with her bad leg, but I managed to lure her down to the beach—or rather, she came because there was nothing else to do. The water was always icy, for the lake was fed by springs, but I swam like a dog, thrashing my arms and legs around at such speed and with such an output of energy that I never grew cold. Finally, when I had had enough, I came out and sat beside Piquette on the sand. When she saw me approaching, her hand squashed flat the sand castle she had been building, and she looked at me sullenly, without speaking.

"Do you like this place?" I asked, after a while, intending to lead on from there into the question of forest lore.

Piquette shrugged. "It's okay. Good as anywhere."

"I love it," I said. "We come here every summer."

"So what?" Her voice was distant, and I glanced at her uncertainly, wondering what I could have said wrong.

"Do you want to come for a walk?" I asked her. "We wouldn't need to go far. If you walk just around the point there, you come to a bay where great big reeds grow in the water, and all kinds of fish hang around there. Want to? Come on."

She shook her head.

"Your dad said I ain't supposed to do no more walking than I got to."

I tried another line.

"I bet you know a lot about the woods and all that, eh?" I began respectfully.

Piquette looked at me from her large dark unsmiling eyes.

"I don't know what in hell you're talkin' about," she replied. "You nuts or somethin'? If you mean where my old man, and me, and all them live, you better shut up, by Jesus, you hear?"

I was startled and my feelings were hurt, but I had a kind of dogged perseverance. I ignored her rebuff.

"You know something, Piquette? There's loons here, on this lake. You can see their nests just up the shore there, behind those logs. At night, you can hear them even from the cottage, but it's better to listen from the beach. My dad says we should listen and try to remember how they sound, because in a few years when more cottages are built at Diamond Lake and more people come in, the loons will go away."

Piquette was picking up stones and snail shells and then dropping them again.

"Who gives a good goddamn?" she said.

It became increasingly obvious that, as an Indian, Piquette was a dead loss. That evening I went out by myself, scrambling through the bushes that overhung the steep path, my feet slipping on the fallen spruce needles that covered the ground. When I reached the shore, I walked along the firm damp sand to the small pier that my father had built, and sat down there. I heard someone else crashing through the undergrowth and the bracken, and for a moment I thought Piquette had changed her mind, but it turned out to be my father. He sat beside me on the pier and we waited, without speaking.

At night the lake was like black glass with a streak of amber which was the path of the moon. All around, the spruce trees grew tall and close-set, branches blackly sharp against the sky, which was lightened by a cold flickering of stars. Then the loons began their calling. They rose like phantom birds from the nests on the shore, and flew out onto the dark still surface of the water.

No one can ever describe that ululating sound, the crying of the loons, and no one who has heard it can ever forget it. Plaintive, and yet with a quality of chilling mockery, those voices belonged to a world separated by aeons from our neat world of summer cottages and the lighted lamps of home.

"They must have sounded just like that," my father remarked, "before any person ever set foot here."

Then he laughed. "You could say the same, of course, about sparrows, or chipmunks, but somehow it only strikes you that way with the loons."

"I know," I said.

Neither of us suspected that this would be the last time we would ever sit here together on the shore, listening. We stayed for perhaps half an hour, and then we went back to the cottage. My mother was reading beside the fireplace. Piquette was looking at the burning birch log, and not doing anything.

"You should have come along," I said, although in fact I was glad she had not.

"Not me," Piquette said. "You wouldn't catch me walkin' way down there jus' for a bunch of squawkin' birds."

Piquette and I remained ill at ease with one another. I felt I had somehow failed my father, but I did not know what was the matter, nor why she would not or could not respond when I suggested exploring the woods or playing house. I thought it was probably her slow and difficult walking that held her back. She stayed most of the time in the cottage with my mother, helping her with the dishes or with Roddie, but hardly ever talking. Then the Duncans arrived at their cottage, and I spent my days with Mavis, who was my best friend. I could not reach Piquette at all, and I soon lost interest in trying. But all that summer she remained as both a reproach and a mystery to me.

That winter my father died of pneumonia, after less than a week's illness. For some time I saw nothing around me, being completely immersed in my own pain and my mother's. When I looked outward once more, I scarcely noticed that Piquette Tonnerre was no longer at school. I do not remember seeing her at all until four years later, one Saturday night when Mavis and I were having Cokes in the Regal Café. The jukebox was booming like tuneful thunder, and beside it, leaning lightly on its chrome and its rainbow glass, was a girl.

Piquette must have been seventeen then, although she looked about twenty. I stared at her, astounded that anyone could have changed so much. Her face, so stolid and expressionless before, was animated now with a gaiety that was almost violent. She laughed and talked very loudly with the boys around her. Her lipstick was bright earmine, and her hair was cut short and frizzily permed. She had not been pretty as a child, and she was not pretty now, for her features were still heavy and blunt. But her dark and slightly slanted eyes were beautiful, and her skin-tight skirt and orange sweater displayed to enviable advantage a soft and slender body.

She saw me, and walked over. She teetered a little, but it was not due to her once-tubercular leg, for her limp was almost gone.

"Hi, Vanessa." Her voice still had the same hoarseness. "Long time no see, eh?"

"Hi." I said. "Where've you been keeping yourself, Piquette?"

"Oh, I been around," she said. "I been away almost two years now. Been all over the place—Winnipeg, Regina, Saskatoon. Jesus, what I could tell you! I come back this summer, but I ain't stayin'. You kids goin' to the dance?"

"No," I said abruptly, for this was a sore point with me. I was fifteen, and thought I was old enough to go to the Saturday-night dances at the Flamingo. My mother, however, thought otherwise.

"Y'oughta come," Piquette said. "I never miss one. It's just about the on'y thing in this jerkwater town that's any fun. Boy, you couldn' catch me stayin' here. I don' give a shit about this place. It stinks."

She sat down beside me, and I caught the harsh over-sweetness of her perfume.

"Listen, you wanna know something, Vanessa?" she confided, her voice only slightly blurred. "Your dad was the only person in Manawaka that ever done anything good to me."

I nodded speechlessly. I was certain she was speaking the truth. I knew a little more than I had that summer at Diamond Lake, but I could not reach her now any more than I had then. I was ashamed, ashamed of my own timidity, the frightened tendency to look the other way. Yet I felt no real warmth towards her—I only felt that I ought to, because of that distant summer and because my father had hoped she would be company for me, or perhaps that I would be for her, but it had not happened that way. At this moment, meeting her again, I had to admit that she repelled and embarrassed me, and I could not help despising the self-pity in her voice. I wished she would go away. I did not want to see her. I did not know what to say to her. It seemed that we had nothing to say to one another.

"I'll tell you something else," Piquette went on. "All the old bitches an' biddies in this town will sure be surprised. I'm gettin' married this fall—my boyfriend, he's an English fella, works in the stockyards in the city there, a very tall guy, got blond wavy hair. Gee, is he ever handsome. Got this real classy name. Alvin Gerald Cummings—some handle, eh? They call him Al."

For the merest instant, then, I saw her. I really did see her, for the first and only time in all the years we had both lived in the same town. Her defiant face, momentarily, became unguarded and unmasked, and in her eyes there was a terrifying hope.

"Gee, Piquette—" I burst out awkwardly, "that's swell. That's really wonderful. Congratulations—good luck—I hope you'll be happy—"

As I mouthed the conventional phrases, I could only guess how great her need must have been, that she had been forced to seek the very things she so bitterly rejected.

When I was eighteen, I left Manawaka and went away to college. At the end of my first year, I came back home for the summer. I spent the first few days in talking non-stop with my mother, as we exchanged all the news that somehow had not found its way into letters—what had happened in my life and what had happened here in Manawaka while I was away. My mother searched her memory for events that concerned people I knew.

"Did I ever write you about Piquette Tonnerre, Vanessa?" she asked one morning.

"No, I don't think so," I replied. "Last I heard of her, she was going to marry some guy in the city. Is she still there?"

My mother looked perturbed, and it was a moment before she spoke, as though she did not know how to express what she had to tell and wished she did not need to try.

"She's dead," she said at last. Then, as I stared at her, "Oh, Vanessa, when it happened, I couldn't help thinking of her as she was that summer—so sullen and gauche and badly dressed. I couldn't help wondering if we could have done something more at that time—but what could we do? She used to be around in the cottage there with me all day, and honestly, it was all I could do to get a word out of her. She didn't even talk to your father very much, although I think she liked him, in her way."

"What happened?" I asked.

"Either her husband left her, or she left him," my mother said. "I don't know which. Anyway, she came back here with two youngsters, both only babies—they must have been born very close together. She kept house, I guess, for Lazarus and her brothers, down in the valley there, in the old Tonnerre place. I used to see her on the street sometimes, but she never spoke to me. She'd put on an awful lot of weight, and she looked a mess, to tell you the truth, a real slattern, dressed any old how. She was up in court a couple of times—drunk and disorderly, of course. One Saturday night last winter, during the coldest weather, Piquette was alone in the shack with the children. The Tonnerres made home brew all the time, so I've

heard, and Lazarus said later she'd been drinking most of the
day when he and the boys went out that evening. They had an
old woodstove there—you know the kind, with exposed
pipes. The shack caught fire. Piquette didn't get out, and neither did the children."

I did not say anything. As so often with Piquette, there did
not seem to be anything to say. There was a kind of silence
around the image in my mind of the fire and the snow, and I
wished I could put from my memory the look that I had seen
once in Piquette's eyes.

I went up to Diamond Lake for a few days that summer,
with Mavis and her family. The MacLeod cottage had been sold
after my father's death, and I did not even go to look at it, not
wanting to witness my long-ago kingdom possessed now by
strangers. But one evening I went down to the shore by myself.

The small pier which my father had built was gone, and in
its place there was a large and solid pier built by the government, for Galloping Mountain was now a national park, and
Diamond Lake had been re-named Lake Wapakata, for it was
felt that an Indian name would have a greater appeal to
tourists. The one store had become several dozen, and the settlement had all the attributes of a flourishing resort—hotels, a
dance-hall, cafés with neon signs, the penetrating odours of
potato chips and hot dogs.

I sat on the government pier and looked out across the
water. At night the lake at least was the same as it had always
been, darkly shining and bearing within its black glass the
streak of amber that was the path of the moon. There was no
wind that evening, and everything was quiet all around me. It
seemed too quiet, and then I realized that the loons were no
longer here. I listened for some time, to make sure, but never
once did I hear that long-drawn call, half mocking and half
plaintive, spearing through the stillness across the lake.

I did not know what had happened to the birds. Perhaps
they had gone away to some far place of belonging. Perhaps
they had been unable to find such a place, and had simply
died out, having ceased to care any longer whether they lived
or not.

I remembered how Piquette had scorned to come along, when my father and I sat there and listened to the lake birds. It seemed to me now that in some unconscious and totally unrecognised way, Piquette might have been the only one, after all, who had heard the crying of the loons.

The Little Match Girl

by
HANS CHRISTIAN ANDERSEN
(1805–1875)

In "The Little Match Girl" a small child is afraid to go home because she hasn't sold any matches and she thinks that her father is going to beat her. Instead, she remains on the street, has a series of visions of warmth and comfort, ending with a vision of her dead grandmother coming down from heaven to save her. The grandmother-saviour is rescuing the child, then, not simply from the cold, but also from her father. "The Little Match Girl" was intended, I think, to give children comfort, to give a feeling of safety and warmth to the child snug in his or her bed. But the story is also a little threatening. There are real dangers for children, the author seems to say, and the story of "The Little Match Girl" seems to me all the more admirable for its evocation of the very real dangers that Hans Christian Andersen perceived.

I t was terribly cold; it snowed and was already almost dark, and evening came on, the last evening of the year. In the cold and gloom a poor little girl, bare-headed and barefoot, was walking through the streets. When she left her own house she certainly had had slippers on; but of what use were they? They were very big slippers, and her mother had used them till then, so big were they. The little maid lost them as she slipped across the road, where two carriages were rattling by terribly fast. One slipper was not to be found again, and a boy had seized the other, and run away with it. He thought he could use it very well as a cradle, some day when he had children of his own. So now the little girl went with her little naked feet, which were quite red and blue with the cold. In an old apron she carried a number of matches, and a bundle of them in her hand. No one had bought anything of her all day, and no one had given her a farthing.

Shivering with cold and hunger she crept along, a picture of misery, poor little girl! The snowflakes covered her long fair hair, which fell in pretty curls over her neck; but she did not think of that now. In all the windows lights were shining, and there was a glorious smell of roast goose, for it was New Year's Eve. Yes, she thought of that!

In a corner formed by two houses, one of which projected beyond the other, she sat down, cowering. She had drawn up her little feet, but she was still colder, and she did not dare to go home, for she had sold no matches, and did not bring a farthing of money. From her father she would certainly receive a beating, and besides, it was cold at home, for they had nothing over them but a roof through which the wind whistled, though the largest rents had been stopped with straw and rags.

Her little hands were almost benumbed with the cold. Ah! a match might do her good, if she could only draw one from the bundle, and rub it against the wall, and warm her hands at it. She drew one out. R-r-atch! how it sputtered and burned! It was a warm, bright flame, like a little candle, when she held her hands over it; it was a wonderful little light! It really seemed to the little girl as if she sat before a great polished stove, with bright brass feet and a brass cover. How the fire burned! how comfortable it was! but the little flame went out, the stove vanished, and she had only the remains of the burned match in her hand.

A second was rubbed against the wall. It burned up, and when the light fell upon the wall it became transparent like a thin veil, and she could see through it into the room. On the table a snow-white cloth was spread; upon it stood a shining dinner service; the roast goose smoked gloriously, stuffed with apples and dried plums. And what was still more splendid to behold, the goose hopped down from the dish, and waddled along the floor, with a knife and fork in its breast, to the little girl. Then the match went out, and only the thick, damp, cold wall was before her. She lighted another match. Then she was sitting under a beautiful Christmas tree; it was greater and more ornamental than the one she had seen through the glass door at the rich merchant's. Thousands of candles burned upon the green branches, and colored pictures like those in the print shops looked down upon them. The little girl stretched forth her hand toward them; then the match went out. The Christmas lights mounted higher. She saw them now as stars in the sky: one of them fell down, forming a long line of fire.

"Now some one is dying," thought the little girl, for her old grandmother, the person who had loved her, and who was now dead, had told her that when a star fell down a soul mounted up to God.

She rubbed another match against the wall; it became bright again, and in the brightness the old grandmother stood clear and shining, mild and lovely.

"Grandmother!" cried the child. "Oh! take me with you! I know you will go when the match is burned out. You will vanish like the warm fire, the warm food, and the great glorious Christmas tree!"

And she hastily rubbed the whole bundle of matches, for she wished to hold her grandmother fast. And the matches burned with such a glow that it became brighter than in the middle of the day; grandmother had never been so large or so beautiful. She took the little girl in her arms, and both flew in brightness and joy above the earth, very, very high, and up there was neither cold, nor hunger, nor care—they were with God!

But in the corner, leaning against the wall, sat the poor girl with red cheeks and smiling mouth, frozen to death on the last evening of the Old Year. The New Year's sun rose upon a little corpse! The child sat there, stiff and cold, with the matches of which one bundle was burned. "She wanted to warm herself," the people said. No one imagined what a beautiful thing she had seen, and in what glory she had gone in with her grandmother to the New Year's Day.

Tobermory

by
SAKI
(H.H. Munro; 1870–1916)

*I first got interested in "Saki" after reading the story of
"Tobermory," and I was determined to find out something
about the author. Hector Hugh Munro was born in Burma to
English parents. After the death of his mother, the two-year-
old Hector was shipped back to England to be brought up by
his two somewhat peculiar aunts, Charlotte and Augusta (or
"Aunt Tom" as Munro called her). The situation must have
been a familiar one for many families living abroad in days of
colonial rule. For little Hector Hugh, however, the situation
was not a happy one. According to Munro, his childhood was
dominated by the bickering of his two aunts, and whether it
was really the aunts who were to blame or Hector Hugh himself, it is certain that the boy turned to satire as a way of com-
bating what he could not control.*

*The name "Saki" was stumbled upon early in his career, and
served to place the author, in name at least, outside the general tenor of English life. Saki was always looking for something
exotic and unusual, and it is this sense of compelling strange-
ness to his work that makes Saki such an intriguing writer. If
you haven't come across Saki before, "Tobermory" is a splendid introduction to his work.*

I t was a chill, rain-washed afternoon of a late August day, that indefinite season when partridges are still in security or cold storage, and there is nothing to hunt—unless one is bounded on the north by the Bristol Channel, in which case one may lawfully gallop after fat red stags. Lady Blemley's house-party was not bounded on the north by the Bristol Channel, hence there was a full gathering of her guests round the tea-table on this particular afternoon. And, in spite of the blankness of the season and the triteness of the occasion, there was no trace in the company of that fatigued restlessness which means a dread of the pianola and a subdued hankering for auction bridge. The undisguised open-mouthed attention of the entire party was fixed on the homely negative personality of Mr. Cornelius Appin. Of all her guests, he was the one who had come to Lady Blemley with the vaguest reputation. Some one had said he was "clever," and he had got his invitation in the moderate expectation, on the part of his hostess, that some portion at least of his cleverness would be contributed to the general entertainment. Until tea-time that day she had been unable to discover in what direction, if any, his cleverness lay. He was neither a wit nor a croquet champion, a hypnotic force nor a begetter of amateur theatricals. Neither did his exterior suggest the sort of man in whom women are willing to pardon a generous measure of mental deficiency. He had subsided into mere Mr. Appin, and the Cornelius seemed a piece of transparent baptismal bluff. And now he was claiming to have launched on the world a discovery beside which the invention of gunpowder, of the printing press, and of steam locomotion were inconsiderable trifles. Science had made bewildering strides in many directions during recent decades, but this thing seemed to belong to the domain of miracle rather than to scientific achievement.

"And do you really ask us to believe," Sir Wilfrid was saying, "that you have discovered a means for instructing animals in the art of human speech, and that dear old Tobermory has proved your first successful pupil?"

"It is a problem at which I have worked for the last seventeen years," said Mr. Appin, "but only during the last eight or nine months have I been rewarded with glimmerings of success. Of course I have experimented with thousands of animals, but latterly only with cats, those wonderful creatures which have assimilated themselves so marvellously with our civilization while retaining all their highly developed feral instincts. Here and there among cats one comes across an outstanding superior intellect, just as one does among the ruck of human beings, and when I made the acquaintance of Tobermory a week ago I saw at once that I was in contact with a 'Beyond-cat' of extraordinary intelligence. I had gone far along the road to success in recent experiments; with Tobermory, as you call him, I have reached the goal."

Mr. Appin concluded his remarkable statement in a voice which he strove to divest of a triumphant inflection. No one said "Rats," though Clovis's lips moved in a monosyllabic contortion which probably invoked those rodents of disbelief.

"And do you mean to say," asked Miss Resker, after a slight pause, "that you have taught Tobermory to say and understand easy sentences of one syllable?"

"My dear Miss Resker," said the wonder-worker patiently, "one teaches little children and savages and backward adults in that piecemeal fashion; when one has once solved the problem of making a beginning with an animal of highly developed intelligence one has no need for those halting methods. Tobermory can speak our language with perfect correctness."

This time Clovis very distinctly said, "Beyond-rats!" Sir Wilfrid was more polite, but equally sceptical.

"Hadn't we better have the cat in and judge for ourselves?" suggested Lady Blemley.

Sir Wilfrid went in search of the animal, and the company settled themselves down to the languid expectation of witnessing some more or less adroit drawing-room ventriloquism.

In a minute Sir Wilfrid was back in the room, his face white beneath its tan and his eyes dilated with excitement.

"By Gad, it's true!"

His agitation was unmistakably genuine, and his hearers started forward in a thrill of awakened interest.

Collapsing into an armchair he continued breathlessly: "I found him dozing in the smoking-room and called out to him to come for his tea. He blinked at me in his usual way, and I said, 'Come on, Toby; don't keep us waiting'; and, by Gad! he drawled out in a most horribly natural voice that he'd come when he dashed well pleased! I nearly jumped out of my skin!"

Appin had preached to absolutely incredulous hearers; Sir Wilfrid's statement carried instant conviction. A Babel-like chorus of startled exclamation arose, amid which the scientist sat mutely enjoying the first fruit of his stupendous discovery.

In the midst of the clamour Tobermory entered the room and made his way with velvet tread and studied unconcern across to the group seated round the tea-table.

A sudden hush of awkwardness and constraint fell on the company. Somehow there seemed an element of embarrassment in addressing on equal terms a domestic cat of acknowledged dental ability.

"Will you have some milk, Tobermory?" asked Lady Blemley in a rather strained voice.

"I don't mind if I do," was the response, couched in a tone of even indifference. A shiver of suppressed excitement went through the listeners, and Lady Blemley might be excused for pouring out the saucerful of milk rather unsteadily.

"I'm afraid I've spilt a good deal of it," she said apologetically.

"After all, it's not my Axminster," was Tobermory's rejoinder.

Another silence fell on the group, and then Miss Resker, in her best district-visitor manner, asked if the human language had been difficult to learn. Tobermory looked squarely at her for a moment and then fixed his gaze serenely on the middle distance. It was obvious that boring questions lay outside his scheme of life.

"What do you think of human intelligence?" asked Mavis Pellington lamely.

"Of whose intelligence in particular?" asked Tobermory coldly.

"Oh, well, mine for instance," said Mavis, with a feeble laugh.

"You put me in an embarrassing position," said Tobermory, whose tone and attitude certainly did not suggest a shred of embarrassment. "When your inclusion in this house-party was suggested Sir Wilfrid protested that you were the most brainless woman of his acquaintance, and that there was a wide distinction between hospitality and the care of the feeble-minded. Lady Blemley replied that your lack of brain-power was the precise quality which had earned you your invitation, as you were the only person she could think of who might be idiotic enough to buy their old car. You know, the one they call 'The Envy of Sisyphus,' because it goes quite nicely up-hill if you push it."

Lady Blemley's protestations would have had greater effect if she had not casually suggested to Mavis only that morning that the car in question would be just the thing for her down at her Devonshire home.

Major Barfield plunged in heavily to effect a diversion.

"How about your carryings-on with the tortoise-shell puss up at the stables, eh?"

The moment he had said it every one realized the blunder.

"One does not usually discuss these matters in public," said Tobermory frigidly. "From a slight observation of your ways since you've been in this house I should imagine you'd find it inconvenient if I were to shift the conversation on to your own little affairs."

The panic which ensued was not confined to the Major.

"Would you like to go and see if cook has got your dinner ready?" suggested Lady Blemley hurriedly, affecting to ignore the fact that it wanted at least two hours to Tobermory's dinner-time.

"Thanks," said Tobermory, "not quite so soon after my tea. I don't want to die of indigestion."

"Cats have nine lives, you know," said Sir Wilfrid heartily.

"Possibly," answered Tobermory, "but only one liver."

"Adelaide!" said Mrs. Cornett, "do you mean to encourage that cat to go out and gossip about us in the servants' hall?"

The panic had indeed become general. A narrow ornamental balustrade ran in front of most of the bedroom windows at the Towers, and it was recalled with dismay that this had formed a favourite promenade for Tobermory at all hours, whence he could watch the pigeons—and heaven knew what else besides. If he intended to become reminiscent in his present outspoken strain the effect would be something more than disconcerting. Mrs. Cornett, who spent much time at her toilet table, and whose complexion was reputed to be of a nomadic though punctual disposition, looked as ill at ease as the Major. Miss Scrawen, who wrote fiercely sensuous poetry and led a blameless life, merely displayed irritation; if you are methodical and virtuous in private you don't necessarily want every one to know it. Bertie van Tahn, who was so depraved at seventeen that he had long ago given up trying to be any worse, turned a dull shade of gardenia white, but he did not commit the error of dashing out of the room like Odo Finsberry, a young gentleman who was understood to be reading for the Church and who was possibly disturbed at the thought of scandals he might hear concerning other people. Clovis had the presence of mind to maintain a composed exterior; privately he was calculating how long it would take to procure a box of fancy mice through the agency of the *Exchange and Mart* as a species of hush-money.

Even in a delicate situation like the present, Agnes Resker could not endure to remain too long in the background.

"Why did I ever come down here?" she asked dramatically.

Tobermory immediately accepted the opening.

"Judging by what you said to Mrs. Cornett on the croquet-lawn yesterday, you were out for food. You described the Blemleys as the dullest people to stay with that you knew, but said they were clever enough to employ a first-rate cook; otherwise they'd find it difficult to get any one to come down a second time."

"There's not a word of truth in it! I appeal to Mrs. Cornett—" exclaimed the discomfited Agnes.

"Mrs. Cornett repeated your remark afterwards to Bertie van Tahn," continued Tobermory, "and said, 'That woman is a regular Hunger Marcher; she'd go anywhere for four square meals a day,' and Bertie van Tahn said—"

At this point the chronicle mercifully ceased. Tobermory had caught a glimpse of the big yellow Tom from the Rectory working his way through the shrubbery towards the stable wing. In a flash he had vanished through the open French window.

With the disappearance of his too brilliant pupil Cornelius Appin found himself beset by a hurricane of bitter upbraiding, anxious inquiry, and frightened entreaty. The responsibility for the situation lay with him, and he must prevent matters from becoming worse. Could Tobermory impart his dangerous gift to other cats? was the first question he had to answer. It was possible, he replied, that he might have initiated his intimate friend the stable puss into his new accomplishment, but it was unlikely that his teaching could have taken a wider range as yet.

"Then," said Mrs. Cornett, "Tobermory may be a valuable cat and a great pet; but I'm sure you'll agree, Adelaide, that both he and the stable cat must be done away with without delay."

"You don't suppose I've enjoyed the last quarter of an hour, do you?" said Lady Blemley bitterly. "My husband and I are very fond of Tobermory—at least, we were before this horrible accomplishment was infused into him; but now, of course, the only thing is to have him destroyed as soon as possible."

"We can put some strychnine in the scraps he always gets at dinner-time," said Sir Wilfrid, "and I will go and drown the stable cat myself. The coachman will be very sore at losing his pet, but I'll say a very catching form of mange has broken out in both cats and we're afraid of its spreading to the kennels."

"But my great discovery!" expostulated Mr. Appin; "after all my years of research and experiment—"

"You can go and experiment on the short-horns at the farm, who are under proper control," said Mrs. Cornett, "or the elephants at the Zoological Gardens. They're said to be highly intelligent, and they have this recommendation, that they don't come creeping about our bedrooms and under chairs, and so forth."

An archangel ecstatically proclaiming the Millennium, and then finding that it clashed unpardonably with Henley and would have to be indefinitely postponed, could hardly have felt more crestfallen than Cornelius Appin at the reception of his wonderful achievement. Public opinion, however, was against him—in fact, had the general voice been consulted on the subject it is probable that a strong minority vote would have been in favour of including him in the strychnine diet.

Defective train arrangements and a nervous desire to see matters brought to a finish prevented an immediate dispersal of the party, but dinner that evening was not a social success. Sir Wilfrid had had rather a trying time with the stable cat and subsequently with the coachman. Agnes Resker ostentatiously limited her repast to a morsel of dry toast, which she bit as though it were a personal enemy; while Mavis Pellington maintained a vindictive silence throughout the meal. Lady Blemley kept up a flow of what she hoped was conversation, but her attention was fixed on the doorway. A plateful of carefully dosed fish scraps was in readiness on the sideboard, but sweets and savoury and dessert went their way, and no Tobermory appeared either in the dining-room or kitchen.

The sepulchral dinner was cheerful compared with the subsequent vigil in the smoking-room. Eating and drinking had at least supplied a distraction and cloak to the prevailing embarrassment. Bridge was out of the question in the general tension of nerves and tempers, and after Odo Finsberry had given a lugubrious rendering of "Mélisande in the Wood" to a frigid audience, music was tacitly avoided. At eleven the servants went to bed, announcing that the small window in the pantry

had been left open as usual for Tobermory's private use. The
guests read steadily through the current batch of magazines,
and fell back gradually on the "Badminton Library" and bound
volumes of Punch. Lady Blemley made periodic visits to the
pantry, returning each time with an expression of listless
depression which forestalled questioning.

At two o'clock Clovis broke the dominating silence.

"He won't turn up tonight. He's probably in the local newspaper office at the present moment, dictating the first install-
ment of his reminiscences. Lady What's-her-name's book won't
be in it. It will be the event of the day."

Having made this contribution to the general cheerfulness,
Clovis went to bed. At long intervals the various members of
the house-party followed his example.

The servants taking round the early tea made a uniform
announcement in reply to a uniform question. Tobermory had
not returned.

Breakfast was, if anything, a more unpleasant function than
dinner had been, but before its conclusion the situation was
relieved. Tobermory's corpse was brought in from the shrubbery, where a gardener had just discovered it. From the bites
on his throat and the yellow fur which coated his claws it was
evident that he had fallen in unequal combat with the big Tom
from the Rectory.

By midday most of the guests had quitted the Towers, and
after lunch Lady Blemley had sufficiently recovered her spirits
to write an extremely nasty letter to the Rectory about the loss
of her valuable pet.

Tobermory had been Appin's one successful pupil, and he
was destined to have no successor. A few weeks later an elephant in the Dresden Zoological Garden, which had shown no
previous signs of irritability, broke loose and killed an
Englishman who had apparently been teasing it. The victim's
name was variously reported in the papers as Oppin and
Eppelin, but his front name was faithfully rendered Cornelius.

"If he was trying German irregular verbs on the poor beast,"
said Clovis, "he deserved all he got."

Death of a Pig

by
E.B. WHITE
(1899–1985)

"Death of a Pig" is the second in a pair of stories involving animal deaths, but unlike poor Tobermory, E.B. White's pig is incapable of human speech. This is probably just as well, for White probes the pig's consciousness in ways that a speaking pig would probably not allow, especially at this particularly critical point in its too-brief existence.

I love reading this story simply for the way that White develops the strange sympathy between man and pig. It is hard to imagine a more unlikely pair. What makes the story such a challenge to read aloud is deciding where to lay the emphasis. A little shift in tone and the meaning alters drastically. I like trying to touch all the bases: to give a sense of White's essential quirkiness, his humour and his warmth.

I spent several days and nights in mid-September with an ailing pig and I feel driven to account for this stretch of time, more particularly since the pig died at last, and I lived, and things might easily have gone the other way round and none left to do the accounting. Even now, so close to the event, I cannot recall the hours sharply and am not ready to say whether death came on the third night or the fourth night. This uncertainty afflicts me with a sense of personal deterioration; if I were in decent health I would know how many nights I had sat up with a pig. The scheme of buying a spring pig in blossomtime, feeding it through summer and fall, and butchering it when the solid cold weather arrives, is a familiar scheme to me and follows an antique pattern. It is a tragedy enacted on most farms with perfect fidelity to the original script. The murder, being pre-meditated, is in the first degree but is quick and skillful, and the smoked bacon and ham provide a ceremonial ending whose fitness is seldom questioned.

Once in a while something slips—one of the actors goes up in his lines and the whole performance stumbles and halts. My pig simply failed to show up for a meal. The alarm spread rapidly. The classic outline of the tragedy was lost. I found myself cast suddenly in the role of pig's friend and physician— a farcical character with an enema bag for a prop. I had a presentiment, the very first afternoon, that the play would never regain its balance and that my sympathies were now wholly with the pig. This was slapstick—the sort of dramatic treatment that instantly appealed to my old dachshund, Fred, who joined the vigil, held the bag, and when all was over, presided at the interment. When we slid the body into the grave, we both were shaken to the core. The loss we felt was not the loss of ham but the loss of pig. He had evidently become precious to me, not that he represented a distant nourishment in a hungry time, but that he had suffered in a suffering world. But I'm running ahead of my story and shall have to go back.

My pigpen is at the bottom of an old orchard below the house. The pigs I have raised have lived in a faded building that once was an icehouse. There is a pleasant yard to move about in, shaded by an apple tree that overhangs the low rail fence. A pig couldn't ask for anything better—or none has, at any rate. The sawdust in the icehouse makes a comfortable bottom in which to root, and a warm bed. This sawdust, however, came under suspicion when the pig took sick. One of my neighbors said he thought the pig would have done better on new ground—the same principle that applies in planting potatoes. He said there might be something unhealthy about that sawdust, that he never thought well of sawdust.

It was about four o'clock in the afternoon when I first noticed that there was something wrong with the pig. He failed to appear at the trough for his supper, and when a pig (or a child) refuses supper a chill wave of fear runs through any household, or ice-household. After examining my pig, who was stretched out in the sawdust inside the building, I went to the phone and cranked it four times. Mr. Dameron answered. "What's good for a sick pig?" I asked. (There is never any identification needed on a country phone; the person on the other end knows who is talking by the sound of the voice and by the character of the question.)

"I don't know, I never had a sick pig," said Mr. Dameron,

"but I can find out quick enough. You hang up and I'll call Henry."

Mr. Dameron was back on the line again in five minutes. "Henry says roll him over on his back and give him two ounces of castor oil or sweet oil, and if that doesn't do the trick give him an injection of soapy water. He says he's almost sure the pig's plugged up, and even if he's wrong, it can't do any harm."

I thanked Mr. Dameron. I didn't go right down to the pig, though. I sank into a chair and sat still for a few minutes to think about my troubles, and then I got up and went to the barn, catching up on some odds and ends that needed tending to. Unconsciously I held off, for an hour, the deed by which I would officially recognize the collapse of the performance of raising a pig; I wanted no interruption in the regularity of feeding, the steadiness of growth, the even succession of days. I wanted no interruption, wanted no oil, no deviation. I just wanted to keep on raising a pig, full meal after full meal, spring into summer into fall. I didn't even know whether there were two ounces of castor oil on the place.

Shortly after five o'clock I remembered that we had been invited out to dinner that night and realized that if I were to dose a pig there was no time to lose. The dinner date seemed a familiar conflict: I move in a desultory society and often a week or two will roll by without my going to anybody's house to dinner or anyone's coming to mine, but when an occasion does arise, and I am summoned, something usually turns up (an hour or two in advance) to make all human intercourse seem vastly inappropriate. I have come to believe that there is in hostesses a special power of divination, and that they deliberately arrange dinners to coincide with pig failure or some other sort of failure. At any rate, it was after five o'clock and I knew I could put off no longer the evil hour.

When my son and I arrived at the pigyard, armed with a small bottle of castor oil and a length of clothesline, the pig had emerged from his house and was standing in the middle of his yard, listlessly. He gave us a slim greeting. I could see that he felt uncomfortable and uncertain. I had brought the

clothesline thinking I'd have to tie him (the pig weighed more
than a hundred pounds) but we never used it. My son reached
down, grabbed both front legs, upset him quickly, and when
he opened his mouth to scream I turned the oil into his
throat—a pink, corrugated area I had never seen before. I had
just time to read the label while the neck of the bottle was in
his mouth. It said Puretest. The screams, slightly muffled by
oil, were pitched in the hysterically high range of pig-sound,
as though torture were being carried out, but they didn't last
long: it was all over rather suddenly, and, his legs released, the
pig righted himself.

In the upset position the corners of his mouth had been
turned down, giving him a frowning expression. Back on his
feet again, he regained the set smile that a pig wears even in
sickness. He stood his ground, sucking slightly at the residue
of oil; a few drops leaked out of his lips while his wicked eyes,
shaded by their coy little lashes, turned on me in disgust and
hatred. I scratched him gently with oily fingers and he
remained quiet, as though trying to recall the satisfaction of
being scratched when in health, and seeming to rehearse in his
mind the indignity to which he had just been subjected. I
noticed, as I stood there, four or five small dark spots on his
back near the tail end, reddish brown in color, each about the
size of a housefly. I could not make out what they were. They
did not look troublesome but at the same time they did not
look like mere surface bruises or chafe marks. Rather they
seemed blemishes of internal origin. His stiff white bristles
almost completely hid them and I had to part the bristles with
my fingers to get a good look.

Several hours later, a few minutes before midnight, having
dined well and at someone else's expense, I returned to the
pighouse with a flashlight. The patient was asleep. Kneeling, I
felt his ears (as you might put your hand on the forehead of a
child) and they seemed cool, and then with the light made a
careful examination of the yard and the house for sign that the
oil had worked. I found none and went to bed.

We had been having an unseasonable spell of weather—hot,
close days, with the fog shutting in every night, scaling for a

few hours in midday, then creeping back again at dark, drifting in first over the trees on the point, then suddenly blowing
across the fields, blotting out the world and taking possession
of houses, men, and animals. Everyone kept hoping for a
break, but the break failed to come. Next day was another hot
one. I visited the pig before breakfast and tried to tempt him
with a little milk in his trough. He just stared at it, while I
made a sucking sound through my teeth to remind him of past
pleasures of the feast. With very small, timid pigs, weanlings,
this ruse is often quite successful and will encourage them to
eat; but with a large, sick pig the ruse is senseless and the
sound I made must have made him feel, if anything, more
miserable. He not only did not crave food, he felt a positive
revulsion to it. I found a place under the apple tree where he
had vomited in the night.

At this point, although a depression had settled over me, I
didn't suppose that I was going to lose my pig. From the lusti-
ness of a healthy pig a man derives a feeling of personal lusti-
ness; the stuff that goes into the trough and is received with
such enthusiasm is an earnest of some later feast of his own,
and when this suddenly comes to an end and the food lies
stale and untouched, souring in the sun, the pig's imbalance
becomes the man's vicariously, and life seems insecure, displaced, transitory.

As my own spirits declined, along with the pig's, the spirits of
my vile old dachshund rose. The frequency of our trips down
the footpath through the orchard to the pigyard delighted him,
although he suffers greatly from arthritis, moves with difficul-
ty, and would be bedridden if he could find anyone willing to
serve him meals on a tray.

He never missed a chance to visit the pig with me, and he
made many professional calls on his own. You could see him
down there at all hours, his white face parting the grass along
the fence as he wobbled and stumbled about, his stethoscope
dangling—a happy quack, writing his villainous prescriptions
and grinning his corrosive grin. When the enema bag
appeared, and the bucket of warm suds, his happiness was

complete, and he managed to squeeze his enormous body between the two lowest rails of the yard and then assumed full charge of the irrigation. Once, when I lowered the bag to check the flow, he reached in and hurriedly drank a few mouthfuls of the suds to test their potency. I have noticed that Fred will feverishly consume any substance that is associated with trouble—the bitter flavor is to his liking. When the bag was above reach, he concentrated on the pig and was everywhere at once, a tower of strength and inconvenience. The pig, curiously enough, stood rather quietly through this colonic carnival, and the enema, though ineffective, was not as difficult as I had anticipated.

I discovered, though, that once having given a pig an enema there is no turning back, no chance of resuming one of life's more stereotyped roles. The pig's lot and mine were inextricably bound now, as though the rubber tube were the silver cord. From then until the time of his death I held the pig steadily in the bowl of my mind; the task of trying to deliver him from his misery became a strong obsession. His suffering soon became the embodiment of all earthly wretchedness. Along toward the end of the afternoon, defeated in physicking, I phoned the veterinary twenty miles away and placed the case formally in his hands. He was full of questions, and when I casually mentioned the dark spots on the pig's back, his voice changed its tone.

"I don't want to scare you," he said, "but when there are spots, erysipelas has to be considered."

Together we considered erysipelas, with frequent interruptions from the telephone operator, who wasn't sure the connection had been established.

"If a pig has erysipelas can he give it to a person?" I asked.

"Yes, he can," replied the vet.

"Have they answered?" asked the operator.

"Yes, they have," I said. Then I addressed the vet again. "You better come over here and examine this pig right away."

"I can't come myself," said the vet, "but McFarland can come this evening if that's all right. Mac knows more about pigs than I do anyway. You needn't worry too much about the spots. To indicate erysipelas they would have to be deep hemorrhagic infarcts."

"Deep hemorrhagic what?" I asked.

"Infarcts," said the vet.

"Have they answered?" asked the operator.

"Well," I said, "I don't know what you'd call these spots, except they're about the size of a housefly. If the pig has erysipelas I guess I have it, too, by this time, because we've been very close lately."

"McFarland will be over," said the vet.

I hung up. My throat felt dry and I went to the cupboard and got a bottle of whiskey. Deep hemorrhagic infarcts—the phrase began fastening its hooks in my head. I had assumed that there could be nothing much wrong with a pig during the months it was being groomed for murder; my confidence in the essential health and endurance of pigs had been strong and deep, particularly in the health of pigs that belonged to me and that were part of my proud scheme. The awakening had been violent and I minded it all the more because I knew that what could be true of my pig could be true also of the rest of my tidy world. I tried to put this distasteful idea from me, but it kept recurring. I took a short drink of the whiskey and then, although I wanted to go down to the yard and look for fresh signs, I was scared to. I was certain I had erysipelas.

It was long after dark and the supper dishes had been put away when a car drove in and McFarland got out. He had a girl with him. I could just make her out in the darkness—she seemed young and pretty. "This is Miss Owen," he said. "We've been having a picnic supper on the shore, that's why I'm late."

McFarland stood in the driveway and stripped off his jacket, then his shirt. His stocky arms and capable hands showed up in my flashlight's gleam as I helped him find his coverall and get zipped up. The rear seat of his car contained an astonishing amount of paraphernalia, which he soon overhauled, selecting a chain, a syringe, a bottle of oil, a rubber tube, and some other things I couldn't identify. Miss Owen said she'd go along with us and see the pig. I led the way down the warm slope of the orchard, my light picking out the path for them, and we all three climbed the fence, entered the pighouse, and squatted by the pig while McFarland took a rectal reading. My flashlight picked up the glitter of an engagement ring on the girl's hand.

"No elevation," said McFarland, twisting the thermometer in the light. "You needn't worry about erysipelas." He ran his hand slowly over the pig's stomach and at one point the pig cried out in pain.

"Poor piggledy-wiggledy!" said Miss Owen.

The treatment I had been giving the pig for two days was then repeated, somewhat more expertly, by the doctor, Miss Owen and I handing him things as he needed them—holding the chain that he had looped around the pig's upper jaw, holding the syringe, holding the bottle stopper, the end of the tube, all of us working in darkness and in comfort, working with the instinctive teamwork induced by emergency conditions, the pig unprotesting, the house shadowy, protecting, intimate. I went to bed tired but with a feeling of relief that I had turned over part of the responsibility of the case to a licensed doctor. I was beginning to think, though, that the pig was not going to live.

He died twenty-four hours later, or it might have been forty-eight—there is a blur in time here, and I may have lost or picked up a day in the telling and the pig one in the dying. At intervals during the last day I took cool fresh water down to him and at such times as he found the strength to get to his feet he would stand with head in the pail and snuffle his snout around. He drank a few sips but no more; yet it seemed to comfort him to dip his nose in water and bobble it about, sucking in and blowing out through his teeth. Much of the time, now, he lay indoors half buried in sawdust. Once, near the last, while I was attending him I saw him try to make a bed for himself but he lacked the strength, and when he set his snout into the dust he was unable to plow even the little furrow he needed to lie down in.

He came out of the house to die. When I went down, before going to bed, he lay stretched in the yard a few feet from the door. I knelt, saw that he was dead, and left him there: his face

had a mild look, expressive neither of deep peace nor of deep
suffering, although I think he had suffered a good deal. I went
back up to the house and to bed, and cried internally—deep
hemorrhagic intears. I didn't wake till nearly eight the next
morning, and when I looked out the open window the grave
was already being dug, down beyond the dump under a wild
apple. I could hear the spade strike against the small rocks
that blocked the way. Never send to know for whom the grave
is dug, I said to myself, it's dug for thee. Fred, I well knew, was
supervising the work of digging, so I ate breakfast slowly.

It was a Saturday morning. The thicket in which I found the
gravediggers at work was dark and warm, the sky overcast.
Here, among alders and young hackmatacks, at the foot of the
apple tree, Lennie had dug a beautiful hole, five feet long,
three feet wide, three feet deep. He was standing in it, remov-
ing the last spadefuls of earth while Fred patrolled the brink in
simple but impressive circles, disturbing the loose earth of the
mound so that it trickled back in. There had been no rain in
weeks and the soil, even three feet down, was dry and pow-
dery. As I stood and stared, an enormous earthworm which
had been partially exposed by the spade at the bottom dug
itself deeper and made a slow withdrawal, seeking even remoter moistures at even lonelier depths. And just as Lennie
stepped out and rested his spade against the tree and lit a cigarette, a small green apple separated itself from a branch overhead and fell into the hole. Everything about this last scene
seemed overwritten—the dismal sky, the shabby woods, the
imminence of rain, the worm (legendary bedfellow of the
dead), the apple (conventional garnish of a pig).

But even so, there was a directness and dispatch about animal burial, I thought, that made it a more decent affair than
human burial: there was no stopover in the undertaker's foul
parlor, no wreath nor spray; and when we hitched a line to the
pig's hind legs and dragged him swiftly from his yard, throwing our weight into the harness and leaving a wake of crushed
grass and smoothed rubble over the dump, ours was a busi-
nesslike procession, with Fred, the dishonorable pallbearer,
staggering along in the rear, his perverse bereavement showing

in every seam in his face; and the post-mortem performed handily and swiftly right at the edge of the grave, so that the inwards that had caused the pig's death preceded him into the ground and he lay at last resting squarely on the cause of his own undoing.

I threw in the first shovelful, and then we worked rapidly and without talk, until the job was complete. I picked up the rope, made it fast to Fred's collar (he is a notorious ghoul), and we all three filed back up the path to the house, Fred bringing up the rear and holding back every inch of the way, feigning unusual stiffness. I noticed that although he weighed far less than the pig, he was harder to drag, being possessed of the vital spark.

The news of the death of my pig traveled fast and far, and I received many expressions of sympathy from friends and neighbors, for no one took the event lightly and the premature expiration of a pig is, I soon discovered, a departure which the community marks solemnly on its calendar, a sorrow in which it feels fully involved. I have written this account in penitence and in grief, as a man who failed to raise his pig, and to explain my deviation from the classic course of so many raised pigs. The grave in the woods is unmarked, but Fred can direct the mourner to it unerringly and with immense good will, and I know he and I shall often revisit it, singly and together, in seasons of reflection and despair, on flagless memorial days of our own choosing.

Meneseteung

by
ALICE MUNRO
(1931–)

There are a few stories that I really like, but which are a little
too complicated to read on radio. "Meneseteung" is one of
these, and I am happy to have the chance to include it here.
Subtle and shifting, Munro's story explores a woman's situation in a Canadian setting of the last century. What I really
like about this story is the way Munro manages to combine the
personal story, Meda's poetry and newspaper accounts to tell
a tale that has many sides. What Munro is trying to say, I
think, is that reality is always more complicated than the history books tell us, and "Meneseteung" is a story far richer and
more personally developed than more conventional histories
would allow. In "Meneseteung," Munro has given us a history
that we very rarely hear.

65

I

Columbine, bloodroot,
And wild bergamot,
Gathering armfuls,
Giddily we go.

Offerings the book is called. Gold lettering on a dull-blue cover. The author's full name underneath: Almeda Joynt Roth. The local paper, the *Vidette*, referred to her as "our poetess." There seems to be a mixture of respect and contempt, both for her calling and for her sex—or for their predictable conjuncture. In the front of the book is a photograph, with the photographer's name in one corner, and the date: 1865. The book was published later, in 1873.

The poetess had a long face; a rather long nose; full, sombre dark eyes, which seem ready to roll down her cheeks like giant tears; a lot of dark hair gathered around her face in droopy rolls and curtains. A streak of grey hair plain to see, although she is, in this picture, only twenty-five. Not a pretty girl but the sort of woman who may age well, who probably won't get fat. She wears a tucked and braid-trimmed dark dress or jacket, with a lacy, floppy arrangement of white material—frills or a bow—filling the deep V at the neck. She also wears a hat, which might be made of velvet, in a dark color to match the dress. It's the untrimmed, shapeless hat, something like a soft beret, that makes me see artistic intentions, or at least a shy and stubborn eccentricity, in this young woman, whose long neck and forward-inclining head indicate as well that she is tall and slender and somewhat awkward. From the waist up, she looks like a young nobleman of another century. But perhaps it was the fashion.

"In 1854," she writes in the preface to her book, "my father brought us—my mother, my sister Catherine, my brother William, and me—to the wilds of Canada West (as it then was). My father was a harness-maker by trade, but a cultivated man who could quote by heart from the Bible, Shakespeare, and the writings of Edmund Burke. He prospered in this newly opened land and was able to set up a harness and leather-goods store, and after a year to build the comfortable house in which I live (alone) today. I was fourteen years old, the eldest of the children, when we came into this country from Kingston, a town whose handsome streets I have not seen again but often remember. My sister was eleven and my brother nine. The third summer that we lived here, my brother and sister were taken ill of a prevalent fever and died within a few days of each other. My dear mother did not regain her spirits after this blow to our family. Her health declined, and after another three years she died. I then became housekeeper to my father and was happy to make his home for twelve years, until he died suddenly one morning at his shop.

"From my earliest years I have delighted in verse and I have occupied myself—and sometimes allayed my griefs, which have been no more, I know, than any sojourner on earth must encounter—with many floundering efforts at its composition. My fingers, indeed, were always too clumsy for crochetwork, and those dazzling productions of embroidery which one sees often today—the overflowing fruit and flower baskets, the little Dutch boys, the bonneted maidens with their watering cans—have likewise proved to be beyond my skill. So I offer instead, as the product of my leisure hours, these rude posies, these ballads, couplets, reflections."

Titles of some of the poems: "Children at Their Games," "The Gypsy Fair," "A Visit to My Family," "Angels in the Snow," "Champlain at the Mouth of the Meneseteung," "The Passing of the Old Forest," and "A Garden Medley." There are other, shorter poems, about birds and wildflowers and snowstorms. There is some comically intentioned doggerel about what people are thinking about as they listen to the sermon in church.

"Children at Their Games": The writer, a child, is playing with her brother and sister—one of those games in which children on different sides try to entice and catch each other. She plays on in the deepening twilight, until she realizes that she is alone, and much older. Still she hears the (ghostly) voices of her brother and sister calling. *Come over, come over, let Meda come over.* (Perhaps Almeda was called Meda in the family, or perhaps she shortened her name to fit the poem.)

"The Gypsy Fair": The Gypsies have an encampment near the town, a "fair," where they sell cloth and trinkets, and the writer as a child is afraid that she may be stolen by them, taken away from her family. Instead, her family has been taken away from her, stolen by Gypsies she can't locate or bargain with.

"A Visit to My Family": A visit to the cemetery, a one-sided conversation.

"Angels in the Snow": The writer once taught her brother and sister to make "angels" by lying down in the snow and moving their arms to create wing shapes. Her brother always jumped up carelessly, leaving an angel with a crippled wing. Will this be made perfect in Heaven, or will he be flying with his own makeshift, in circles?

"Champlain at the Mouth of the Meneseteung": This poem celebrates the popular, untrue belief that the explorer sailed down the eastern shore of Lake Huron and landed at the mouth of the major river.

"The Passing of the Old Forest": A list of all the trees—their names, appearance, and uses—that were cut down in the original forest, with a general description of the bears, wolves, eagles, deer, waterfowl.

"A Garden Medley": Perhaps planned as a companion to the forest poem. Catalogue of plants brought from European countries, with bits of history and legend attached, and final Canadianness resulting from this mixture.

The poems are written in quatrains or couplets. There are a couple of attempts at sonnets, but mostly the rhyme scheme is simple—*a b a b* or *a b c b*. The rhyme used is what was once called "masculine" ("shore"/"before"), though once in a while it is "feminine" ("quiver"/"river"). Are those terms familiar anymore? No poem is unrhymed.

II

White roses cold as snow
Bloom where those "'angels" lie.
Do they but rest below
Or, in God's wonder, fly?

In 1879, Almeda Roth was still living in the house at the corner of Pearl and Dufferin streets, the house her father had built for his family. The house is there today; the manager of the liquor store lives in it. It's covered with aluminium siding; a closed-in porch has replaced the veranda. The woodshed, the fence, the gates, the privy, the barn—all these are gone. A photograph taken in the eighteen-eighties shows them all in place. The house and fence look a little shabby, in need of paint, but perhaps that is just because of the bleached-out look of the brownish photograph. The lace-curtained windows look like white eyes. No big shade tree is in sight, and, in fact, the tall elms that overshadowed the town until the nineteen-fifties, as well as the maples that shade it now, are skinny young trees with rough fences around them to protect them from the cows. Without the shelter of those trees, there is a great exposure—back yards, clotheslines, woodpiles, patchy shed and barns and privies—all bare, exposed, provisional-looking. Few houses would have anything like a lawn, just a patch of plantains and anthills and raked dirt. Perhaps petunias growing on top of a stump, in a round box. Only the main street is gravelled; the other streets are dirt roads, muddy or dusty according to season. Yards must be fenced to keep animals out. Cows are tethered in vacant lots or pastured in back yards, but sometimes they get loose. Pigs get loose, too, and dogs roam free or nap in a lordly way on the boardwalks. The town has

taken root, it's not going to vanish, yet it still has some of the
look of an encampment. And, like a encampment, it's busy all
the time—full of people, who, within the town, usually walk
wherever they're going; full of animals, which leave horse
buns, cow pats, dog turds that ladies have to hitch up their
skirts for; full of the noise of building and of drivers shouting
at their horses and of the trains that come in several times a
day.

I read about that life in the *Vidette*.

The population is younger than it is now, than it will ever
be again. People past fifty usually don't come to a raw, new
place. There are quite a few people in the cemetery already,
but most of them died young, in accidents or childbirth or
epidemics. It's youth that's in evidence in town. Children—
boys—rove through the streets in gangs. School is compulsory
for only four months a year, and there are lots of occasional
jobs that even a child of eight or nine can do—pulling flax,
holding horses, delivering groceries, sweeping the boardwalk
in front of stores. A good deal of time they spend looking for
adventures. One day they follow an old woman, a drunk nick-
named Queen Aggie. They get her into a wheelbarrow and
trundle her all over town, then dump her into a ditch to sober
her up. They also spend a lot of time around the railway station. They jump on shunting cars and dart between them and
dare each other to take chances, which once in a while result
in their getting maimed or killed. And they keep an eye out for
any strangers coming into town. They follow them, offer to
carry their bags, and direct them (for a five-cent piece) to a
hotel. Strangers who don't look so prosperous are taunted and
tormented. Speculation surrounds all of them—it's like a cloud
of flies. Are they coming to town to start up a new business, to
persuade people to invest in some scheme, to sell cures or
gimmicks, to preach on the street corners? All these things are
possible any day of the week. Be on your guard, the *Vidette*
tells people. These are times of opportunity and danger.
Tramps, confidence men, hucksters, shysters, plain thieves are
travelling the roads, and particularly the railroads. Thefts are
announced: money invested and never seen again, a pair of

trousers taken from the clothesline, wood from the woodpile, eggs from the henhouse. Such incidents increase in the hot weather.

Hot weather brings accidents, too. More horses run wild then, upsetting buggies. Hands caught in the wringer while doing the washing, a man lopped in two at the sawmill, a leaping boy killed in a fall of lumber at the lumberyard. Nobody sleeps well. Babies wither with summer complaint, and fat people can't catch their breath. Bodies must be buried in a hurry. One day a man goes through the streets ringing a cowbell and calling, "Repent! Repent!" It's not a stranger this time, it's a young man who works at the butcher shop. Take him home, wrap him in cold wet cloths, give him some nerve medicine, keep him in bed, pray for his wits. If he doesn't recover, he must go to the asylum.

Almeda Roth's house faces on Dufferin Street, which is a street of considerable respectability. On this street, merchants, a mill owner, an operator of salt wells have their houses. But Pearl Street, which her back windows overlook and her back gate opens onto, is another story. Workmen's houses are adjacent to hers. Small but decent row houses—that is all right. Things deteriorate toward the end of the block, and the next, last one becomes dismal. Nobody but the poorest people, the unrespectable and undeserving poor, would live there at the edge of a boghole (drained since then), called the Pearl Street Swamp. Bushy and luxuriant weeds grow there, makeshift shacks have been put up, there are piles of refuse and debris and crowds of runty children, slops are flung from doorways. The town tries to compel these people to built privies, but they would just as soon go in the bushes. If a gang of boys goes down there in search of adventure, it's likely they'll get more than they bargained for. It is said that even the town constable won't go down Pearl Street on a Saturday night. Almeda Roth has never walked past the row housing. In one of those houses lives the young girl Annie, who helps her with her housecleaning. That young girl herself, being a decent girl, has never walked down to the last block or the swamp. No decent woman ever would.

But the same swamp, lying to the east of Almeda Roth's house, presents a fine sight at dawn. Almeda sleeps at the back of the house. She keeps to the same bedroom she once shared with her sister Catherine—she would not think of moving to the large front bedroom, where her mother used to lie in bed all day, and which was later the solitary domain of her father. From her window she can see the sun rising, the swamp mist filling with light, the bulky, nearest trees floating against that mist and the trees behind turning transparent. Swamp oaks, soft maples, tamarack, bitternut.

III

*Here where the river meets the
inland sea,
Spreading her blue skirts from the
solemn wood,
I think of birds and beasts and
vanished men,
Whose pointed dwellings on these
pale sands stood.*

One of the strangers who arrived at the railway station a few years ago was Jarvis Poulter, who now occupies the next house to Almeda Roth's—separated from hers by a vacant lot, which he has bought, on Dufferin Street. The house is plainer than the Roth house and has no fruit trees or flowers planted around it. It is understood that this is a natural result of Jarvis Poulter's being a widower and living alone. A man may keep his house decent, but he will never—if he is a proper man— do much to decorate it. Marriage forces him to live with more ornament as well as sentiment, and it protects him, also, from the extremities of his own nature—from a frigid parsimony or a luxuriant sloth, from squalor, and from excessive sleeping or reading, drinking, smoking, or freethinking.

In the interests of economy, it is believed, a certain estimable gen-tleman of our town persists in fetching water from the public tap and supplementing his fuel supply by picking up the loose coal

along the railway track. Does he think to repay the town or the
railway company with a supply of free salt?

This is the *Vidette,* full of shy jokes, innuendo, plain accusa-
tion that no newspaper would get away with today. It's Jarvis
Poulter they're talking about—though in other passages he is
spoken of with great respect, as a civil magistrate, an employ-
er, a churchman. He is close, that's all. An eccentric, to a
degree. All of which may be a result of his single condition, his
widower's life. Even carrying his water from the town tap and
filling his coal pail along the railway track. This is a decent cit-
izen, prosperous: a tall—slightly paunchy?—man in a dark
suit with polished boots. A beard? Black hair streaked with
gray. A severe and self-possessed air, and a large pale wart
among the bushy hairs of one eyebrow? People talk about a
young, pretty, beloved wife, dead in childbirth or some horrible accident, like a house fire or a railway disaster. There is no
ground for this, but it adds interest. All he has told them is
that his wife is dead.

He came to this part of the country looking for oil. The first
oil well in the world was sunk in Lambton County, south of
here, in the eighteen-fifties. Drilling for oil, Jarvis Poulter discovered salt. He set to work to make the most of that. When
he walks home from church with Almeda Roth, he tells her
about his salt wells. They are twelve hundred feet deep.
Heated water is pumped down into them, and that dissolves
the salt. Then the brine is pumped to the surface. It is poured
into great evaporator pans over slow, steady fires, so that the
water is steamed off and the pure, excellent salt remains. A
commodity for which the demand will never fail.

"The salt of the earth," Almeda says.

"Yes," he says, frowning. He may think this disrespectful.
She did not intend it so. He speaks of competitors in other
towns who are following his lead and trying to hog the mar-
ket. Fortunately, their wells are not drilled so deep, or their
evaporating is not done so efficiently. There is salt everywhere
under this land, but it is not so easy to come by as some people think.

Does this not mean, Almeda says, that there was once a great sea?

Very likely, Jarvis Poulter says. Very likely. He goes on to tell her about other enterprises of his—a brickyard, a limekiln. And he explains to her how this operates, and where the good clay is found. He also owns two farms, whose woodlots supply the fuel for his operations.

Among the couples strolling home from church on a recent, sunny Sabbath morning we noted a certain salty gentleman and literary lady, not perhaps in their first youth but by no means blighted by the frosts of age. May we surmise?

This kind of thing pops up in the *Vidette* all the time.

May they surmise, and is this courting? Almeda Roth has a bit of money, which her father left her, and she has her house. She is not too old to have a couple of children. She is a good enough housekeeper, with the tendency toward fancy iced cakes and decorated tarts that is seen fairly often in old maids. (Honorable mention at the Fall Fair.) There is nothing wrong with her looks, and naturally she is in better shape than most married women of her age, not having been loaded down with work and children. But why was she passed over in her earlier, more marriageable years, in a place that needs women to be partnered and fruitful? She was a rather gloomy girl—that may have been the trouble. The deaths of her brother and sister, and then of her mother, who lost her reason, in fact, a year before she died, and lay in her bed talking nonsense—those weighed on her, so she was not lively company. And all that reading and poetry—it seemed more of a drawback, a barrier, an obsession, in the young girl than in the middle-aged woman, who needed something, after all, to fill her time. Anyway, it's five years since her book was published, so perhaps she has got over that. Perhaps it was the proud, bookish father encouraging her?

Everyone takes it for granted that Almeda Roth is thinking of Jarvis Poulter as a husband and would say yes if he asked her. And she is thinking of him. She doesn't want to get her hopes up too much, she doesn't want to make a fool of herself. She would like a signal. If he attended church on Sunday evening, there would be a chance, during some months of the year, to walk home after dark. He would carry a lantern. (There is yet no street lighting in town.) He would swing the lantern to light the way in front of the lady's feet and observe their narrow and delicate shape. He might catch her arm as they step off the boardwalk. But he does not go to church at night.

Nor does he call for her, and walk with her to church on Sunday mornings. That would be a declaration. He walks her home, past his gate as far as hers; he lifts his hat then and leaves her. She does not invite him to come in—a woman living alone could never do such a thing. As soon as a man and woman of almost any age are alone together within four walls, it is assumed that anything may happen. Spontaneous combustion, instant fornication, an attack of passion. Brute instinct, triumph of the senses. What possibilities men and women must see in each other to infer such dangers. Or, believing in the dangers, how often they must think about the possibilities.

When they walk side by side, she can smell his shaving soap, the barber's oil, his pipe tobacco, the wool and linen and leather smell of his manly clothes. The correct, orderly, heavy clothes are like those she used to brush and starch and iron for her father. She misses that job—her father's appreciation, his dark, kind authority. Jarvis Poulter's garments, his smell, his movements all cause the skin on the side of her body next to him to tingle hopefully, and a meek shiver raises the hairs on her arms. Is this to be taken as a sign of love? She thinks of him coming into her—*their*—bedroom in his long underwear and his hat. She knows this outfit is ridiculous, but in her mind he does not look so; he has the solemn effrontery of a figure in a dream. He comes into the room and lies down on the bed beside her, preparing to take her in his arms. Surely he removes his hat? She doesn't know, for at this point a fit of welcome and submission overtakes her, a buried gasp. He would be her husband.

One thing she has noticed about married women, and that is how many of them have to go about creating their husbands. They have to start ascribing preferences, opinions, dictatorial ways. Oh, yes, they say, my husband is very particular. He won't touch turnips. He won't eat fried meat. (Or he will only eat fried meat.) He likes me to wear blue (brown) all the time. He can't stand organ music. He hates to see a woman go out bareheaded. He would kill me if I took one puff of tobacco. This way, bewildered, sidelong-looking men are made over, made into husbands, heads of households. Almeda Roth cannot imagine herself doing that. She wants a man who doesn't have to be made, who is firm already and determined and mysterious to her. She does not look for companionship. Men—except for her father—seem to her deprived in some way, incurious. No doubt that is necessary, so that they will do what they have to do. Would she herself, knowing that there was salt in the earth, discover how to get it out and sell it? Not likely. She would be thinking about the ancient sea. That kind of speculation is what Jarvis Poulter has, quite properly, no time for.

Instead of calling for her and walking her to church, Jarvis Poulter might make another, more venturesome declaration. He could hire a horse and take her for a drive out to the country. If he did this, she would be both glad and sorry. Glad to be beside him, driven by him, receiving this attention from him in front of the world. And sorry to have the countryside removed for her—filmed over, in a way, by his talk and preoccupations. The countryside that she has written about in her poems actually takes diligence and determination to see. Some things must be disregarded. Manure piles, of course, and boggy fields full of high, charred stumps, and great heaps of brush waiting for a good day for burning. The meandering creeks have been straightened, turned into ditches with high, muddy banks. Some of the crop fields and pasture fields are fenced with big, clumsy uprooted stumps; others are held in a crude stitchery of rail fences. The trees have all been cleared back to the woodlots. And the woodlots are all second growth. No trees along the roads or lanes or around the farmhouses, except a few that are newly planted, young and weedy-look-ing. Clusters of log barns—the grand barns that are to domi-nate the countryside for the next hundred years are just begin-ning to be built—and mean-looking log houses, and every four or five miles a ragged little settlement with a church and school and store and a blacksmith shop. A raw countryside just wrenched from the forest, but swarming with people. Every hundred acres is a farm, every farm has a family, most families have ten or twelve children. (This is the country that will send out wave after wave of settlers—it's already starting to send them—to northern Ontario and the West.) It's true that you can gather wildflowers in spring in the woodlots, but you'd have to walk through herds of horned cows to get to them.

IV

The Gypsies have departed.
Their camping-ground is bare.
Oh, boldly would I bargain now
At the Gypsy Fair.

Almeda suffers a good deal from sleeplessness, and the doctor has given her bromides and nerve medicine. She takes the bro-mides, but the drops gave her dreams that were too vivid and disturbing, so she has put the bottle by for an emergency. She told the doctor her eyeballs felt dry, like hot glass, and her joints ached. Don't read so much, he said, don't study; get yourself good and tired out with housework, take exercise. He believes that her troubles would clear up if she got married. He believes this in spite of the fact that most of his nerve med-icine is prescribed for married women.

So Almeda cleans house and helps clean the church, she lends a hand to friends who are wallpapering or getting ready for a wedding, she bakes one of her famous cakes for the Sunday-school picnic. On a hot Saturday in August, she decides to make some grape jelly. Little jars of grape jelly will make fine Christmas presents, or offerings to the sick. But she started late in the day and the jelly is not made by nightfall. In fact, the hot pulp has just been dumped into the cheesecloth bag to strain out the juice. Almeda drinks some tea and eats a slice of cake with butter (a childish indulgence of hers), and that's all she wants for supper. She washes her hair at the sink and sponges off her body to be clean for Sunday. She doesn't light a lamp. She lies down on the bed with the window wide open and a sheet just up to her waist, and she does feel wonderfully tired. She can even feel a little breeze.

When she wakes up, the night seems fiery hot and full of threats. She lies sweating on her bed, and she has the impression that the noises she hears are knives and saws and axes—all angry implements chopping and jabbing and boring within her head. But it isn't true. As she comes further awake, she recognizes the sounds that she has heard sometimes before—the fracas of a summer Saturday night on Pearl Street. Usually the noise centers on a fight. People are drunk, there is a lot of protest and encouragement concerning the fight, somebody will scream, "Murder!" Once, there was a murder. But it didn't happen in a fight. An old man was stabbed to death in his shack, perhaps for a few dollars he kept in the mattress.

She gets out of bed and goes to the window. The night sky is clear, with no moon and with bright stars. Pegasus hangs straight ahead, over the swamp. Her father taught her that constellation—automatically, she counts its stars. Now she can make out distinct voices, individual contributions to the row. Some people, like herself, have evidently been wakened from sleep. "Shut up!" they are yelling. "Shut up that caterwauling or I'm going to come down and tan the arse off yez!"

But nobody shuts up. It's as if there were a ball of fire rolling up Pearl Street, shooting off sparks—only the fire is noise; it's yells and laughter and shrieks and curses, and the sparks are voices that shoot off alone. Two voices gradually distinguish themselves—a rising and falling howling cry and a steady throbbing, low-pitched stream of abuse that contains all those words which Almeda associates with danger and depravity and foul smells and disgusting sights. Someone—the person crying out, "Kill me! Kill me now!"—is being beaten. A woman is being beaten. She keeps crying, "Kill me! Kill me!" and sometimes her mouth seems choked with blood. Yet there is something taunting and triumphant about her cry. There is something theatrical about it. And the people around are calling out, "Stop it! Stop that!" or "Kill her! Kill her!" in a frenzy, as if at the theatre or a sporting match or a prizefight. Yes, thinks Almeda, she has noticed that before—it is always partly a charade with these people; there is a clumsy sort of parody, an exaggeration, a missed connection. As if anything they did—even a murder—might be something they didn't quite believe but were powerless to stop.

Now there is the sound of something thrown—a chair, a plank?—and of a woodpile or part of a fence giving way. A lot of newly surprised cries, the sound of running, people getting out of the way, and the commotion has come much closer. Almeda can see a figure in a light dress, bent over and running. That will be the woman. She has got hold of something like a stick of wood or a shingle, and she turns and flings it at the darker figure running after her.

"Ah, go get her!" the voices cry. "Go baste her one!"

Many fall back now; just the two figures come on and grapple, and break loose again, and finally fall down against Almeda's fence. The sound they make becomes very confused—gagging, vomiting, grunting, pounding. Then a long, vibrating, choking sound of pain and self-abasement, self-abandonment, which could come from either or both of them.

Almeda has backed away from the window and sat down on the bed. Is that the sound of murder she has heard? What is to be done, what is she to do? She must light a lantern, she must go downstairs. Into the yard. The lantern. She falls over on her bed and pulls the pillow to her face. In a minute. The stairs, the lantern. She sees herself already down there, in the back hall, drawing the bolt of the back door. She falls asleep.

She wakes, startled, in the early light. She thinks there is a big crow sitting on her windowsill, talking in a disapproving but unsurprised way about the events of the night before. "Wake up and move the wheelbarrow!" it says to her, scolding, and she understands that it means something else by "wheelbarrow"—something foul and sorrowful. Then she is awake and sees that there is no such bird. She gets up at once and looks out the window.

Down against her fence there is a pale lump pressed—a body.

Wheelbarrow.

She puts a wrapper over her nightdress and goes downstairs. The front rooms are still shadowy, the blinds down in the kitchen. Something goes *plop, plup*, in a leisurely, censorious way, reminding her of the conversation of the crow. It's just the grape juice, straining overnight. She pulls the bolt and goes out the back door. Spiders have draped their webs over the doorway in the night, and the hollyhocks are drooping, heavy with dew. By the fence, she parts the sickly hollyhocks and looks down and she can see.

A woman's body heaped up there, turned on her side with her face squashed down into the earth. Almeda can't see her face. But there is a bare breast let loose, brown nipple pulled long like a cow's teat, and a bare haunch and leg, the haunch showing a bruise as big as a sunflower. The unbruised skin is grayish, like a plucked, raw drumstick. Some kind of night-gown or all-purpose dress she has on. Smelling of vomit. Urine, drink, vomit.

Barefoot, in her nightgown and flimsy wrapper, Almeda runs away. She runs around the side of her house between the apple trees and the veranda; she opens the front gate and flees down Dufferin Street to Jarvis Poulter's house, which is the nearest to hers. She slaps the flat of her hand many times against the door.

"There is the body of a woman," she says when Jarvis Poulter appears at last. He is in his dark trousers, held up with braces, and his shirt is half unbuttoned, his face unshaven, his hair standing up on his head. "Mr. Poulter, excuse me. A body of a woman. At my back gate."

He looks at her fiercely. "Is she dead?"

His breath is dank, his face creased, his eyes bloodshot.

"Yes. I think murdered," says Almeda. She can see a little of his cheerless front hall. His hat on a chair. "In the night I woke up. I heard a racket down on Pearl Street," she says, struggling to keep her voice low and sensible. "I could hear this—pair. I could hear a man and a woman fighting."

He picks up his hat and puts it on his head. He closes and locks the front door, and puts the key in his pocket. They walk along the boardwalk and she sees that she is in her bare feet. She holds back what she feels a need to say next—that she is responsible, she could have run out with a lantern, she could have screamed (but who needed more screams?), she could have beat the man off. She could have run for help then, not now.

They turn down Pearl Street, instead of entering the Roth yard. Of course the body is still there. Hunched up, half bare, the same as before.

Jarvis Poulter doesn't hurry or halt. He walks straight over to the body and looks down at it, nudges the leg with the toe of his boot, just as you'd nudge a dog or a sow.

"You," he says, not too loudly but firmly, and nudges again.

Almeda tastes bile at the back of her throat.

"Alive," says Jarvis Poulter, and the woman confirms this. She stirs, she grunts weakly.

Almeda says, "I will get the doctor." If she had touched the woman, if she had forced herself to touch her, she would not have made such a mistake.

"Wait," says Jarvis Poulter. "Wait. Let's see if she can get up."

"Get up, now," he says to the woman. "Come on. Up, now. Up."

Now a startling thing happens. The body heaves itself onto all fours, the head is lifted—the hair all matted with blood and vomit—and the woman begins to bang this head, hard and rhythmically, against Almeda Roth's picket fence. As she bangs her head, she finds her voice and lets out an openmouthed yowl, full of strength and what sounds like an anguished pleasure.

"Far from dead," says Jarvis Poulter. "And I wouldn't bother the doctor."

"There's blood," says Almeda as the woman turns her smeared face.

"From her nose," he says. "Not fresh." He bends down and

catches the horrid hair close to the scalp to stop the head-banging.

"You stop that, now," he says. "Stop it. Gwan home, now. Gwan home, where you belong." The sound coming out of the woman's mouth has stopped. He shakes her head slightly, warning her, before he lets go of her hair. "Gwan home!"

Released, the woman lunges forward, pulls herself to her feet. She can walk. She weaves and stumbles down the street, making intermittent, cautious noises of protest. Jarvis Poulter watches her for a moment to make sure that she's on her way. Then he finds a large burdock leaf, on which he wipes his hand. He says, "There goes your dead body!"

The back gate being locked, they walk around to the front. The front gate stands open. Almeda still feels sick. Her abdomen is bloated; she is hot and dizzy.

"The front door is locked," she says faintly. "I came out by the kitchen." If only he would leave her, she could go straight to the privy. But he follows. He follows her as far as the back door and into the back hall. He speaks to her in a tone of harsh joviality that she has never before heard from him. "No need for alarm," he says. "It's only the consequences of drink. A lady oughtn't to be living alone so close to a bad neighborhood." He takes hold of her arm just above the elbow. She can't open her mouth to speak to him, to say thank you. If she opened her mouth, she would retch.

What Jarvis Poulter feels for Almeda Roth at this moment is just what he has not felt during all those circumspect walks and all his own solitary calculations of her probable worth, undoubted respectability, adequate comeliness. He has not been able to imagine her as a wife. Now that is possible. He is sufficiently stirred by her loosened hair—prematurely gray but thick and soft—her flushed face, her light clothing, which nobody but a husband should see. And by her indiscretion, her agitation, her foolishness, her need?

"I will call on you later," he says to her. "I will walk with you to church."

At the corner of Pearl and Dufferin streets last Sunday morning

*there was discovered, by a lady resident there, the body of a certain
woman of Pearl Street, thought to be dead but only, as it turned out,
dead drunk. She was roused from her heavenly—or otherwise—
stupor by the firm persuasion of Mr. Poulter, a neighbour and a
Civil Magistrate, who had been summoned by the lady resident.
Incidents of this sort, unseemly, troublesome, and disgraceful to our
town, have of late become all too common.*

V

*I sit at the bottom of sleep,
As on the floor of the sea.
And fanciful Citizens of the Deep
Are graciously greeting me.*

As soon as Jarvis Poulter has gone and she has heard her front
gate close, Almeda rushes to the privy. Her relief is not complete, however, and she realizes that the pain and fullness in
her lower body come from an accumulation of menstrual
blood that has not yet started to flow. She closes and locks the
back door. Then, remembering Jarvis Poulter's words about
church, she writes on a piece of paper, "I am not well, and
wish to rest today." She sticks this firmly into the outside
frame of the little window in the front door. She locks that
door, too. She is trembling, as if from a great shock or danger.
But she builds a fire, so that she can make tea. She boils water,
measures the tea leaves, makes a large pot of tea, whose steam
and smell sicken her further. She pours out a cup while the tea
is still quite weak and adds to it several dark drops of nerve
medicine. She sits to drink it without raising the kitchen
blind. There, in the middle of the floor, is the cheesecloth bag
hanging on its broom handle between the two chairbacks. The
grape pulp and juice has stained the swollen cloth a dark purple. *Plop, plup,* into the basin beneath. She can't sit and look at
such a thing. She takes her cup, the teapot, and the bottle of
medicine into the dining room.

   She is still sitting there when the horses start to go by on
the way to church, stirring up clouds of dust. The roads will
be getting hot as ashes. She is there when the gate is opened

and a man's confident steps sound on her veranda. Her hearing is so sharp she seems to hear the paper taken out of the frame and unfolded—she can almost hear him reading it, hear the words in his mind. Then the footsteps go the other way, down the steps. The gate closes. An image comes to her of tombstones—it makes her laugh. Tombstones are marching down the street on their little booted feet, their long bodies inclined forward, their expressions preoccupied and severe. The church bells are ringing.

Then the clock in the hall strikes twelve and an hour has passed.

The house is getting hot. She drinks more tea and adds more medicine. She knows that the medicine is affecting her. It is responsible for her extraordinary languor, her perfect immobility, her unresisting surrender to her surroundings. That is all right. It seems necessary.

Her surroundings—some of her surroundings—in the dining room are these: walls covered with dark-green garlanded wallpaper, lace curtains and mulberry velvet curtains on the windows, a table with a crocheted cloth and a bowl of wax fruit, a pinkish-gray carpet with nosegays of blue and pink roses, a sideboard spread with embroidered runners and holding various patterned plates and jugs and the silver tea things. A lot of things to watch. For every one of these patterns, decorations seems charged with life, ready to move and flow and alter. Or possibly to explode. Almeda Roth's occupation throughout the day is to keep an eye on them. Not to prevent their alteration so much as to catch them at it—to understand it, to be a part of it. So much is going on in this room that there is no need to leave it. There is not even the thought of leaving it.

Of course, Almeda in her observations cannot escape words. She may think she can, but she can't. Soon this glowing and swelling begins to suggest words—not specific words but a flow of words somewhere, just about ready to make themselves known to her. Poems, even. Yes, again, poems. Or one poem. Isn't that the idea—one very great poem that will contain everything and, oh, that will make all the other poems, the poems she has written, inconsequential, mere trial and error, mere rags? Stars and flowers and birds and trees and angels in the snow and dead children at twilight—that is not the half of it. You have to get in the obscene racket on Pearl Street and the polished toe of Jarvis Poulter's boot and the plucked-chicken haunch with its blue-black flower. Almeda is a long way now from human sympathies or fears or cozy household considerations. She doesn't think about what could be done for that woman or about keeping Jarvis Poulter's dinner warm and hanging his long underwear on the line. The basin of grape juice has overflowed and is running over her kitchen floor, staining the boards of the floor, and the stain will never come out.

She has to think of so many things at once—Champlain and the naked Indians and the salt deep in the earth, but as well as the salt the money, the money-making intent brewing forever in heads like Jarvis Poulter's. Also the brutal storms of winter and the clumsy and benighted deeds on Pearl Street. The changes of climate are often violent, and if you think about it there is no peace even in the stars. All this can be borne only if it is channelled into a poem, and the word "channelled" is appropriate, because the name of the poem will be—it *is*—"The Meneseteung." The name of the poem is the name of the river. No, in fact it is the river, the Meneseteung, that is the poem—with its deep holes and rapids and blissful pools under the summer trees and its grinding blocks of ice thrown up at the end of winter and its desolating spring floods. Almeda looks deep, deep into the river of her mind and into the tablecloth, and she sees the crocheted roses floating. They look bunchy and foolish, her mother's crocheted roses—they don't look much like real flowers. But their effort, their floating independence, their pleasure in their silly selves do seem to her so admirable. A hopeful sign. *Meneseteung.*

She doesn't leave the room until dusk, when she goes out to the privy again and discovers that she is bleeding, her flow has started. She will have to get a towel, strap it on, bandage herself up. Never before, in health, has she passed a whole day in her nightdress. She doesn't feel any particular anxiety about this. On her way through the kitchen, she walks through the pool of grape juice. She knows that she will have to mop it up, but not yet, and she walks upstairs leaving purple footprints and smelling her escaping blood and the sweat of her body that has sat all day in the closed hot room.

No need for alarm.

For she hasn't thought that crocheted roses could float away or that tombstones could hurry down the street. She doesn't mistake that for reality, and neither does she mistake anything else for reality, and that is how she knows that she is sane.

VI

I dream of you by night,
I visit you by day.
Father, Mother,
Sister, Brother,
Have you no word to say?

April 22, 1903. At her residence, on Tuesday last, between three and four o'clock in the afternoon, there passed away a lady of talent and refinement whose pen, in days gone by, enriched our local literature with a volume of sensitive, eloquent verse. It is a sad misfortune that in later years the mind of this fine person had become somewhat clouded and her behaviour, in consequence, somewhat rash and unusual. Her attention to decorum and to the care and adornment of her person had suffered, to the degree that she had become, in the eyes of those unmindful of her former pride and daintiness, a familiar eccentric, or even, sadly, a figure of fun. But now all such lapses pass from memory and what is recalled is her excellent published verse, her labours in former days in the Sunday school, her dutiful care of her parents, her noble womanly nature, charitable concerns, and unfailing religious faith. Her last illness was of mercifully short duration. She caught cold, after having become thoroughly wet from a ramble in the Pearl Street bog. (It has been said that some urchins chased her into the water, and such is the boldness and cruelty of some of our youth, and their observed persecution of this lady, that the tale cannot be entirely discounted.)

The cold developed into pneumonia, and she died, attended at the last by a former neighbour, Mrs. Bert (Annie) Friels, who witnessed her calm and faithful end.

January, 1904. One of the founders of our community, an early maker and shaker of this town, was abruptly removed from our midst on Monday morning last, whilst attending to his correspondence in the office of his company. Mr. Jarvis Poulter possessed a keen and lively commercial spirit, which was instrumental in the creation of not one but several local enterprises, bringing the benefits of industry, productivity, and employment to our town.

So the *Vidette* runs on, copious and assured. Hardly a death goes undescribed, or a life unevaluated.

I looked for Almeda Roth in the graveyard. I found the family stone. There was just one name on it—Roth. Then I noticed two flat stones in the ground, a distance of a few feet—six feet?—from the upright stone. One of these said "Papa," the other "Mama." Farther out from these I found two other flat stones, with the names William and Catherine on them. I had to clear away some overgrowing grass and dirt to see the full name of Catherine. No birth or death dates for anybody, nothing about being dearly beloved. It was a private sort of memorializing, not for the world. There were no roses, either—no sign of a rosebush. But perhaps it was taken out. The grounds keeper doesn't like such things; they are a nuisance to the lawnmower, and if there is nobody left to object he will pull them out.

I thought that Almeda must have been buried somewhere else. When this plot was bought—at the time of the two children's deaths—she would still have been expected to marry, and to lie finally beside her husband. They might not have left room for her here. Then I saw that the stones in the ground fanned out from the upright stone. First the two for the parents, then the two for the children, but these were placed in such a way that there was room for a third, to complete the fan. I paced out from "Catherine" the same number of steps that it took to get from "Catherine" to "William," and at this spot I began pulling grass and scrabbling in the dirt with my bare hands. Soon I felt the stone and knew that I was right. I worked away and got the whole stone clear and I read the name "Meda." There it was with the others, staring at the sky.

I made sure I had got to the edge of the stone. That was all the name there was—Meda. So it was true that she was called by that name in the family. Not just in the poem. Or perhaps she chose her name from the poem, to be written on her stone.

I thought that there wasn't anybody alive in the world but me who would know this, who would make the connection. And I would be the last person to do so. But perhaps this isn't so. People are curious. A few people are. They will be driven to find things out, even trivial things. They will put things together. You see them going around with notebooks, scraping the dirt off gravestones, reading microfilm, just in the hope of seeing this trickle in time, making a connection, rescuing one thing from the rubbish.

And they may get it wrong, after all. I may have got it wrong. I don't know if she ever took laudanum. Many ladies did. I don't know if she ever made grape jelly.

The Ant
and the
Grasshopper

by
SOMERSET MAUGHAM
(1874–1965)

I'm sure that everyone has some book from their past that has been read over and over, as if to commit to memory. For me, one of those books was Somerset Maugham's Of Human Bondage. I think this was probably because it was the first vaguely "adult" book that I happened to come across at an early age, and so it held new problems for me that I somehow wanted to solve. "The Ant and the Grasshopper" reminds me of those early days spent reading Of Human Bondage and, like Maugham, I think that I would also come up on the side of the grasshopper. Winter always seems a long way away until it is actually with us.

When I was a very small boy I was made to learn by heart certain of the fables of La Fontaine, and the moral of each was carefully explained to me. Among those learned was "The Ant and the Grasshopper," which is devised to bring home to the young the useful lesson that in an imperfect world industry is rewarded and giddiness punished. In this admirable fable (I apologise for telling something which everyone is politely, but inexactly, supposed to know) the ant spends a laborious summer gathering its winter store, while the grasshopper sits on a blade of grass singing to the sun. Winter comes and the ant is comfortably provided for, but the grasshopper has an empty larder; he goes to the ant and begs for a little food. Then the ant gives him her classic answer:

"What were you doing in the summer time?"

"Saving your presence, I sang. I sang all day, all night."

"You sang. Why, then go and dance."

I do not ascribe it to perversity on my part, but rather to the inconsequence of childhood, which is deficient in moral sense, that I could never quite reconcile myself to the lesson. My sympathies were with the grasshopper and for some time I never saw an ant without putting my foot on it. In this summary (and as I have discovered since, entirely human) fashion I sought to express my disapproval of prudence and commonsense.

I could not help thinking of this fable when the other day I saw George Ramsay lunching by himself in a restaurant. I never saw anyone wear an expression of such deep gloom. He was staring into space. He looked as though the burden of the whole world sat upon his shoulders. I was sorry for him: I suspected at once that his unfortunate brother had been causing trouble again. I went up to him and held out my hand.

"How are you?" I asked.

"I'm not in hilarious spirits," he answered.

"Is it Tom again?"

He sighed.

"Yes, it's Tom again."

"Why don't you chuck him? You've done everything in this world for him. You must know by now that he's quite hopeless."

I suppose every family has a black sheep. Tom had been a sore trial to his for twenty years. He had begun life decently enough: he went into business, married and had two children. The Ramsays were perfectly respectable people and there was every reason to suppose that Tom Ramsay would have a useful and honourable career. But one day, without warning, he announced that he didn't like work and that he wasn't suited for marriage. He wanted to enjoy himself. He would listen to no expostulations. He left his wife and his office. He had a little money and he spent two happy years in various capitals in Europe. Rumours of his doings reached his relations from time to time and they were profoundly shocked. He certainly had a very good time. They shook their heads and asked what would happen when his money was spent. They soon found out: he borrowed. He was charming and unscrupulous. I have never met anyone to whom it was more difficult to refuse a loan. He made a steady income from his friends and he made friends easily. But he always said that the money you spent on necessities was boring; the money that was amusing to spend was the money you spent on luxuries. For this he depended on his brother George. He did not waste his charm on him. George was respectable. Once or twice he fell to Tom's promises of amendment and gave him considerable sums in order that he might make a fresh start. On these Tom bought a motorcar and some very nice jewellery. But when circumstances forced George to realise that his brother would never settle down and he washed his hands of him, Tom, without a qualm, began to blackmail him. It was not very nice for a respectable lawyer to find his brother shaking cocktails behind the bar of his favourite restaurant or to see him waiting on the box-seat of a taxi outside his club. Tom said that to serve in a bar or to drive a taxi was a perfectly decent occupation, but if George could oblige him with a couple of hundred pounds he didn't mind for the honour of the family giving it up. George paid.

Once Tom nearly went to prison. George was terribly upset. He went into the whole discreditable affair. Really Tom had gone too far. He had been wild, thoughtless and selfish, but he had never before done anything dishonest, by which George meant illegal; and if he were prosecuted he would assuredly be convicted. But you cannot allow your only brother to go to gaol. The man Tom had cheated, a man called Cronshaw, was vindictive. He was determined to take the matter into court; he said Tom was a scoundrel and should be punished. It cost George an infinite deal of trouble and five hundred pounds to settle the affair. I have never seen him in such a rage as when he heard that Tom and Cronshaw had gone off together to Monte Carlo the moment they cashed the cheque. They spent a happy month there.

For twenty years Tom raced and gambled, philandered with the prettiest girls, danced, ate in the most expensive restaurants, and dressed beautifully. He always looked as if he had just stepped out of a bandbox. Though he was forty-six you would never have taken him for more than thirty-five. He was a most amusing companion and though you knew he was perfectly worthless you could not but enjoy his society. He had high spirits, an unfailing gaiety and incredible charm. I never grudged the contributions he regularly levied on me for the

necessities of his existence. I never lent him fifty pounds without feeling that I was in his debt. Tom Ramsay knew everyone
and everyone knew Tom Ramsay. You could not approve of
him, but you could not help liking him.

Poor George, only a year older than his scapegrace brother,
looked sixty. He had never taken more than a fortnight's holiday in the year for a quarter of a century. He was in his office
every morning at nine-thirty and never left it till six. He was
honest, industrious and worthy. He had a good wife, to whom
he had never been unfaithful even in thought, and four daughters to whom he was the best of fathers. He made a point of
saving a third of his income and his plan was to retire at fifty-
five to a little house in the country where he proposed to culti-
vate his garden and play golf. His life was blameless. He was
glad that he was growing old because Tom was growing old
too. He rubbed his hands and said:

"It was all very well when Tom was young and good-looking,
but he's only a year younger than I am. In four years he'll be
fifty. He won't find life too easy then. I shall have thirty thousand pounds by the time I'm fifty. For twenty-five years I've said
that Tom would end in the gutter. And we shall see how he
likes that. We shall see if it really pays best to work or be idle."

Poor George! I sympathised with him. I wondered now as I
sat down beside him what infamous thing Tom had done.
George was evidently very much upset.

"Do you know what's happened now?" he asked me.

I was prepared for the worst. I wondered if Tom had got
into the hands of the police at last. George could hardly bring
himself to speak.

"You're not going to deny that all my life I've been hard
working, decent, respectable and straightforward. After a life of
industry and thrift I can look forward to retiring on a small
income in gilt-edged securities. I've always done my duty in
that state of life in which it has pleased Providence to place me."

"True."

"And you can't deny that Tom has been an idle, worthless,
dissolute and dishonourable rogue. If there were any justice
he'd be in the workhouse."

"True."

George grew red in the face.

"A few weeks ago he became engaged to a woman old enough to be his mother. And now she's died and left him everything she had. Half a million pounds, a yacht, a house in London and a house in the country."

George Ramsay beat his clenched fist on the table.

"It's not fair, I tell you, it's not fair. Damn it, it's not fair."

I could not help it. I burst into a shout of laughter as I looked at George's wrathful face. I rolled in my chair, I very nearly fell on the floor. George never forgave me. But Tom often asks me to excellent dinners in his charming house in Mayfair, and if he occasionally borrows a trifle from me, that is merely from force of habit. It is never more than a sovereign.

An Orange from Portugal

by
HUGH MACLENNAN
(1907–1990)

For me it is especially at Christmas time that the reading of stories becomes one of life's most pleasurable traditions. "An Orange from Portugal," in addition to being a wonderful story of Christmas giving, also forms a nice sort of bridge between contemporary Canada and the more traditional world of Dickens and the classics. It is a Canadian Christmas story. It is also a story that describes the last glimpse of a changing world, of old Halifax, and the orange of the title seems to me to be a nice, brightly coloured symbol of a new world to come.

I suppose all of us, when we think of Christmas, recall Charles Dickens and our own childhood. So, today, from an apartment in Montreal, looking across to a new neon sign, I think back to Dickens and Halifax and the world suddenly becomes smaller, shabbier and more comfortable, and one more proof is registered that comfort is a state of mind, having little to do with the number of springs hidden inside your mattress or the upholstery in your car.

Charles Dickens should have lived in Halifax. If he had, that brown old town would have acquired a better reputation in Canada than it now enjoys, for all over the world people would have known what it was like. Halifax, especially a generation or two ago, was a town Dickens could have used.

There were dingy basement kitchens all over the town where rats were caught every day. The streets were full of teamsters, hard-looking men with lean jaws, most of them, and at the entrance to the old North Street station cab drivers in long coats would mass behind a heavy anchor chain and terrify travellers with bloodcurdling howls as they bid for fares. Whenever there was a southeast wind, harbor bells moaned behind the wall of fog that cut the town off from the rest of the world. Queer faces peered at you suddenly from doorways set flush with the streets. When a regiment held a smoker in the old Masonic Hall you could see a line beginning to form in the early morning, waiting for the big moment at midnight when the doors would be thrown open to the town and any man could get a free drink who could reach the hogsheads.

For all these things Dickens would have loved Halifax, even for the pompous importers who stalked to church on Sunday mornings, swinging their canes and complaining that they never had a chance to hear a decent sermon. He would have loved it for the waifs and strays and beachcombers and discharged soldiers and sailors whom the respectable never seemed to notice, for all the numerous aspects of the town that made Halifax deplorable and marvelous.

If Dickens had been given a choice of a Canadian town in which to spend Christmas, that's where I think he would have gone, for his most obvious attitude toward Christmas was that it was necessary. Dickens was no scientist or organizer. Instead of liking The People, he simply liked people. And so inevitably, he liked places where accidents were apt to happen. In Halifax accidents were happening all the time. Think of the way he writes about Christmas—a perfect Christmas for him was always a chapter of preposterous accidents. Now, I don't think he would have chosen to spend his Christmas in Westmount or Toronto, for he'd be fairly sure that neither of those places needed it.

Today we know too much. Having become democratic by ideology, we are divided into groups which eye each other like dull strangers at a dull party, polite in public and nasty when each other's backs are turned. Today we are informed by those who know that if we tell children about Santa Claus we will probably turn them into neurotics. Today we believe in universal justice and in universal war to effect it, and because Santa Claus gives the rich more than he gives the poor, lots of us think it better that there should be no Santa Claus at all. Today we are technicians, and the more progressive among us see no reason why love and hope should not be organized in a department of the government, planned by a politician and administered by trained specialists. Today we have a super-colossal Santa Claus for The Customer; he sits in the window of department stores in a cheap red suit, stringy whiskers and a mask which is a caricature of a face, and for a month before every Christmas he laughs continually with a vulgar roar. The sounds of his laughter come from a record played over and over, and the machine in his belly that produces the bodily contortions has a number in the patent office in Washington.

In the old days in Halifax we never thought about the meaning of the word democracy; we were all mixed up together in a general deplorability. So the only service any picture of those days can render is to help prove how far we have advanced since then. The first story I have to tell has no importance and not even much of a point. It is simply the record of how one boy felt during a Christmas that now seems remote enough to belong to the era of Bob Cratchit. The second story is about the same. The war Christmases I remember in Halifax were not jolly ones. In a way they were half-tragic, but there may be some significance in the fact that they are literally the only ones I can still remember. Indirectly, the war was part of them both. It was a war nobody down there understood. We were simply a part of it, swept into it from the mid-Victorian Age in which we were all living until 1914.

On Christmas Eve in 1915 a cold northeaster was blowing through the town with the smell of coming snow on the wind. All day our house was hushed for a reason I didn't understand, and I remember being sent out to play with some other boys in the middle of the afternoon. Supper was a silent meal. And then, immediately after we had finished, my father put on the greatcoat of his new uniform and went to the door and I saw the long tails of the coat blowing out behind him in the flicker of a faulty arc light as he half-ran up to the corner.

We heard bagpipes, and almost immediately a company of soldiers appeared swinging down Spring Garden Road from old Dalhousie. It was very cold as we struggled up to the corner after my father, and he affected not to notice us. Then the pipes went by playing "The Blue Bonnets," the lines of khaki men went past in the darkness and my father fell in behind the last rank and faded off down the half-lit street, holding his head low against the wind to keep his flat military cap from blowing off, and my mother tried to hide her feelings by saying what a shame the cap didn't fit him properly. She told my sister and me how nice it was of the pipers to have turned out on such a cold day to see the men off, for pipe music was the only kind my father liked. It was all very informal. The men of that unit—almost entirely a local one—simply left their homes the way my father had done and joined the column and the column marched down Spring Garden Road to the ship along the familiar route most of them had taken to church all their lives.

An hour later we heard tugboat whistles and then the foghorn of the transport and we knew he was on his way. As my sister and I hung up our stockings on the mantelpiece I wondered whether the vessel was no farther out than Thrum Cap or whether it had already reached Sambro.

It was a bleak night for children to hang up their stockings and wait for Santa Claus, but next morning we found gifts in them as usual, including a golden orange in each toe. It was strange to think that the very night my father had left the house, a strange old man, remembering my sister and me, had come into it. We thought it was a sign of good luck.

That was 1915, and sometime during the following year a boy at school told me there was no Santa Claus and put his case so convincingly that I believed him.

Strictly speaking, this should have been the moment of my first step toward becoming a neurotic. Maybe it was, but there were so many other circumstances to compete with it, I don't know whether Santa Claus was responsible for what I'm like now or not. For about a week after discovering the great deception I wondered how I could develop a line of conduct that would prevent my mother from finding out that I knew who filled our stockings on Christmas Eve. I hated to disappoint her in what I knew was a great pleasure. After a while I forgot all about it. Then, shortly before Christmas a cable arrived saying that my father was on his way home. He hadn't been killed like the fathers of other boys at school; he was being invalided home as a result of excessive work as a surgeon in the hospital.

We had been living with my grandmother in Cape Breton, so my mother rented a house in Halifax sight unseen; we got down there in time to meet his ship when it came in, and then we all went to the new house. This is the part of my story that reminds me of Charles Dickens again. Five minutes after we entered the house it blew up. This was not the famous Halifax explosion; we had to wait another year for that. This was our own private explosion. It smashed half the windows in the other houses along the block; it shook the ground like an earthquake and it was heard for a mile.

I have seen many queer accidents in Halifax, but none that gave the reporters more satisfaction than ours did. For a house to blow up suddenly in our district was unusual, so the press felt some explanation was due to the public. Besides, it was nearly Christmas and local news was hard to find. The moment the first telephone call reached the newspaper offices to report the accident, they knew the cause. Gas had been leaking in our district for years and a few people had even complained about it. In our house, gas had apparently backed in from the city mains, filling partitions between the walls and lying stagnant in the basement. But this was the first time anyone could prove that gas had been leaking. The afternoon paper gave the story:

DOCTOR HUNTS GAS LEAK WITH BURNING MATCH—FINDS IT!

When my father was able to talk, which he couldn't do for several days because the skin had been burned off his hands and face, he denied the story about the match. According to modern theory this denial should have precipitated my second plunge toward neurosis, for I had distinctly seen him with the match in his hand, going down to the basement to look for the gas and complaining about how careless people were. However, those were ignorant times and I didn't realize I might get a neurosis. Instead of brooding and deciding to close my mind to reality from then on to preserve my belief in the

veracity and faultlessness of my father, I wished to God he had
been able to tell his story sooner and stick to it. After all, he
was a first-class doctor, but what would prospective patients
think if every time they heard his name they saw a picture of
an absent-minded veteran looking for a gas leak in a dark
basement with a lighted match?

It took two whole days for the newspaper account of our
accident to settle. In the meantime the house was temporarily
ruined, school children had denuded the chandelier in the living room of its prisms, and it was almost Christmas. My sister
was still away at school, so my mother, my father and I found
ourselves in a single room in an old residential hotel in
Barrington Street. I slept on a cot and they nursed their burns
in a huge bed which opened out of the wall. The bed had a
mirror on the bottom of it, and it was equipped with such a
strong spring that it crashed into place in the wall whenever
they got out of it. I still remember my father sitting up in it
with one arm in a sling from the war, and his face and head in
white bandages. He was philosophical about the situation,
including the vagaries of the bed, for it was his Calvinistic way
to permit himself to be comfortable only when things were
going badly.

The hotel was crowded and our meals were brought to us
by a boy called Chester, who lived in the basement near the
kitchen. That was all I knew about Chester at first; he brought
our meals, he went to school only occasionally, and his mother
was ill in the basement. But as long as my memory lasts, that
Christmas of 1916 will be Chester's Christmas.

He was a waif of a boy. I never knew his last name, and
wherever he is now, I'm certain he doesn't remember me. But
for a time I can say without being sentimental that I loved
him.

He was white-faced and thin, with lank hair on top of a
head that broke back at right angles from a high narrow forehead. There were always holes in his black stockings, his
handed-down pants were so badly cut that one leg was several
inches longer than the other and there was a patch on the
right seat of a different color from the rest of the cloth. But he

was proud of his clothes; prouder than anyone I've ever seen over a pair of pants. He explained that they were his father's and his father had worn them at sea.

For Chester, nobody was worth considering seriously unless he was a seaman. Instead of feeling envious of the people who lived upstairs in the hotel, he seemed to feel sorry for them because they never went to sea. He would look at the old ladies with the kind of eyes that Dickens discovered in children's faces in London: huge eyes as trusting as a bird-dog's, but old, as though they had forgotten how to cry long ago.

I wondered a lot about Chester—what kind of a room they had in the basement, where they ate, what his mother was like. But I was never allowed in the basement. Once I walked behind the hotel to see if I could look through the windows, but they were only six or eight inches above the ground and they were covered with snow. I gathered that Chester liked it down there because it was warm, and once he was down nobody ever bothered him.

The days went past, heavy and grey and cold. Soon it was the day before Christmas again, and I was still supposed to believe in Santa Claus. I found myself confronted by a double crisis.

I would have to hang up my stocking as usual, but how could my parents, who were still in bed, manage to fill it? And how would they feel when the next morning came and my stocking was still empty? This worry was overshadowed only by my concern for Chester.

On the afternoon of Christmas Eve he informed me that this year, for the first time in his life, Santa Claus was really going to remember him. "I never ett a real orange and you never did neether because you only get real oranges in Portugal. My old man says so. But Santy Claus is going to bring me one this year. That means the old man's still alive."

"Honest, Chester? How do you know?" Everyone in the hotel knew that his father, who was a quartermaster, was on a slow convoy to England.

"Mrs. Urquhart says so."

Everyone in the hotel also knew Mrs. Urquhart. She was a

tiny old lady with a harsh voice who lived in the room opposite ours on the ground floor with her unmarried sister. Mrs.
Urquhart wore a white lace cap and carried a cane. Both old
ladies wore mourning—Mrs. Urquhart for two dead husbands,
her sister for Queen Victoria. They were a trial to Chester
because he had to carry hot tea upstairs for them every morning at seven.

"Mrs. Urquhart says if Santy Claus bring me real oranges it
means he was talkin' to the old man and the old man told him
I wanted one. And if Santy Claus was talkin' to the old man, it
means the old man's alive, don't it?"

Much of this was beyond me until Chester explained further.

"Last time the old man was home I see'd some oranges in a
store window, but he wouldn't get me one because if he buys
stuff in stores he can't go on being a seaman. To be a seaman
you got to wash out your insides with rum every day and rum
costs lots of money. Anyhow, store oranges ain't real."

"How do you know they aren't?"

"My old man says so. He's been in Portugal and he picks
real ones off trees. That's where they come from. Not from
stores. Only my old man and the people who live in Portugal
has ever ett real oranges."

Someone called and Chester disappeared into the basement.
An hour or so later, after we had eaten the supper he brought
to us on a tray, my father told me to bring the wallet from the
pocket of his uniform, which was hanging in the cupboard.
He gave me some small change and sent me to buy grapes for
my mother at a corner fruit store. When I came back with the
grapes I met Chester in the outer hall. His face was beaming
and he was carrying a parcel wrapped in brown paper.

"Your old man give me a two-dollar bill," he said. "I got my
old lady a Christmas present."

I asked him if it was medicine.

"She don't like medicine," he said. "When she's feelin' bad
she wants rum."

When I got back to our room I didn't tell my father what
Chester had done with his two dollars. I hung up my stocking

on the old-fashioned mantelpiece, the lights were put out and I was told to go to sleep.

An old flickering arc light hung in the street almost directly in front of the hotel, and as I lay in the dark pretending to be asleep the ceiling seemed to be quivering, for the shutters fitted badly and the room could never be completely darkened. After a time I heard movement in the room, then saw a shadowy figure near the mantelpiece. I closed my eyes tightly, heard the swish of tissue paper, then the sounds of someone getting back into bed. A fog bell, blowing in the harbor and heralding bad weather, was audible.

After what seemed to me a long time I heard heavy breathing from the bed. I got up, crossed the room carefully and felt the stocking in the dark. My fingers closed on a round object in its toe. Well, I thought, one orange would be better than none.

In those days hardly any children wore pyjamas, at least not in Nova Scotia. And so a minute later, when I was sneaking down the dimly lit hall of the hotel in a white nightgown, heading for the basement stairs with the orange in my hand, I was a fairly conspicuous object. Just as I was putting my hand to the knob of the basement door I heard a tapping sound and ducked under the main stairs that led to the second floor of the hotel. The tapping came nearer, stopped, and I knew somebody was standing still, listening, only a few feet away.

A crisp voice said, "You naughty boy, come out of there."

I waited a moment and then moved into the hall. Mrs. Urquhart was standing before me in her black skirt and white cap, one hand on the handle of her cane.

"You ought to be ashamed of yourself, at this hour of the night. Go back to your room at once!"

As I went back up the hall I was afraid the noise had wakened my father. The big door creaked as I opened it and looked up at the quivering maze of shadows on the ceiling. Somebody on the bed was snoring and it seemed to be all right. I slipped into my cot and waited for several minutes, then got up again and replaced the orange in the toe of the stocking and carefully put the other gifts on top of it. As soon as I reached my cot again I fell asleep with the sudden fatigue of children.

The room was full of light when I woke up; not sunlight but the grey luminosity of filtered light reflected off snow. My parents were sitting up in bed and Chester was standing inside the door with our breakfast. My father was trying to smile under his bandages and Chester had a grin so big it showed the gap in his front teeth. The moment I had been worrying about was finally here.

The first thing I must do was display enthusiasm for my parents' sake. I went to my stocking and emptied it on my cot while Chester watched me out of the corner of his eye. Last of all the orange rolled out.

"I bet it ain't real," Chester said.

My parents said nothing as he reached over and held it up to the light.

"No," he said. "It ain't real," and dropped it on the cot again. Then he put his hand into his pocket and with an effort managed to extract a medium-sized orange. "Look at mine," he said. "Look what it says right here."

On the skin of the orange, printed daintily with someone's pen, were the words, PRODUCE OF PORTUGAL.

"So my old man's been talkin' to Santy Claus, just like Mrs. Urquhart said."

There was never any further discussion in our family about whether Santa Claus was or was not real. Perhaps Mrs. Urquhart was the actual cause of my neurosis. I'm not a scientist, so I don't know.

The Highwayman

by
ALFRED NOYES
(1880–1958)

Some poems and stories simply beg to be read aloud. "The Highwayman" is one of these. Preferably the poem should be read in a large room with high moulded ceilings and a large stone fireplace. The fire should be low, just a few embers. A little rain at the window would be nice. Perhaps even some thunder and an occasional bolt of lightning. The reader's voice should roll and echo around the room, rising in the darkness as the highwayman comes riding, riding...

Part One

I

The wind was a torrent of darkness among the gusty trees.
The moon was a ghostly galleon tossed upon cloudy seas.
The road was a ribbon of moonlight over the purple moor,
And the highwayman came riding—
     Riding—riding—
The highwayman came riding, up to the old inn-door.

II

He'd a French cocked-hat on his forehead, a bunch of lace at
     his chin,
A coat of claret velvet, and breeches of brown doe-skin.
They fitted with never a wrinkle. His boots were up to the
     thigh.
And he rode with a jewelled twinkle,
     His pistol butts a-twinkle,
His rapier hilt a-twinkle, under the jewelled sky.

III

Over the cobbles he clattered and clashed in the dark inn-yard.
He tapped with his whip on the shutters, but all was locked
     and barred.
He whistled a tune to the window, and who should be waiting
     there
But the landlord's black-eyed daughter,
     Bess, the landlord's daughter,
Plaiting a dark red love-knot into her long black hair.

IV

And dark in the dark old inn-yard a stable-wicket creaked
Where Tim the ostler listened. His face was white and peaked.
His eyes were hollows of madness, his hair like mouldy hay,
But he loved the landlord's daughter,
     The landlord's red-lipped daughter,
Dumb as a dog he listened, and he heard the robber say—

V

"One kiss, my bonny sweetheart, I'm after a prize to-night,
But I shall be back with the yellow gold before the morning
    light;
Yet, if they press me sharply, and harry me through the day,
Then look for me by moonlight,
      Watch for me by moonlight,
I'll come to thee by moonlight, though hell should bar the
    way."

VI

He rose upright in the stirrups. He scarce could reach her
    hand,
But she loosened her hair in the casement. His face burnt like
    a brand
As the black cascade of perfume came tumbling over his breast;
And he kissed its waves in the moonlight,
      (O, sweet black waves in the moonlight!)
Then he tugged at his rein in the moonlight, and galloped
    away to the west.

Part Two

I

He did not come in the dawning. He did not come at noon;
And out of the tawny sunset, before the rise of the moon,
When the road was a gipsy's ribbon, looping the purple moor,
A red-coat troop came marching—
      Marching—marching—
King George's men came marching, up to the old inn-door.

II

They said no word to the landlord. They drank his ale instead.
But they gagged his daughter, and bound her, to the foot of
  her narrow bed.
Two of them knelt at her casement, with muskets at their side!
There was death at every window;
      And hell at one dark window;
For Bess could see, through her casement, the road that *he*
  would ride.

III

They had tied her up to attention, with many a sniggering jest.
They had bound a musket beside her, with the muzzle beneath
  her breast!
"Now, keep good watch!" and they kissed her. She heard the
  doomed man say—
Look for me by moonlight;
      Watch for me by moonlight;
I'll come to thee by moonlight, though hell should bar the way!

IV

She twisted her hands behind her; but all the knots held good!
She writhed her hands till her fingers were wet with sweat or
  blood!
They stretched and strained in the darkness, and the hours
  crawled by like years,
Till, now, on the stroke of midnight,
      Cold, on the stroke of midnight,
The tip of one finger touched it! The trigger at least was hers!

V

The tip of one finger touched it. She strove no more for the
  rest.
Up, she stood up to attention, with the muzzle beneath her
  breast,
She would not risk their hearing; she would not strive again;

For the road lay bare in the moonlight;
    Blank and bare in the moonlight;
And the blood of her veins, in the moonlight, throbbed to her
    love's refrain.

VI

Tlot-tlot; tlot-tlot! Had they heard it? The horse-hoofs ringing
    clear;
Tlot-tlot, tlot-tlot, in the distance? Were they deaf that they did
    not hear?
Down the ribbon of moonlight, over the brow of the hill,
The highwayman came riding—
    Riding—riding—
The red-coats looked to their priming! She stood up, straight
    and still.

VII

Tlot-tlot, in the frosty silence! *Tlot-tlot* in the echoing night!
Nearer he came and nearer! Her face was like a light.
Her eyes grew wide for a moment; she drew one last deep
    breath,
Then her finger moved in the moonlight,
    Her musket shattered in the moonlight,
Shattered her breast in the moonlight and warned him—with
    her death.

VIII

He turned; he spurred to the west; he did not know who
    stood
Bowed, with her head o'er the musket, drenched with her own
    blood!
Not till the dawn he heard it, and his face grew grey to hear
How Bess, the landlord's daughter,
    The landlord's black-eyed daughter,
Had watched for her love in the moonlight, and died in the
    darkness there.

IX

Back, he spurred like a madman, shouting a curse to the sky,
With the white road smoking behind him and his rapier bran-
    dished high!
Blood-red were his spurs in the golden noon; wine-red was his
    velvet coat;
When they shot him down on the highway,
    Down like a dog on the highway,
And he lay in his blood on the highway, with the bunch of lace
    at his throat.

X

And still of a winter's night, they say, when the wind is in the trees,
When the moon is a ghostly galleon tossed upon cloudy seas,
When the road is a ribbon of moonlight over the purple moor,
A highwayman comes riding—
    Riding—riding—
A highwayman comes riding, up to the old inn-door.

XI

Over the cobbles he clatters and clangs in the dark inn-yard;
He taps with his whip on the shutters; but all is locked and barred.
He whistles a tune to the window, and who should be waiting there
But the landlord's black-eyed daughter,
    Bess, the landlord's daughter,
Plaiting a dark red love-knot in her long black hair.

An Occurrence at Owl Creek Bridge

by
AMBROSE BIERCE
(1842–1914?)

I have read this story many times, and I am never quite sure what really happens. That is the trick: to learn to see beneath the surface. Someone once told me that storytelling is all about deceiving, about leading the poor believing reader astray. My guess is that writers are a little like magicians, and reading "An Occurrence at Owl Creek Bridge" is like entering into a house of mirrors at a carnival. What you see depends on where you're standing.

At Owl Creek Bridge

I

A man stood upon a railroad bridge in Northern Alabama, looking down into the swift waters twenty feet below. The man's hands were behind his back, the wrists bound with a cord. A rope loosely encircled his neck. It was attached to a stout cross-timber above his head, and the slack fell to the level of his knees. Some loose boards laid upon the sleepers supporting the metals of the railway supplied a footing for him and his executioners—two private soldiers of the Federal army, directed by a sergeant, who in civil life may have been a deputy sheriff. At a short remove upon the same temporary platform was an officer in the uniform of his rank, armed. He was a captain. A sentinel at each end of the bridge stood with his rifle in position known as "support," that is to say, vertical in front of the left shoulder, the hammer resting on the forearm thrown straight across the chest—a formal and unnatural position, enforcing an erect carriage of the body. It did not appear to be the duty of these two men to know what was occurring at the centre of the bridge; they merely blockaded the two ends of the foot plank which traversed it.

Beyond one of the sentinels nobody was in sight; the railroad ran straight away into a forest for a hundred yards, then, curving, was lost to view. Doubtless there was an outpost further along. The other bank of the stream was open ground—a gentle acclivity crowned with a stockade of vertical tree trunks, loop-holed for rifles, with a single embrasure through which protruded the muzzle of a brass cannon commanding the bridge. Midway of the slope between bridge and fort were the spectators—a single company of infantry in line, at "parade rest," the butts of the rifles on the ground, the barrels inclining slightly backward against the right shoulder, the hands crossed upon the stock. A lieutenant stood at the right of the line, the point of his sword upon the ground, his left hand resting upon his right. Excepting the group of four at the centre of the bridge not a man moved. The company faced the bridge, staring stonily, motionless. The sentinels, facing the banks of the stream, might have been statues to adorn the bridge. The captain stood with folded arms, silent, observing the work of his subordinates but making no sign. Death is a dignitary who, when he comes announced, is to be received with formal manifestations of respect, even by those most familiar with him. In the code of military etiquette silence and fixity are forms of deference.

The man who was engaged in being hanged was apparently about thirty-five years of age. He was a civilian, if one might judge from his dress, which was that of a planter. His features were good—a straight nose, firm mouth, broad forehead, from which his long, dark hair was combed straight back, falling behind his ears to the collar of his well-fitting frock coat. He wore a moustache and pointed beard, but no whiskers; his eyes were large and dark grey and had a kindly expression which one would hardly have expected in one whose neck was in the hemp. Evidently this was no vulgar assassin. The liberal military code makes provision for hanging many kinds of people, and gentlemen are not excluded.

The preparations being complete, the two private soldiers stepped aside and drew away the plank upon which he had been standing. The sergeant turned to the captain, saluted and placed himself immediately behind the officer, who in turn moved apart one pace. These movements left the condemned man and the sergeant standing on the two ends of the same plank, which spanned three of the cross-ties of the bridge. The end upon which the civilian stood almost, but not quite, reached a fourth. This plank had been held in place by the weight of the captain; it was now held by that of the sergeant. At a signal from the former, the latter would step aside, the plank would tilt and the condemned man go down between two ties. The arrangement commended itself to his judgment as simple and effective. His face had not been covered nor his eyes bandaged. He looked a moment at his "unsteadfast footing," then let his gaze wander to the swirling water of the stream racing madly beneath his feet. A piece of dancing driftwood caught his attention and his eyes followed it down the current. How slowly it appeared to move! What a sluggish stream!

He closed his eyes in order to fix his last thoughts upon his wife and children. The water, touched to gold by the early sun, the brooding mists under the banks at some distance down the stream, the fort, the soldiers, the piece of drift—all had distracted him. And now he became conscious of a new disturbance. Striking through the thought of his dear ones was a sound which he could neither ignore nor understand, a sharp, distinct, metallic percussion like the stroke of a blacksmith's hammer upon the anvil; it had the same ringing quality. He wondered what it was, and whether immeasurably distant or near by—it seemed both. Its recurrence was regular, but as slow as the tolling of a death knell. He awaited each stroke with impatience and—he knew not why—apprehension. The intervals of silence grew progressively longer, the delays became maddening. With their greater infrequency the sounds increased in strength and sharpness. They hurt his ear like the thrust of a knife; he feared he would shriek. What he heard was the ticking of his watch.

He unclosed his eyes and saw again the water below him. "If I could free my hands," he thought, "I might throw off the noose and spring into the stream. By diving I could evade the bullets, and, swimming vigorously, reach the bank, take to the woods, and get away home. My home, thank God, is as yet outside their lines; my wife and little ones are still beyond the invader's farthest advance."

As these thoughts, which have here to be set down in words, were flashed into the doomed man's brain rather than evolved from it, the captain nodded to the sergeant. The sergeant stepped aside.

II

Peyton Farquhar was a well-to-do planter, of an old and high-ly-respected Alabama family. Being a slave owner, and, like other slave owners, a politician, he was naturally an original secessionist and ardently devoted to the Southern cause. Circumstances of an imperious nature which it is unnecessary to relate here, had prevented him from taking service with the gallant army which had fought the disastrous campaigns ending with the fall of Corinth, and he chafed under the inglorious restraint, longing for the release of his energies, the larger life of the soldier, the opportunity for distinction. That opportunity, he felt, would come, as it comes to all in war time. Meanwhile he did what he could. No service was too humble for him to perform in aid of the South, no adventure too perilous for him to undertake if consistent with the character of a civilian who was at heart a soldier, and who in good faith and without too much qualification assented to at least a part of the frankly villainous dictum that all is fair in love and war.

One evening while Farquhar and his wife were sitting on a rustic bench near the entrance to his grounds, a grey-clad soldier rode up to the gate and asked for a drink of water. Mrs. Farquhar was only too happy to serve him with her own white hands. While she was gone to fetch the water, her husband approached the dusty horseman and inquired eagerly for news from the front.

"The Yanks are repairing the railroads," said the man, "and are getting ready for another advance. They have reached the Owl Creek bridge, put it in order, and built a stockade on the other bank. The commandant has issued an order, which is posted everywhere, declaring that any civilian caught interfering with the railroad, its bridges, tunnels, or trains, will be summarily hanged. I saw the order."

"How far is it to the Owl Creek bridge?" Farquhar asked.

"About thirty miles."

"Is there no force on this side the creek?"

"Only a picket post half a mile out, on the railroad, and a single sentinel at this end of the bridge."

"Suppose a man—a civilian and student of hanging— should elude the picket post and perhaps get the better of the sentinel," said Farquhar, smiling, "what could he accomplish?"

The soldier reflected. "I was there a month ago," he replied. "I observed that the flood of last winter had lodged a great quantity of driftwood against the wooden pier at this end of the bridge. It is now dry and would burn like tow."

The lady had now brought the water, which the soldier drank. He thanked her ceremoniously, bowed to her husband, and rode away. An hour later, after nightfall, he repassed the plantation, going northward in the direction from which he had come. He was a Federal scout.

III

As Peyton Farquhar fell straight downward through the bridge, he lost consciousness and was as one already dead. From this state he was awakened—ages later, it seemed to him—by the pain of a sharp pressure upon his throat, followed by a sense of suffocation. Keen, poignant agonies seemed to shoot from his neck downward through every fibre of his body and limbs. These pains appeared to flash along well-defined lines of ramification, and to beat with an inconceivably rapid periodicity. They seemed like streams of pulsating fire beating him to an intolerable temperature. As to his head, he was conscious of nothing but a feeling of fullness—of congestion. These sensations were unaccompanied by thought. The intellectual part of his nature was already effaced; he had power only to feel, and feeling was torment. He was conscious of motion. Encompassed in a luminous cloud, of which he was now merely the fiery heart, without material substance, he swung through unthinkable arcs of oscillation, like a vast pendulum. Then all at once, with terrible suddenness, the light about him shot upward with the noise of a loud plash; a frightful roaring was in his ears, and all was cold and dark. The power of thought was restored; he knew that the rope had broken and he had fallen into the stream. There was no additional strangulation; the noose about his neck was already suffocating him, and kept the water from his lungs. To die of hanging at the bottom of a river!—the idea seemed to him ludicrous. He opened his eyes in the blackness and saw above him a gleam of light, but how distant, how inaccessible! He was still sinking, for the light became fainter and fainter until it was a mere glimmer. Then it began to grow and brighten, and he knew that he was rising toward the surface—knew it with reluctance, for he was now very comfortable. "To be hanged and drowned," he thought, "that is not so bad; but I do not wish to be shot. No; I will not be shot; that is not fair."

He was not conscious of an effort, but a sharp pain in his wrist apprised him that he was trying to free his hands. He gave the struggle his attention, as an idler might observe the feat of a juggler, without interest in the outcome. What splendid effort!—what magnificent, what superhuman strength! Ah, that was a fine endeavour! Bravo! The cord fell away; his arms parted and floated upward, the hands dimly seen on each side in the growing light. He watched them with a new interest as first one and then the other pounced upon the noose at his neck. They tore it away and thrust it fiercely aside, its undulations resembling those of a water-snake. "Put it back, put it back!" He thought he shouted these words to his hands, for the undoing of the noose had been succeeded by the direst pang which he had yet experienced. His neck ached horribly; his brain was on fire; his heart, which had been fluttering faintly, gave a great leap, trying to force itself out at his mouth. His whole body was racked and wrenched with an insupportable anguish! But his disobedient hands gave no heed to the command. They beat the water vigorously with quick, downward strokes, forcing him to the surface. He felt his head emerge; his eyes were blinded by the sunlight; his chest expanded convulsively, and with a supreme and crowning agony his lungs engulfed a great draught of air, which instantly he expelled in a shriek!

He was now in full possession of his physical senses. They were, indeed, preternaturally keen and alert. Something in the awful disturbance of his organic system had so exalted and refined them that they made record of things never before perceived. He felt the ripples upon his face and heard their separate sounds as they struck. He looked at the forest on the bank of the stream, saw the individual trees, the leaves and the veining of each leaf—the very insects upon them, the locusts, the brilliant-bodied flies, the grey spiders stretching their webs from twig to twig. He noted the prismatic colors in all the dewdrops upon a million blades of grass. The humming of the gnats that danced above the eddies of the stream, the beating of the dragon flies' wings, the strokes of the water spiders' legs, like oars which had lifted their boat—all these made audible music. A fish slid along beneath his eyes and he heard the rush of its body parting the water.

He had come to the surface facing down the stream; in a moment the visible world seemed to wheel slowly round, himself the pivotal point, and he saw the bridge, the fort, the soldiers upon the bridge, the captain, the sergeant, the two privates, his executioners. They were in silhouette against the blue sky. They shouted and gesticulated, pointing at him; the captain had drawn his pistol, but did not fire; the others were unarmed. The movements were grotesque and horrible, the forms gigantic.

Suddenly he heard a sharp report and something struck the water smartly within a few inches of his head, spattering his face with spray. He heard a second report, and saw one of the sentinels with his rifle at his shoulder, a light cloud of blue smoke rising from the muzzle. The man in the water saw the eye of the man on the bridge gazing into his own through the sights of the rifle. He observed that it was a grey eye and remembered having read that grey eyes were keenest and that all famous marksmen had them. Nevertheless, this one had missed.

A counter swirl had caught Farquhar and turned him half round; he was again looking into the forest on the bank opposite the fort. The sound of a clear, high voice in a monotonous singsong now rang out behind him and came across the water with a distinctness that pierced and subdued all other sounds, even the beating of the ripples in the ears. Although no soldier, he had frequented camps enough to know the dread significance of that deliberate, drawling, aspirated chant; the lieutenant on shore was taking a part in the morning's work. How coldly and pitilessly—with what an even, calm intonation, presaging and enforcing tranquillity, in the men—with what accurately-measured intervals fell those cruel words:

"Attention, company...Shoulder arms...Ready...Aim...Fire."

Farquhar dived—dived as deeply as he could. The water roared in his ears like the voice of Niagara, yet he heard the dulled thunder of the volley, and rising again toward the surface, met shining bits of metal, singularly flattened, oscillating slowly downward. Some of them touched him on the face and hands, then fell away, continuing their descent. One lodged between his collar and neck; it was uncomfortably warm, and he snatched it out.

As he rose to the surface, gasping for breath, he saw that he had been a long time under water; he was perceptibly farther down stream—nearer to safety. The soldiers had almost finished reloading; the metal ramrods flashed all at once in the sunshine as they were drawn from the barrels, turning in the air, and thrust into their sockets. The two sentinels fired again, independently and ineffectually.

The hunted man saw all this over his shoulder; he was now swimming vigorously with the current. His brain was as energetic as his arms and legs; he thought with the rapidity of lightning.

"The officer," he reasoned, "will not make that martinet's error a second time. It is as easy to dodge a volley as a single shot. He was probably already given the command to fire at will. Gold help me, I cannot dodge them all!"

An appalling plash within two yards of him, followed by a loud rushing sound, *diminuendo*, which seemed to travel back through the air to the fort and died in an explosion which stirred the very river to its deeps! A rising sheet of water, which curved over him, fell down upon him, blinded him, strangled him! The cannon had taken a hand in the game. As he shook his head free from the commotion of the smitten water, he heard the deflected shot humming through the air ahead, and in an instant it was cracking and smashing the branches in the forest beyond.

"They will not do that again," he thought; "the next time they will use a charge of grape. I must keep my eye upon the gun; the smoke will apprise me—the report arrives too late; it lags behind the missile. It is a good gun."

Suddenly he felt himself whirled round and round—spinning like a top. The water, the banks, the forest, the now distant bridge, fort and men—all were commingled and blurred. Objects were represented by their colors only; circular horizontal streaks of color—that was all he saw. He had been caught in a vortex and was being whirled on with a velocity of advance and gyration which made him giddy and sick. In a few moments he was flung upon the gravel at the foot of the left bank of the stream—the southern bank—and behind a projecting point which concealed him from his enemies. The sudden arrest of his motion, the abrasion of one of his hands on the gravel, restored him and he wept with delight. He dug his fingers into the sand, threw it over himself in handfuls and audibly blessed it. It looked like gold, like diamonds, rubies, emeralds; he could think of nothing beautiful which it did not resemble. The trees upon the bank were giant garden plants; he noted a definite order in their arrangement, inhaled the fragrance of their blooms. A strange, roseate light shone through the spaces among their trunks, and the wind made in their branches the music of æolian harps. He had no wish to perfect his escape, was content to remain in that enchanting spot until retaken.

A whizz and rattle of grapeshot among the branches high above his head roused him from his dream. The baffled cannoneer had fired him a random farewell. He sprang to his feet, rushed up the sloping bank, and plunged into the forest.

All that day he travelled, laying his course by the rounding sun. The forest seemed interminable, nowhere did he discover a break in it, not even a woodman's road. He had not known that he lived in so wild a region. There was something uncanny in the revelation.

By nightfall he was fatigued, footsore, famishing. The thought of his wife and children urged him on. At last he found a road which led him in what he knew to be the right direction. It was as wide and straight as a city street, yet it seemed untravelled. No fields bordered it, no dwelling anywhere. Not so much as the barking of a dog suggested human habitation. The black bodies of the great trees formed a straight wall on both sides, terminating on the horizon in a point, like a diagram in a lesson in perspective. Overhead, as he looked up through this rift in the wood, shone great golden stars looking unfamiliar and grouped in strange constellations. He was sure they were arranged in some order which had a secret and malign significance. The wood on either side was full of singular noises, among which—once, twice, and again—he distinctly heard whispers in an unknown tongue.

His neck was in pain, and, lifting his hand to it, he found it horribly swollen. He knew that it had a circle of black where the rope had bruised it. His eyes felt congested; he could no longer close them. His tongue was swollen with thirst; he relieved its fever by thrusting it forward from between his teeth into the cool air. How softly the turf had carpeted the untravelled avenue! He could no longer feel the roadway beneath his feet!

Doubtless, despite his suffering, he fell asleep while walking, for now he sees another scene—perhaps he has merely recovered from a delirium. He stands at the gate of his own home. All is as he left it, and all bright and beautiful in the morning sunshine. He must have travelled the entire night. As he pushes open the gate and passes up the wide white walk, he sees a flutter of female garments; his wife, looking fresh and cool and sweet, steps down from the verandah to meet him. At the bottom of the steps she stands waiting, with a smile of ineffable joy, an attitude of matchless grace and dignity. Ah, how beautiful she is! He springs forward with extended arms. As he is about to clasp her, he feels a stunning blow upon the back of the neck; a blinding white light blazes all about him, with a sound like the shock of a cannon—then all is darkness and silence!

Peyton Farquhar was dead; his body, with a broken neck, swung gently from side to side beneath the timbers of the Owl Creek bridge.

Everyday Use

by
ALICE WALKER
(1944–   )

"Everyday Use" is one of those stories about Aunt Ruth's favourite teacup. You know what I mean, about those little heirlooms that every family has: about how and when to pass them on, and whether to use things or to put them behind glass, like in a museum. I've always been for everyday use myself, for enjoying things rather than simply polishing them up for show.

I will wait for her in the yard that Maggie and I made so clean and wavy yesterday afternoon. A yard like this is more comfortable than most people know. It is not just a yard. It is like an extended living room. When the hard clay is swept clean as a floor and the fine sand around the edges lined with tiny, irregular grooves, anyone can come and sit and look up into the elm tree and wait for the breezes that never come inside the house.

Maggie will be nervous until after her sister goes: she will stand hopelessly in corners, homely and ashamed of the burn scars down her arms and legs, eying her sister with a mixture of envy and awe. She thinks her sister has held life in the palm of one hand, that "no" is a word the world never learned to say to her.

You've no doubt seen those TV shows where the child who has "made it" is confronted, as a surprise, by her own mother and father, tottering in weakly from backstage. On TV mother and child embrace and smile into each other's faces. Sometimes the mother and father weep, the child wraps them in her arms and leans across the table to tell how she would not have made it without their help. I have seen these programs.

Sometimes I dream a dream in which Dee and I are suddenly brought together on a TV program of this sort. Out of a dark and soft-seated limousine I am ushered into a bright room filled with many people. There I meet a smiling, gray, sporty man like Johnny Carson who shakes my hand and tells me what a fine girl I have. Then we are on the stage and Dee is embracing me with tears in her eyes. She pins on my dress a large orchid, even though she has told me once that she thinks orchids are tacky flowers.

In real life I am a large, big-boned woman with rough, man-working hands. In the winter I wear flannel nightgowns to bed and overalls during the day. I can kill and clean a hog as mercilessly as a man. My fat keeps me hot in zero weather. I can work outside all day, breaking ice to get water for washing; I can eat pork liver cooked over the open fire minutes after it comes steaming from the hog. One winter I knocked a bull calf straight in the brain between the eyes with a sledge hammer and had the meat hung up to chill before nightfall. But of course all this does not show on television. I am the way my daughter would want me to be: a hundred pounds lighter, my skin like an uncooked barley pancake. My hair glistens in the hot bright lights. Johnny Carson has much to do to keep up with my quick and witty tongue.

But that is a mistake. I know even before I wake up. Who ever knew a Johnson with a quick tongue? Who can even imagine me looking a strange white man in the eye? It seems to me I have talked to them always with one foot raised in flight, with my head turned in whichever way is farthest from them. Dee, though. She would always look anyone in the eye. Hesitation was no part of her nature.

"How do I look, Mama?" Maggie says, showing just enough of her thin body enveloped in pink skirt and red blouse for me to know she's there, almost hidden by the door.

"Come out into the yard," I say.

Have you ever seen a lame animal, perhaps a dog run over by some careless person rich enough to own a car, sidle up to someone who is ignorant enough to be kind to him? That is the way my Maggie walks. She has been like this, chin to chest, eyes on ground, feet in shuffle, ever since the fire that burned the other house to the ground.

Dee is lighter than Maggie, with nicer hair and a fuller figure. She's a woman now, though sometimes I forget. How long ago was it that the other house burned? Ten, twelve years? Sometimes I can still hear the flames and feel Maggie's arms sticking to me, her hair smoking and her dress falling off her in little black papery flakes. Her eyes seemed stretched open, blazed open by the flames reflected in them. And Dee. I see her standing off under the sweet gum tree she used to dig gum out of; a look of concentration on her face as she watched the last dingy gray board of the house fall in toward the red-hot brick chimney. Why don't you do a dance around the ashes? I'd wanted to ask her. She had hated the house that much.

I used to think she hated Maggie, too. But that was before we raised the money, the church and me, to send her to Augusta to school. She used to read to us without pity; forcing words, lies, other folks' habits, whole lives upon us two, sitting trapped and ignorant underneath her voice. She washed us in a river of make-believe, burned us with a lot of knowledge we didn't necessarily need to know. Pressed us to her with the serious way she read, to shove us away at just the moment, like dimwits, we seemed about to understand.

Dee wanted nice things. A yellow organdy dress to wear to her graduation from high school; black pumps to match a green suit she'd made from an old suit somebody gave me. She was determined to stare down any disaster in her efforts. Her eyelids would not flicker for minutes at a time. Often I fought off the temptation to shake her. At sixteen she had a style of her own: and knew what style was.

I never had an education myself. After second grade the school was closed down. Don't ask me why: in 1927 colored asked fewer questions than they do now. Sometimes Maggie reads to me. She stumbles along good-naturedly but can't see well. She knows she is not bright. Like good looks and money, quickness passed her by. She will marry John Thomas (who has mossy teeth in an earnest face) and then I'll be free to sit here and I guess just sing church songs to myself. Although I never was a good singer. Never could carry a tune. I was always better at a man's job. I used to love to milk till I was hooked in the side in '49. Cows are soothing and slow and don't bother you, unless you try to milk them the wrong way.

I have deliberately turned my back on the house. It is three rooms, just like the one that burned, except that the roof is tin; they don't make shingle roofs any more. There are no real windows, just some holes cut in the sides, like the portholes in a ship, but not round and not square, with rawhide holding the shutters up on the outside. This house is in a pasture, too, like the other one. No doubt when Dee sees it she will want to tear it down. She wrote me once that no matter where we "choose" to live, she will manage to come see us. But she will never bring her friends. Maggie and I thought about this and Maggie asked me, "Mama, when did Dee ever *have* any friends?"

She had a few. Furtive boys in pink shirts hanging about on washday after school. Nervous girls who never laughed. Impressed with her they worshipped the well-turned phrase, the cute shape, the scalding humor that erupted like bubbles in lye. She read to them.

When she was courting Jimmy T she didn't have much time to pay to us, but turned all her faultfinding power on him. He *flew* to marry a cheap city girl from a family of ignorant flashy people. She hardly had time to recompose herself.

When she comes I will meet—but there they are!

Maggie attempts to make a dash for the house, in her shuffling way, but I stay her with my hand. "Come back here," I say. And she stops and tries to dig a well in the sand with her toe.

It is hard to see them clearly through the strong sun. But even the first glimpse of leg out of the car tells me it is Dee. Her feet were always neat-looking, as if God himself had shaped them with a certain style. From the other side of the car comes a short, stocky man. Hair is all over his head a foot

long and hanging from his chin like a kinky mule tail. I hear
Maggie suck in her breath. "Uhnnnh," is what it sounds like.
Like when you see the wriggling end of a snake just in front of
your foot on the road. "Uhnnnh."

Dee next. A dress down to the ground, in this hot weather.
A dress so loud it hurts my eyes. There are yellows and
oranges enough to throw back the light of the sun. I feel my
whole face warming from the heat waves it throws out.
Earrings gold, too, and hanging down to her shoulders.
Bracelets dangling and making noises when she moves her
arm up to shake the folds of the dress out of her armpits. The
dress is loose and flows, and as she walks closer, I like it. I
hear Maggie go "Uhnnnh" again. It is her sister's hair. It stands
straight up like the wool on a sheep. It is black as night and
around the edges are two long pigtails that rope about like
small lizards disappearing behind her ears.

"Wa-su-zo-Tean-o!" she says, coming on in that gliding way
the dress makes her move. The short stocky fellow with the
hair to his navel is all grinning and he follows up with
"Asalamalakim,* my mother and sister!" He moves to hug
Maggie but she falls back, right up against the back of my
chair. I feel her trembling there and when I look up I see the
perspiration falling off her chin.

"Don't get up," says Dee. Since I am stout it takes something
of a push. You can see me trying to move a second or two
before I make it. She turns, showing white heels through her
sandals, and goes back to the car. Out she peeks next with a
Polaroid. She stoops down quickly and lines up picture after
picture of me sitting there in front of the house with Maggie
cowering behind me. She never takes a shot without making
sure the house is included. When a cow comes nibbling
around the edge of the yard she snaps it and me and Maggie
and the house. Then she puts the Polaroid in the back seat of
the car, and comes up and kisses me on the forehead.

Meanwhile Asalamalakin is going through motions with
Maggie's hand. Maggie's hand is as limp as a fish, and probably
as cold, despite the sweat, and she keeps trying to pull it back.
It looks like Asalamalakim wants to shake hands but wants to

do it fancy. Or maybe he don't know how people shake hands. Anyhow, he soon gives up on Maggie.

"Well," I say. "Dee."

"No, Mama," she says. "Not 'Dee,' Wangero Leewanika Kemanjo!"

"What happened to 'Dee'?" I wanted to know.

"She's dead," Wangero said. "I couldn't bear it any longer, being named after the people who oppress me."

"You know as well as me you was named after your aunt Dicie," I said. Dicie is my sister. She named Dee. We called her "Big Dee" after Dee was born.

"But who was *she* named after?" asked Wangero.

"I guess after Grandma Dee," I said.

"And who was she named after?" asked Wangero.

"Her mother," I said, and saw Wangero was getting tired. "That's about as far back as I can trace it," I said. Though, in fact, I probably could have carried it back beyond the Civil War through the branches.

"Well," said Asalamalakim, "there you are."

"Uhnnnh," I heard Maggie say.

"There I was not," I said, "before 'Dicie' cropped up in our family, so why should I try to trace it that far back?"

He just stood there grinning, looking down on me like somebody inspecting a Model A car. Every once in a while he and Wangero sent eye signals over my head.

"How do you pronounce this name?" I asked.

"You don't have to call me by it if you don't want to," said Wangero.

"Why shouldn't I?" I asked. "If that's what you want us to call you, we'll call you."

"I know it might sound awkward at first," said Wangero.

"I'll get used to it," I said. "Ream it out again."

Well, soon we got the name out of the way. Asalamalakim had a name twice as long and three times as hard. After I tripped over it two or three times he told me to just call him Hakim-a-barber. I wanted to ask him was he a barber, but I didn't really think he was, so I didn't ask.

"You must belong to those beef-cattle peoples down the

road," I said. They said "Asalamalakim" when they met you, too, but they didn't shake hands. Always too busy: feeding the cattle, fixing the fences, putting up salt-lick shelters, throwing down hay. When the white folks poisoned some of the herd the men stayed up all night with rifles in their hands. I walked a mile and a half just to see the sight.

Hakim-a-barber said, "I accept some of their doctrines, but farming and raising cattle is not my style." (They didn't tell me, and I didn't ask, whether Wangero (Dee) had really gone and married him.)

We sat down to eat and right away he said he didn't eat collards and pork was unclean. Wangero, though, went on through the chitlins and corn bread, the greens and everything else. She talked a blue streak over the sweet potatoes. Everything delighted her. Even the fact that we still used the benches her daddy made for the table when we couldn't afford to buy chairs.

"Oh, Mama!" she cried. Then turned to Hakim-a-barber. "I never knew how lovely these benches are. You can feel the rump prints," she said, running her hands underneath her and along the bench. Then she gave a sigh and her hand closed over Grandma Dee's butter dish. "That's it!" she said. "I knew there was something I wanted to ask you if I could have." She jumped up from the table and went over in the corner where the churn stood, the milk in it clabber by now. She looked at the churn and looked at it.

"This churn top is what I need," she said. "Didn't Uncle Buddy whittle it out of a tree you all used to have?"

"Yes," I said.

"Uh huh," she said happily. "And I want the dasher, too."

"Uncle Buddy whittle that, too?" asked the barber.

Dee (Wangero) looked at me.

"Aunt Dee's first husband whittled the dash," said Maggie so low you almost couldn't hear her. "His name was Henry, but they called him Stash."

"Maggie's brain is like a elephant's," Wangero said, laughing. "I can use the churn top as a centerpiece for the alcove table," she said, sliding a plate over the churn, "and I'll think of something artistic to do with the dasher."

When she finished wrapping the dasher the handle stuck out. I took it for a moment in my hands. You didn't even have to look close to see where hands pushing the dasher up and down to make butter had left a kind of sink in the wood. In fact, there were a lot of small sinks; you could see where thumbs and fingers had sunk into the wood. It was beautiful light yellow wood, from a tree that grew in the yard where Big Dee and Stash had lived.

After dinner Dee (Wangero) went to the trunk at the foot of my bed and started rifling through it. Maggie hung back in the kitchen over the dishpan. Out came Wangero with two quilts. They had been pieced by Grandma Dee and then Big Dee and me had hung them on the quilt frames on the front porch and quilted them. One was in the Lone Star pattern. The other was Walk Around the Mountain. In both of them were scraps of dresses Grandma Dee had worn fifty and more years ago. Bits and pieces of Grandpa Jarrell's Paisley shirts. And one teeny faded blue piece, about the size of a penny matchbox, that was from Great Grandpa Ezra's uniform he wore in the Civil War.

"Mama," Wangero said sweet as a bird. "Can I have these old quilts?"

I heard something fall in the kitchen, and a minute later the kitchen door slammed.

"Why don't you take one or two of the others?" I asked. "These old things was just done by me and Big Dee from some tops your grandma pieced before she died."

"No," said Wangero. "I don't want those. They are stitched around the borders by machine."

"That'll make them last better," I said.

"That's not the point," said Wangero. "These are all pieces of dresses Grandma used to wear. She did all this stitching by hand. Imagine!" She held the quilts securely in her arms, stroking them.

"Some of the pieces, like those lavender ones, come from old clothes her mother handed down to her," I said, moving up to touch the quilts. Dee (Wangero) moved back just enough so that I couldn't reach the quilts. They already belonged to her.

"Imagine!" she breathed again, clutching them closely to her bosom.

"The truth is," I said, "I promised to give them quilts to Maggie, for when she marries John Thomas."

She gasped like a bee had stung her.

"Maggie can't appreciate these quilts!" she said. "She'd probably be backward enough to put them to everyday use."

"I reckon she would," I said. "God knows I been saving 'em for long enough with nobody using 'em. I hope she will!" I didn't want to bring up how I had offered Dee (Wangero) a quilt when she went away to college. Then she had told me they were old-fashioned, out of style.

"But they're *priceless*!" she was saying now, furiously; for she has a temper. "Maggie would put them on the bed and in five years they'd be in rags. Less than that!" "She can always make some more," I said. "Maggie knows how to quilt."

Dee (Wangero) looked at me with hatred. "You just will not understand. The point is these quilts, *these* quilts!"

"Well," I said, stumped. "What would *you* do with them?"

"Hang them," she said. As if that was the only thing you *could* do with quilts.

Maggie by now was standing in the door. I could almost hear the sound her feet made as they scraped over each other.

"She can have them, Mama," she said, like somebody used to never winning anything, or having anything reserved for her. "I can 'member Grandma Dee without the quilts."

I looked at her hard. She had filled her bottom lip with checkerberry snuff and it gave her face a kind of dopey, hangdog look. It was Grandma Dee and Big Dee who taught her how to quilt herself. She stood there with her scarred hands hidden in the folds of her skirt. She looked at her sister with something like fear but she wasn't mad at her. This was Maggie's portion. This was the way she knew God to work.

When I looked at her like that something hit me in the top of my head and ran down to the soles of my feet. Just like when I'm in church and the spirit of God touches me and I get happy and shout. I did something I never had done before: hugged Maggie to me, then dragged her on into the room, snatching the quilts out of Miss Wangero's hands and dumped them into Maggie's lap. Maggie just sat there on my bed with her mouth open.

"Take one or two of the others," I said to Dee.

But she turned without a word and went out to Hakim-a-barber.

"You just don't understand," she said, as Maggie and I came out to the car.

"What don't I understand?" I wanted to know.

"Your heritage," she said. And then she turned to Maggie, kissed her, and said, "You ought to try to make something of yourself, too, Maggie. It's really a new day for us. But from the way you and Mama still live you'd never know it."

She put on some sunglasses that hid everything above the tip of her nose and her chin.

Maggie smiled; maybe at the sunglasses. But a real smile, not scared. After we watched the car dust settle I asked Maggie to bring me a dip of snuff. And then the two of us sat there just enjoying, until it was time to go in the house and go to bed.

* Phonetic rendering of a Muslim greeting.

After Twenty Years

by
O. HENRY
(William Sydney Porter; 1862–1910)

The stories of O. Henry have long been a staple of my read-ings. In fact, it was a reading of O. Henry's "The Gift of the Magi" that first made me think, "Hey, I know how to do this." But it really wasn't me who knew what I was doing at the time. It was O. Henry. Reading aloud, I soon discovered, requires a certain type of story. Unlike reading, listening to a story does not leave a person a lot of time to reflect. The story must capture the imagination immediately, and move along quickly, without getting bogged down. This is what O. Henry does so well. He always has a good story to tell, and he tells the story simply—for the sake of the story alone.

T he policeman on the beat moved up the avenue impressively. The impressiveness was habitual and not for show, for spectators were few. The time was barely 10 o'clock at night, but chilly gusts of wind with a taste of rain in them had well nigh depeopled the streets.

Trying doors as he went, twirling his club with many intricate and artful movements, turning now and then to cast his watchful eye adown the pacific thoroughfare, the officer, with his stalwart form and slight swagger, made a fine picture of a guardian of the peace. The vicinity was one that kept early hours. Now and then you might see the lights of a cigar store or of an all-night lunch counter; but the majority of the doors belonged to business places that had long since been closed.

When about midway of a certain block the policeman suddenly slowed his walk. In the doorway of a darkened hardware store a man leaned, with an unlighted cigar in his mouth. As the policeman walked up to him the man spoke up quickly.

"It's all right, officer," he said, reassuringly. "I'm just waiting for a friend. It's an appointment made twenty years ago. Sounds a little funny to you, doesn't it? Well, I'll explain if you'd like to make certain it's all straight. About that long ago there used to be a restaurant where this store stands—'Big Joe' Brady's restaurant."

"Until five years ago," said the policeman. "It was torn down then."

The man in the doorway struck a match and lit his cigar. The light showed a pale, square-jawed face with keen eyes, and a little white scar near his right eyebrow. His scarfpin was a large diamond, oddly set.

"Twenty years ago tonight," said the man, "I dined here at 'Big Joe' Brady's with Jimmy Wells, my best chum, and the finest chap in the world. He and I were raised here in New York, just like two brothers, together. I was eighteen and Jimmy was twenty. The next morning I was to start for the West to make my fortune. You couldn't have dragged Jimmy out of New York; he thought it was the only place on earth. Well, we agreed that night that we would meet here again exactly twenty years from that date and time, no matter what our conditions might be or from what distance we might have to come. We figured that in twenty years each of us ought to have our destiny worked out and our fortunes made, whatever they were going to be."

"It sounds pretty interesting," said the policeman. "Rather a long time between meets, though, it seems to me. Haven't you heard from your friend since you left?"

"Well, yes, for a time we corresponded," said the other. "But after a year or two we lost track of each other. You see, the West is a pretty big proposition, and I kept hustling around over it pretty lively. But I know Jimmy will meet me here if he's alive, for he always was the truest, stanchest old chap in the world. He'll never forget. I came a thousand miles to stand in this door to-night, and it's worth it if my old partner turns up."

The waiting man pulled out a handsome watch, the lids of it set with small diamonds.

"Three minutes to ten," he announced. "It was exactly ten o'clock when we parted here at the restaurant door."

"Did pretty well out West, didn't you?" asked the policeman.

"You bet! I hope Jimmy has done half as well. He was a kind of plodder, though, good fellow as he was. I've had to compete with some of the sharpest wits going to get my pile. A man gets in a groove in New York. It takes the West to put a razor-edge on him."

The policeman twirled his club and took a step or two.

"I'll be on my way. Hope your friend comes around all right. Going to call time on him sharp?"

"I should say not!" said the other. "I'll give him half an hour at least. If Jimmy is alive on the earth he'll be here by that time. So long, officer."

"Good-night, sir," said the policeman, passing on along his beat, trying doors as he went.

There was now a fine, cold drizzle falling, and the wind had risen from its uncertain puffs into a steady blow. The few foot passengers astir in that quarter hurried dismally and silently along with coat collars turned high and pocketed hands. And in the door of the hardware store the man who had come a thousand miles to fill an appointment, uncertain almost to absurdity, with the friend of his youth, smoked his cigar and waited.

About twenty minutes he waited, and then a tall man in a long overcoat, with collar turned up to his ears, hurried across from the opposite side of the street. He went directly to the waiting man.

"Is that you, Bob?" he asked, doubtfully.

"It that you, Jimmy Wells?" cried the man in the door.

"Bless my heart!" exclaimed the new arrival, grasping both the other's hands with his own. "It's Bob, sure as fate. I was certain I'd find you here if you were still in existence. Well, well, well!—twenty years is a long time. The old restaurant's gone, Bob; I wish it had lasted, so we could have had another dinner there. How has the West treated you, old man?"

"Bully; it has given me everything I asked it for. You've changed lots, Jimmy. I never thought you were so tall by two or three inches."

"Oh, I grew a bit after I was twenty."

"Doing well in New York, Jimmy?"

"Moderately. I have a position in one of the city departments. Come on, Bob; we'll go around to a place I know of, and have a good long talk about old times."

The two men started up the street, arm in arm. The man from the West, his egotism enlarged by success, was beginning to outline the history of his career. The other, submerged in his overcoat, listened with interest.

At the corner stood a drug store, brilliant with electric lights. When they came into this glare each of them turned simultaneously to gaze upon the other's face.

The man from the West stopped suddenly and released his arm.

"You're not Jimmy Wells," he snapped. "Twenty years is a long time, but not long enough to change a man's nose from a Roman to a pug."

"It sometimes changes a good man into a bad one," said the tall man. "You've been under arrest for ten minutes, 'Silky' Bob. Chicago thinks you may have dropped over our way and wires us she wants to have a chat with you. Going quietly, are you? That's sensible. Now, before we go to the station here's a note I was asked to hand to you. You may read it here at the window. It's from Patrolman Wells."

The man from the West unfolded the little piece of paper handed him. His hand was steady when he began to read, but it trembled a little by the time he had finished. The note was rather short.

Bob: I was at the appointed place on time. When you struck the match to light your cigar I saw it was the face of the man wanted in Chicago. Somehow I couldn't do it myself, so I went around and got a plain clothes man to do the job.

Jimmy

Bicycle

by

LYNDA SHORTEN

(1955–   )

There's a nice little anecdote about reading this story that I would like to tell. "Bicycle" is from a book called Without Reserve, Stories from Urban Natives, *a collection of stories by native storytellers that was compiled by Lynda Shorten. When the book first came out it was circulated around the CBC, the way things sometimes are. I think "Morningside" was considering doing something with it before we decided to do a reading on "As it Happens." I eventually chose the "Bicycle" story, I think, because it was a little more upbeat than some of the others in the collection. It had that sense of hope that some of the other more serious stories lacked. It is also a very funny story. Anyway, I guess it was about two years later that Lynda Shorten came to work at "As it Happens." She told me when we met how she had sat at home on Canada Day two years previously, pregnant with her first child, and listened to my reading, and how much it had meant to me. I very much hope that the character of "Sky," the originator of the story, also had a chance to hear my reading of "Bicycle." It is a story that I'm very fond of.*

There's this old guy riding a bicycle east from Enoch down Highway 16 toward the Alamo Motel. The Alamo Motel squats brown and square just off the highway, ugly, near empty and for sale. By the time you're at the Alamo, you've almost made Edmonton. Just the Windmill, the Parkland, the Royal Scot, the Siesta, the All Star American Bar to go and bingo—you've hit the city.

The old man has a way to go yet before he reaches the Alamo. He's wearing a grey raincoat and a peaked cap and his bicycle is tinny and rusted. His head is bent, staring down at his pedals, and in my rear-view mirror I can just catch his knees pumping—up, down, up, down—going like billyho.

The old man is coming from Enoch, the Stony Plain Indian reserve fifteen minutes west of downtown Edmonton, about ten minutes away, by a back road, from West Edmonton Mall. In fact the mall, some say, is built on reserve land sold off by a shortsighted band council years ago.

Some on the reserve claim the name "Enoch" was given by a Catholic missionary whose inspiration was a Sodom-type town in the Bible. It's not as bad as it sounds, they say; the town, the one in the Bible, pulled itself up by its boot straps

and that's what the missionary had in mind for Enoch. Some
say the reserve is named after Enoch, son of Cain, second from
Adam. Or after Enoch, seventh from Adam, a prophet who
walked the earth with God for 365 years and begat many sons
and daughters. Someone else says in the early 1900s a man
named Enoch Lapatac enticed a few families from the
Papaschase Reserve onto this new, fertile reserve to farm.
Lapatac was the reserve's first chief, they say; the name follows.

The last story is true. The boot straps story is the one Sky
believes. As a consequence, so do I.

Sky and I pass the old man on the bike pedalling down the
right shoulder, the wrong side of the road, going with and not
against the cars like he is supposed to. Sky was born in North
Dakota in 1955 but grew up in Manitoba and spent twenty
years in Prince Albert and Stony Mountain penitentiaries. He
ended up in Edmonton because when he was released, finally,
he happened to be in the Edmonton Maximum Institution. He
lives on Enoch because he couldn't handle the city after a few
weeks of living in his car, sleeping on concrete, watching his
people, he said, picking out of garbage cans.

I'm driving because Sky's got no car. His 1977 grey El
Dorado with red leather interior was stolen, just two days after
he spent a thousand dollars installing a new motor and a
stereo. Sky had big hopes for that car, once it was fixed up.

Sky believes the two kids who stole his El Dorado started
out intending just to lift his black leather jacket, the one he
bought from the bleached blond Christian wolf-trainer at the
Leather Ranch at West Edmonton Mall. This woman told Sky
that when she is not selling coats or training wolves she
writes books about how to train dogs, although she is having
some trouble with her publisher right now. She also show-
jumps horses and sews saddles by hand. When Sky walked
into the Leather Ranch she saw his deerskin shirt, the one he
designed himself, the one he wore at the Sun Dance, and
approached him to design shirts for her. She said she'd sell
his shirts at the new store she and her partners, silent partners, are just about to open. Just as soon as the negotiations

over space are complete. By God, she tells Sky, she knows her leathers. She tells him she believes in God.

Sky says he knew right away he could not trust that woman. She would pay him for one design, then copy it herself and make lots of money and never pay him again. It's happened to him before, he says. God or no God, he doesn't take her up on her offer.

The kids who broke through a basement window to steal his leather jacket, Sky says, found car keys in his pocket and forgot about the jacket. Then they found his medicine bundle in the car. They opened it. They took out his sacred pipe and smoked hash in it. Then they drove the El Dorado across fields, sped through small towns. When the RCMP started chasing them on the highway outside Morinville, they lost control of the car and drove into two concrete pillars. They ended up on the TV news. They hurt themselves bad. Now they're in jail.

Sky says that, at first, after his car was stolen, he was pretty much numb. After he got over being numb he started to wish those two kids had broken their necks. Then he started to think about being in a Manitoba prison when he was a kid, serving his first federal time. So he went to a sweat lodge and made offerings to the grandfathers of those kids, asking that the kids would learn something and something good would come of him losing his pipe and his medicine bundle and his car.

Sky says he realizes now he was thinking about those possessions too much—his medicine bundle and his car. They were the only two things he owned, he says, so the grandfathers, the spirits took them away to show him the foolishness of cherishing things over people.

Sky's El Dorado is parked now in a muddy tow yard outside an Edmonton bedroom community. The medicine bundle and the stereo are gone for good. Sky has to pay the towing charge plus daily fees to get his El Dorado back. The tow yard is run by an ex-con, a man who oils back his hair with Brylcreem, a man who fancies black leather studded with silver spangles, and gold skull rings with diamonds for eyes. The tow yard office is papered with tire-store madonnas. Sky's car sits in the

mud smiling—the concrete pillars the two kids hit convinced
the front end to grin, and hay pokes out from under the grill
like unshaved stubble.

It's the end of October and none too warm. Sky and I are on
our way into the city because he wants to pick up some fish
and chips from a strip-mall restaurant before we fetch his car.
We've been to the restaurant before; in fact we watched the
San Francisco earthquake on the restaurant's TV. Sky took the
earthquake with a shrug. It is simply one of the prophesies
come true, he said. The white man does not respect the earth,
and the earth takes her revenge. The french fries were served
in their skins on wicker plates. A hand-lettered sign posted
beside the till read: "Fish is brain food and the smarter you
are, the richer we are." Sky likes the place, and I don't mind.

It is driving down the highway from Enoch to the fish and
chip joint that Sky spots the man on the bicycle. "There's that
old man," he says. Sky leans forward to look at the man's reflection in the side mirror as we pass. He laughs, "Yep, that's him."

I think, incorrectly, that I know which old man Sky means. I
am often wrong when I assume I know what Sky means. I
think he means the man we were supposed to go talk to about
residential schools but who wasn't at home in his motel strip
reserve house when we pulled up. I say, "You wanna stop for
him?"

Sky says, "Nah. The old man's OK. Just keep going." He
leans back, pulls his long hair out from where it's stuck
between his shoulders and the bucket seat, and settles in.

Then he tells this story.

"That old man, he a drinker, eh. One day he was feeling
really sick from his drinking. Real hung over. So he says to his
son, 'Son, you gotta ride the bicycle into Edmonton and buy
me some beer.'

"The son say, 'Forget it, old man. You want beer you can get
it yourself.'

"That old man, he still feeling pretty sick. But he really
wants his beer. Trouble is, he's feeling so sick he doesn't know
if he can ride the bicycle. So he pulls it out of the shed and
hauls it into the kitchen. He gets on that bicycle and rides

around the kitchen a few times. That seems to work OK. So the old man figures he'll just ride into the city and buy his own beer.

"The old man gets onto the highway and starts riding. He rides along for about three miles. Everything is going fine. The old man is feeling pretty good, all things considered. And then the bicycle chain falls off.

"The old man doesn't know what to do. He doesn't know how to fix the bicycle chain. Edmonton is still a long ways away. But he knows he wants his beer. So he decides he'll push the bicycle into Edmonton, buy his beer and then figure things out.

"He's pushing the bicycle along the highway when pretty soon a car stops. This young guy gets out and says, 'What you doing, old man?' And the old man says, 'I'm going to Edmonton.' The young guy looks at the old man, and then looks at the bike. 'Come on,' he says. 'I'll give you a ride.'

"So the two of them, they try to put the bike in the trunk. It won't fit. They try to put it into the back seat. It won't fit. They try tying it onto the roof, but the young guy only has one rope and the bike won't stay put.

"Finally the young guy says, 'I'll tell you what, old man. I'll tie the front of your bike to my bumper and I'll tow you into Edmonton.'

"The old man isn't sure this is such a good idea. 'No thanks,' he tells the young guy. 'You drive too fast.' And he grabs the handlebars and gets set to start pushing again.

"But the young guy says, 'Don't worry. I'll drive real slow. If I start to go too fast, you just ring the bell on that bicycle and I'll slow down.'

"This sounds not too bad to the old man. So they tie the front of his bike to the young guy's bumper and the two of them start into town, the car towing the bike with the old man perched up there behind the car, sitting on the bicycle seat holding onto his handlebars for dear life.

"So, before too long another car pulls up beside the young guy and starts gunning it. This other car jumps ahead and falls back, and guns ahead and falls back. The young guy just can't resist. Pretty soon the two cars are dragging, racing down the highway side by side. By the time they make Edmonton they've hit at least ninety miles an hour. Maybe a hundred. Maybe more.

"Just outside of Edmonton, just past the Alamo, the Windmill, the Royal Scot, an unmarked RCMP cruiser picks up two speeding cars on radar. The cop turns on his siren and straps on his bubble light. He gives chase and pulls the speeders over. The cop writes out the tickets, then walks back to his car and radios in.

"'You won't believe it,' the cop says to the radio. 'I just picked two guys up for speeding. And the damndest thing. There was some old Indian on a bicycle behind them, ringing his bell like crazy, trying to pass.'"

When I stop laughing, Sky looks out the car window. He tells me: "I used to know a lot of stories like that. At one time I knew a lot of stories like that."

Trap Lines

by
THOMAS KING
(1943–   )

I think that I've probably learned a few things about myself by putting together these stories. What one generation gives to the next, the traditions, the memories, the stories, is clearly important to me. I don't think that I realized this quite so concretely before. Still, it's hard to miss when it's staring you in the face: as a major theme in almost every tale. But what I really like about "Trap Lines" is the sense of progression between the generations in the story. Things are passed along but things also move forward. The ambitions of one generation are not necessarily those of the next. In "Trap Lines," people seek progress while cherishing the traditions of the past.

When I was twelve, thirteen at most, and we were still living on the reserve, I asked my grandmother and she told me my father sat in the bathroom in the dark because it was the only place he could go to get away from us kids. What does he do in the bathroom, I wanted to know. Sits, said my grandmother. That's it? Thinks, she said, he thinks. I asked her if he went to the bathroom, too, and she said that was adult conversation, and I would have to ask him. It seemed strange at the time, my father sitting in the dark, thinking, but rather than run the risk of asking him, I was willing to believe my grandmother's explanation.

At forty-six, I am sure it was true, though I have had some trouble convincing my son that sitting in the bathroom with the lights out is normal. He has, at eighteen, come upon language, much as a puppy comes upon a slipper. Unlike other teenagers his age who slouch in closets and basements, mute and desolate, Christopher likes to chew on conversation, toss it in the air, bang it off the walls. I was always shy around language. Christopher is fearless.

"Why do you sit in the bathroom, Dad?"

"My father used to sit in the bathroom."

"How many bathrooms did you have in the olden days?"

"We lived on the reserve then. We only had the one."

"I thought you guys lived in a teepee or something. Where was the bathroom?"

"That was your great grandfather. We lived in a house."

"It's a good thing we got two bathrooms," he told me.

The house on the reserve had been a government house, small and poorly made. When we left and came to the city, my father took a picture of it with me and my sisters standing in front. I have the picture in a box somewhere. I want to show it to Christopher, so he can see just how small the house was.

"You're always bragging about that shack."

"It wasn't a shack."

"The one with all the broken windows?"

"Some of them had cracks."

"And it was cold, right?"

"In the winter it was cold."

"And you didn't have television."

"That's right."

"Jerry says that every house built has cable built in. It's a law or something."

"We didn't have cable or television."

"Is that why you left?"

"My father got a job here. I've got a picture of the house. You want to see it?"

"No big deal."

"I can probably find it."

"No big deal."

Some of these conversations were easy. Others were hard. My conversations with my father were generally about the weather or trapping or about fishing. That was it.

"Jerry says his father has to sit in the bathroom, too."

"Shower curtain was bundled up again. You have to spread it out so it can dry."

"You want to know why?"

"Be nice if you cleaned up the water you leave on the floor."

"Jerry says it's because his father's constipated."

"Lawn has to be mowed. It's getting high."

"He says it's because his father eats too much junk food."

"Be nice if you cleaned the bottom of the mower this time. It's packed with grass."

"But that doesn't make any sense, does it? Jerry and I eat junk food all the time, and we're not constipated."

"Your mother wants me to fix the railing on the porch. I'm going to need your help with that."

"Are you constipated?"

Alberta wasn't much help. I could see her smiling to herself whenever Christopher started chewing. "It's because we're in the city," she said. "If we had stayed on the reserve, Christopher would be out on a trap line with his mouth shut and you wouldn't be constipated."

"Nobody runs a trap line anymore."

"My grandfather said the outdoors was good for you."

"We could have lived on the reserve, but you didn't want to."

"And he was never constipated."

"My father ran a trap line. We didn't leave the reserve until I was sixteen. Your folks have always lived in the city."

"Your father was a mechanic."

"He ran a trap line, just like his father."

"Your grandfather was a mechanic."

"Not in the winter."

My father never remarried. After my mother died, he just looked after the four of us. He seldom talked about himself, and, slowly, as my sisters and I got older, he became a mystery. He remained a mystery until his death.

"You hardly even knew my father," I said. "He died two years after we were married."

Alberta nodded her head and stroked her hair behind her ears. "Your grandmother told me."

"She died before he did."

"My mother told me. She knew your grandmother."

"So, what did your mother tell you?"

"She told me not to marry you."

"She told me I was a damn good catch. Those were her exact words, 'damn good.'"

"She said that just to please you. She said you had a smart

mouth. She wanted me to marry Sid."

"So, why didn't you marry Sid?"

"I didn't love Sid."

"What else did she say?"

"She said that constipation ran in your family."

After Christopher graduated from high school, he pulled up in front of the television and sat there for almost a month.

"You planning on going to university?" I asked him.

"I guess."

"You going to do it right away or you going to get a job?"

"I'm going to rest first."

"Seems to me, you got to make some decisions."

"Maybe I'll go in the bathroom later on and think about it."

"You can't just watch television."

"I know."

"You're an adult now."

"I know."

Alberta called these conversations father and son talks, and you could tell the way she sharpened her tongue on "father and son" that she didn't think much of them.

"You ever talk to him about important things?"

"Like what?"

"You know."

"Sure."

"Okay, what do you tell him?"

"I tell him what he needs to know."

"My mother talked to my sisters and me all the time. About everything."

"We have good conversations."

"Did he tell you he isn't going to college."

"He just wants some time to think."

"Not what he told me."

I was in a bookstore looking for the new Audrey Thomas novel. The Ts were on the third shelf down and I had to bend over and cock my head to one side in order to read the titles. As I stood there, bent over and twisted, I felt my face start to slide. It was a strange sensation. Everything that wasn't anchored to bone just slipped off the top half of my head, slopped into the lower half, and hung there like a bag of jello. When I arrived home, I got myself into the same position in front of the bathroom mirror. That evening, I went downstairs and sat on the couch with Christopher and waited for a commercial.

"How about turning off the sound?"

"We going to have another talk?"

"I thought we could talk about the things that you're good at doing."

"I'm not good at anything."

"That's not true. You're good at computers."

"I like the games."

"You're good at talking to people. You could be a teacher."

"Teaching looks boring. Most of my teachers were boring."

"Times are tougher now," I said. "When your grandfather was a boy, he worked on a trap line up north. It was hard work, but you didn't need a university degree. Now you have to have one. Times are tougher."

"Mr. Johnson was the boringest of all."

"University is the key. Lot of kids go there not knowing what they want to do, and, after two or three years, they figure it out. Have you applied to any universities yet?"

"Commercial's over."

"No money in watching television."

"Commercial's over."

Alberta caught me bent over in front of the mirror. "You lose something?"

"Mirror's got a defect in it. You can see it just there."

"At least you're not going bald."

"I talked to Christopher about university."

"My father never looked a day over forty." Alberta grinned at herself in the mirror so she could see her teeth. "You know," she said, "When you stand like that, your face hangs funny."

I don't remember my father growing old. He was fifty-six when he died. We never had long talks about life or careers. When I was a kid—I forget how old—we drove into Medicine

River to watch the astronauts land on the moon. We sat in the American Hotel and watched it on the old black and white that Morris Rough Dog kept in the lobby. Morris told my father that they were checking the moon to see if it had any timber, water, valuable minerals, or game, and, if it didn't, they planned to turn it into a reserve and move all the Cree up there. Hey, he said to my father, what's that boy of yours going to be when he grows up? Beats me, said my father. Well, said Morris, there's damn little money in the hotel business and sure as hell nothing but scratch and splinters in being an Indian.

For weeks after, my father told Morris's story about the moon and the astronauts. My father laughed when he told the story. Morris had told it straight-faced.

"What do you really do in the bathroom, Dad?"

"I think."

"That all?"

"Just thinking."

"Didn't know thinking smelled so bad."

My father liked the idea of fishing. There were always fishing magazines around the house, and he would call me and my sisters over to show us a picture of a rainbow trout breaking water, or a northern pike rolled on its side or a tarpon sailing out of the blue sea like a silver missile. At the back of the magazines were advertisements for fishing tackle that my father would cut out and stick on the refrigerator door. When they got yellow and curled up, he would take them down and put up fresh ones.

I was in the downstairs bathroom. Christopher and Jerry were in Christopher's room. I could hear them playing video games and talking.

"My father wants me to go into business with him," said Jerry.

"Yeah."

"Can you see it? Me, selling cars the rest of my life?"

"Good money?"

"Sure, but what a toady job. I'd rather go to university and see what comes up."

"I'm thinking about that, too."

"What's your dad want you to do," said Jerry.

It was dark in the bathroom and cool, and I sat there trying not to breathe.

"Take a guess."

"Doctor?" said Jerry. "Lawyer?"

"Nope."

"An accountant? My dad almost became an accountant."

"You'll never guess. You could live to be a million years old and you'd never guess."

"Sounds stupid."

"A trapper. He wants me to work a trap line."

"You got to be kidding."

"God's truth. Just like my grandfather."

"Your dad is really weird."

"You ought to live with him."

We only went fishing once. It was just before my mother died. We all got in the car and drove up to a lake just off the reserve. My dad rented a boat and took us kids on in pairs. My mother stayed on the docks and lay in the sun.

Towards the end of the day, my sisters stayed on the dock with my mother, and my father and I went out in the boat alone. He had a new green tackle box he had bought at the hardware store on Saturday. Inside was an assortment of hooks and spinners and lures and a couple of red things with long trailing red and white skirts. He snorted and showed me a clipping that had come with the box for a lure that could actually call the fish.

Used to be beaver all around here, he told me, but they've been trapped out. Do you know why the beavers were so easy to catch, he asked me. It's because they always do the same thing. You can count on beavers to be regular. They're not stupid. They're just predictable, so you always set the trap in the same place and you always use the same bait, and pretty soon, they're gone.

Trapping was good money when your grandfather was here, but not now. No money in being a mechanic either. Better think of something else to do. Maybe I'll be an astronaut, I said. Have more luck trying to get pregnant, he said. Maybe I'll be a fisherman. No sir, he said. All the money's in making junk like this, and he squeezed the advertisement into a ball and set it afloat on the lake.

Christopher was in front of the television when I got home from work on Friday. There was a dirty plate under the coffee table and a box of crackers sitting on the cushions.

"What do you say we get out of the house this weekend and do something?"

"Like what?"

"I don't know. What would you like to do?"

"We could go to that new movie."

"I meant outdoors."

"What's to do outdoors besides work?"

"We could go fishing."

"Fishing?"

"Sure, I used to go fishing with my father all the time."

"This one of those father, son things?"

"We could go to the lake and rent a boat."

"I may have a job."

"Great. Where?"

"Let you know later."

"What's the secret?"

"No secret. I'll just tell you later."

"What about the fishing trip?"

"Better stick around the house in case someone calls."

Christopher slumped back into the cushions and turned up the sound on the television.

"What about the dirty plate?"

"It's not going anywhere."

"That box is going to spill if you leave it like that."

"It's empty."

My father caught four fish that day. I caught two. He sat in the

stern with the motor. I sat in the bow with the anchor. When
the sun dropped into the trees, he closed his tackle box and
gave the starter rope a pull. The motor sputtered and died. He
pulled it again. Nothing. He moved his tackle box out of the
way, stood up, and put one foot on the motor and gave the
rope a hard yank. It broke in his hand and he tumbled over
backwards, the boat tipping and slopping back and forth.
Damn, he said, and he pulled himself back up on the seat.
Well, son, he said, I've got a job for you, and he set the oars in
the locks and leaned against the motor. He looked around the
lake at the trees and the mountains and the sky. And he
looked at me. Try not to get me wet, he said.

Alberta was in the kitchen peeling a piece of pizza away from
the box. "Christopher got a job at that new fast food place. Did
he tell you?"
    "No. He doesn't tell me those things."
    "You should talk with him more."
    "I talk with him all the time."
    "He needs to know you love him."
    "He knows that."
    "He just wants to be like you."

Once when my sister and I were fighting, my father broke us
up and sent us out in the woods to get four sticks apiece about
as round as a finger. So we did. And when we brought them
back, he took each one and broke it over his knee. Then he
sent us out to get some more.

"Why don't you take him fishing?"
    "I tried. He didn't want to go."
    "What did you and your father do?"
    "We didn't do much of anything."
    "Okay, start there."

When we came home with the sticks, my father wrapped them
all together with some cord. Try to break these, he said. We
jumped on the sticks and we kicked them. We put the bundle

between two rocks and hit it with a board. But the sticks
didn't break. Finally, my father took the sticks and tried to
break them across his knee. You kids get the idea, he said.
After my father went back into the house, my youngest sister
kicked the sticks around the yard some more and said it was
okay but she'd rather have a ball.

Christopher's job at the fast food place lasted three weeks.
After that he resumed his place in front of the television.

"What happened with the job?"

"It was boring."

"Lots of jobs are boring."

"Don't worry, I'll get another."

"I'm not worried," I said, and I told him about the sticks. "A
stick by itself is easy to break, but it's impossible to break them
when they stand together. You see what I mean?"

"Chainsaw," said my son.

"What?"

"Use a chainsaw."

I began rowing for the docks, and my father began to sing.
Then he stopped and leaned forward as though he wanted to
tell me something. Son, he said, I've been thinking . . . And
just then a gust of wind blew his hat off, and I had to swing
the boat around so we could get it before it sank. The hat was
waterlogged. My father wrung it out as best he could, and
then he settled in against the motor again and started singing.

My best memory of my father was that day on the lake. He
lived alone, and, after his funeral, my sisters and I went back
to his apartment and began packing and dividing the things as
we went. I found his tackle box in the closet at the back.

"Christopher got accepted to university."

"When did that happen?"

"Last week. He said he was going to tell you."

"Good."

"He and Jerry both got accepted. Jerry's father gave Jerry a
car and they're going to drive over to Vancouver and see about

getting jobs before school starts."

"Vancouver, huh?"

"Not many more chances."

"What?"

"For talking to your son."

Jerry came by on a Saturday, and Alberta and I helped Christopher pack his things in the station wagon.

"Nice car," said Alberta.

"It's a pig," said Jerry. "My father couldn't sell it because of the color. But it'll get us there."

"Bet your father and mother are going to miss you."

"My father wanted me to stick around and help with the business. Gave me this big speech about traditions."

"Nothing wrong with traditions," Alberta said.

"Yeah, I guess. Look at this." Jerry held up a red metal tool box. "It's my grandfather's first tool box. My father gave it to me. You know, father to son and all that."

"That's nice," said Alberta.

"I guess."

"Come on," said Christopher. "Couple more things and we can get going."

Alberta put her arm around my waist and she began to poke me. Not so you could see. Just a sharp, annoying poke. "For Christ's sake," she whispered, "say something."

Christopher came out of the house carrying his boots and a green metal box. "All set," he said.

"Where'd you get the box?" I asked.

"It's an old fishing tackle box."

"I know."

"It's been sitting in the closet for years. Nobody uses it."

"It was my father's box."

"Yeah. It's got some really weird stuff in it. Jerry says that there's good fishing in B.C."

"That's right," said Jerry. "You should see some of those salmon."

"You don't fish."

"You never took me."

"My father gave me that box. It was his father's."

"You never use it."

"No, it's okay. I was going to give it to you anyway."

"No big deal. I can leave it here."

"No, it's yours."

"I'll take care of it."

"Maybe after you get settled out there, we can come out. Maybe you and I can do some fishing."

"Sure."

"Love you, honey," said Alberta and she put her arms around Christopher and held him. "I'm going to miss you. Call us if you need anything. And watch what you eat so you don't wind up like your father."

"Sure."

Alberta and I stood in the yard for a while after the boys drove off. "You could have told him you loved him," she said.

"I did. In my own way."

"Oh, he's supposed to figure that out because you gave him that old fishing box."

"That's the way my father did it."

"I thought you told me you found the box when you and your sisters were cleaning out his place."

After supper, Alberta went grocery shopping. I sat in the bathroom and imagined what my father had been going to say just before the wind took his hat, something important I guessed, something I could have shared with my son.

The *Fable* of the *Man* with the *Golden Brain*

ALPHONSE DAUDET
(1840–1897)

Alphonse Daudet is a wonderful storyteller. It seems a pity he isn't read more often. There is a sort of charming simplicity and warmth about this story. Like most fables "The Fable of the Man with the Golden Brain" has a moral, but what I like about Daudet is that things are never quite as simple as they seem. Yes, the man who leads a reckless life is made to pay for his recklessness, but it is Daudet's larger sense of sympathy that remains with you after the story is finished. This is one of those stories that was either written for children and intended for adults, or written for adults and intended for children. It doesn't really matter. "The Fable of the Man with the Golden Brain" works equally well with a brandy or hot chocolate.

165

To the Lady who asks for light-hearted stories

When I read your letter, madam, I had a twinge of something like remorse. I blamed myself for the sombre hue of my stories, and promised myself I would offer you something joyful today, something light-heartedly joyful.

After all, why should I be sad? I live a thousand leagues from Paris, on a sun-soaked hill, in the country of tambourines and muscat wine. Around me all is sunshine and music. I have orchestras of wheatears and choirs of tomtits. In the morning the curlews call. In the afternoon, the cicadas. Then the herdsmen come, playing the fife, and the beautiful, dark-haired girls who can be heard laughing among the vines.

In truth, the place is the least conducive to melancholy. I ought rather to be dispatching rose-coloured poems and basketfuls of love stories.

Alas, no! I am still too near to Paris. Every day, even among my pine trees, the murky splashes of her miseries reach me. At the very moment that I am writing this, I have just learnt of the miserable death of poor Charles Barbara;* and my mill is in deep mourning. Farewell, curlews and cicadas! I have heart no more for anything light and gay. That is why, madam, instead of the merry little tale I had promised to give you, you will today receive once again a melancholy fable.

Once upon a time there was a man who had a brain of gold. Yes, madam, a brain of pure gold. When he was born, the doctors thought he would not live, so heavy was his head and so enormous his skull. But live he did, and grew in the sunshine like a healthy young olive tree. His huge head, however, was always getting him into difficulties. It was pitiful to see him bumping into the furniture as he walked about. He fell over often. One day he rolled right down a flight of stairs, knocked his forehead against a marble step, and his skull rang like an ingot. They thought he was dead, but, on picking him up, only a slight cut was found, with two or three little drops of gold clotted in his fair hair. It was thus his parents learnt that the child had a brain of gold.

The matter was kept secret; the poor little boy himself suspected nothing. From time to time, he would ask why they no longer allowed him to run about in the street in front of the house with the other boys.

'You would be stolen, my treasure!' his mother would reply.

Then the child became very frightened of being stolen. He used to stay inside, playing all alone, saying nothing, dragging himself from one room to another.

Not until he was eighteen did his parents reveal to him the monstrous gift he had received from fate. And as they had fed and clothed and cared for him to that age, they asked him in return for a little of his gold. The boy did not hesitate; the very same moment—how and by what means the fable does not tell—he plucked out of his skull a piece of solid gold, as big as a walnut, and threw it proudly into his mother's lap. Then, quite dazzled by the riches he carried in his head, mad with ambitions, drunk with his power, he left his father's house and went out into the world squandering his treasure.

At the rate he lived, royally and recklessly, his treasure might have been thought inexhaustible. But exhaustible it was, and gradually his eyes were seen to become duller and his cheeks hollower. One day at last, the morning after a night of sense-less debauchery, the wretched youth, left alone among the wreckage of the banquet and the fading light of the chande-liers, was struck with panic at the tremendous breach he had already made in his ingot of gold. It was time to stop.

From that moment he began a new life. The man with the brain of gold went away to live alone and by the work of his hands, suspicious and fearful like a miser, out of reach of temp-tations, trying to make himself forget those fateful riches which he no longer wished to use...Unfortunately a friend had fol-lowed him into his solitude, and this friend knew his secret.

One night the poor man was suddenly awakened with a pain, an excruciating pain, in his head. He jumped up dis-tracted and by the light of the moon he saw the friend running away hiding something under his cloak...

A little more of his brain had been taken from him!...

Some time after that, the man with the golden brain fell in love, and this time all was over. With all his heart, he loved a little fair-haired girl who loved him also, but who loved even more frilly dresses, white feathers, and pretty bronze tassels around her little shoes.

In the hands of this dainty creature—half bird, half doll—it was a pleasure to see the pieces of gold melt away. She was full of caprice, and he could deny her nothing. For fear of upset-ting her, he even to the very end hid from her the sad secret of his wealth.

'We are very rich, then?' she used to say.

And the poor man would reply,

'Oh, yes...yes, very rich!'

And he would smile with love at the little blue bird that was innocently eating his brain. But, sometimes, fear overwhelmed him and he tried to spend less. Yet then his little wife would come hopping up to him, saying,

'My rich, rich husband! Buy me something very expensive!'

And he would buy her something very expensive.

This went on for two years. Then, one morning, his little wife died, without any apparent cause, just like a bird...The treasure was nearly exhausted; with what he had left the widower arranged a beautiful funeral for his beloved one. A full peal of bells, heavy coaches draped with black velvet hangings— nothing was too fine for her. What did his gold matter to him now? He gave it to the church, to the pall-bearers, to the women who provided the wreaths. He gave it everywhere heedlessly. So, when he left the cemetery, almost nothing remained of that marvellous brain, scarcely a few grains on the lining of the brain-pan.

Then he was seen wandering the streets distractedly, grop- ing his way with his hands, staggering like a drunkard. In the evening, when the shops were lighting up, he stopped in front of a shop-window filled with a jumble of fabrics and finery glistening in the lights, and remained there for a long time, looking at two little blue satin boots lined with swan's down. 'I know someone to whom those little boots would give a lot of pleasure,' he said to himself, smiling. And no longer even remembering that his little wife was dead, he went in to buy them.

The shop-keeper, in the back room of her shop, heard a great cry. She ran in and drew back with fear on seeing a man leaning sideways against the counter, staring at her as if in ter- rible pain. He was grasping in one hand the little blue boots lined with swan's down, and holding out to her his other hand, all covered with blood but with scrapings of gold on his finger-nails.

Such, madam, is the fable of the man with the brain of gold.

Although it sounds an unbelievable story, this fable is true from beginning to end. There are in this world unfortunate people who pay in fine gold, with their marrow and their very substance, for the least things in life. For them, life is a daily renewal of pain; and then, when they are weary of suffering...

* A now forgotten French novelist. The reference dates this story exactly since Barbara died on 19 September 1866.

Back for Christmas

by
JOHN COLLIER
(1901-1980)

There are some stories that you see in your mind's eye when reading them. "Back for Christmas" is a little like the screenplay for an old Hitchcock movie: there is the opening scene that is strangely felt to be somehow suspect, and then the camera begins to take a darker roll. The whole story is curiously visual and, like Hitchcock, "Back for Christmas" has its quirky, comic side. I always used to think that if the CBC gave me an open mandate and some money, it would be fun to make a film, and "Back for Christmas" is a movie I'd very much like to make.

Doctor," said Major Sinclair, "we certainly must have you with us for Christmas." Tea was being poured, and the Carpenters' living room was filled with friends who had come to say last-minute farewells to the Doctor and his wife.

"He shall be back," said Mrs. Carpenter. "I promise you."

"It's hardly certain," said Dr. Carpenter. "I'd like nothing better, of course."

"After all," said Mr. Hewitt, "you've contracted to lecture only for three months."

"Anything may happen," said Dr. Carpenter.

"Whatever happens," said Mrs. Carpenter, beaming at them, "he shall be back for Christmas. You may all believe me."

They all believed her. The Doctor himself almost believed her. For ten years she had been promising him for dinner parties, garden parties, committees, heaven knows what, and the promises had always been kept.

The farewells began. There was a fluting of compliments on dear Hermione's marvelous arrangements. She and her husband would drive to Southampton that evening. They would embark the following day. No trains, no bustle, no last-minute worries. Certainly the Doctor was marvelously looked after. He would be a great success in America. Especially with Hermione to see to everything. She would have a wonderful time, too. She must see the skyscrapers. Nothing like that in Little Godwearing. But she must be very sure to bring him back. "Yes, I will bring him back. You may rely upon it!" He mustn't be persuaded. No extensions. No wonderful post at some super-American hospital. Our infirmary needs him. And he must be back by Christmas. "Yes," Mrs. Carpenter called to the last departing guest, "I shall see to it. He shall be back by Christmas."

The final arrangements for closing the house were very well managed. The maids soon had the tea things washed up; they came in, said good-bye, and were in time to catch the afternoon bus to Devizes.

Nothing remained but odds and ends, locking doors, seeing that everything was tidy. "Go upstairs," said Hermione, "and change into your brown tweeds. Empty the pockets of that suit before you put it in your bag. I'll see to everything else. All you have to do is not to get in the way."

The Doctor went upstairs and took off the suit he was wearing, but, instead of the brown tweeds, he put on an old, dirty bathrobe, which he took from the back of his wardrobe. Then, after making one or two little arrangements, he leaned over the head of the stairs and called to his wife, "Hermione! Have you a moment to spare?"

"Of course, dear. I'm just finished."

"Just come up here for a moment. There's something rather extraordinary up here."

Hermione immediately came up. "Good heavens, my dear man!" she said when she saw her husband. "What are you lounging about in that filthy old thing for? I told you to have it burned long ago."

"Who in the world," said the Doctor, "has dropped a gold chain down the bathtub drain?"

"Nobody has, of course," said Hermione. "Nobody wears such a thing."

"Then what is it doing there?" said the Doctor. "Take this

flashlight. If you lean right over, you can see it shining, deep down."

"Some Woolworth's bangle off one of the maids," said Hermione. "It can be nothing else." However, she took the flashlight and leaned over, squinting into the drain. The Doctor, raising a short length of lead pipe, struck two or three times with great force and precision, and tilting the body by the knees, tumbled it into the tub.

He then slipped off the bathrobe and, standing completely naked, unwrapped a towel full of implements and put them into the washbasin. He spread several sheets of newspaper on the floor and turned once more to his victim.

She was dead, of course—horribly doubled up, like a somersaulter, at one end of the tub. He stood looking at her for a very long time, thinking of absolutely nothing at all. Then he saw how much blood there was and his mind began to move again.

First he pushed and pulled until she lay straight in the bath, then he removed her clothing. In the narrow bathtub this was an extremely clumsy business, but he managed it at last and then turned on the taps. The water rushed into the tub, then dwindled, then died away, and the last of it gurgled down the drain.

"Good God!" he said. "She turned it off at the main."

There was only one thing to do: the Doctor hastily wiped his hands on a towel, opened the bathroom door with a clean corner of the towel, threw it back onto the bath stool, and ran downstairs, barefoot, light as a cat. The cellar door was in a corner of the entrance hall, under the stairs. He knew just where the cut-off was. He had reason to: he had been pottering about down there for some time past—trying to scrape out a bin for wine, he had told Hermione. He pushed open the cellar door, went down the steep steps, and just before the closing door plunged the cellar into pitch darkness, he put his hand on the tap and turned it on. Then he felt his way back along the grimy wall till he came to the steps. He was about to ascend them when the bell rang.

The Doctor was scarcely aware of the ringing as a sound. It

was like a spike of iron pushed slowly up through his stomach. It went on until it reached his brain. Then something broke. He threw himself down in the coal dust on the floor and said, "I'm done for. Done for!"

"They've got no *right* to come," he said. Then he heard himself panting. "None of this," he said to himself. "None of this."

He began to revive. He got to his feet, and when the bell rang again the sound passed through him almost painlessly. "Let them go away," he said. Then he heard the front door open. He said, "I don't care." His shoulder came up, like that of a boxer, to shield his face. "I give up," he said.

He heard people calling. "Herbert!" "Hermione!" It was the Wallingfords. "Damn them! They come butting in. People anxious to get off. All naked! And blood and coal dust! I'm done! I'm through! I can't do it."

"Herbert!"

"Hermione!"

"Where the dickens can they be?"

"The car's there."

"Maybe they've popped round to Mrs. Liddell's."

"We must see them."

"Or to the shops, maybe. Something at the last minute."

"Not Hermione. I say, listen! Isn't that someone having a bath? Shall I shout? What about whanging on the door?"

"Sh-h-h! Don't. It might not be tactful."

"No harm in a shout."

"Look, dear. Let's come in on our way back. Hermione said they wouldn't be leaving before seven. They're dining on the way, in Salisbury."

"Think so? All right. Only I want a last drink with old Herbert. He'd be hurt."

"Let's hurry. We can be back by half past six."

The Doctor heard them walk out and the front door close quietly behind them. He thought, "Half past six. I can do it."

He crossed the hall, sprang the latch of the front door, went upstairs, and, taking his instruments from the washbasin, finished what he had to do. He came down again, clad in his bathrobe, carrying parcel after parcel of toweling or newspaper neatly secured with safety pins. These he packed carefully into the narrow, deep hole he had made in the corner of the cellar, shoveled in the soil, spread coal dust over all, satisfied himself that everything was in order, and went upstairs again. He then thoroughly cleaned the bath, and himself, and the bath again, dressed, and took his wife's clothing and his bathrobe to the incinerator.

One or two more little touches and everything was in order. It was only a quarter past six. The Wallingfords were always late; he had only to get into the car and drive off. It was a pity he couldn't wait till after dusk, but he could make a detour to avoid passing through the main street, and even if he was seen driving alone, people would only think Hermione had gone on ahead for some reason, and they would forget about it.

Still, he was glad when he had finally got away, entirely unobserved, on the open road, driving into the gathering dusk. He had to drive very carefully; he found himself unable to judge distances, his reactions were abnormally delayed, but that was a detail. When it was quite dark he allowed himself to stop the car on the top of the downs, in order to think.

The stars were superb. He could see the lights of one or two little towns far away on the plain below him. He was exultant. Everything that was to follow was perfectly simple. Marion was waiting in Chicago. She already believed him to be a widower. The lecture people could be put off with a word. He had nothing to do but establish himself in some thriving out-of-the-way town in America and he was safe forever. There were Hermione's clothes, of course, in the suitcases; they could be disposed of through the porthole. Thank heaven she wrote her letters on the typewriter—a little thing like handwriting might have prevented everything. "But there you are," he said. "She was up-to-date, efficient all along the line. Managed everything. Managed herself to death, damn her!"

"There's no reason to get excited," he thought. "I'll write a few letters for her, then fewer and fewer. Write myself—always expecting to get back, never quite able to. Keep the house one year, then another, then another; they'll get used to it. Might even come back alone in a year or two and clear it up properly.

Nothing easier. But not for Christmas!" He started up the engine and was off.

In New York he felt free at last, really free. He was safe. He could look back with pleasure—at least after a meal, lighting his cigarette, he could look back with a sort of pleasure—to the minute he had passed in the cellar listening to the bell, the door, and the voices. He could look forward to Marion.

As he strolled through the lobby of his hotel, the clerk, smiling, held up letters for him. It was the first batch from England. Well, what did it matter? It would be fun dashing off the typewritten sheets in Hermione's downright style, signing them with her squiggle, telling everyone what a success his first lecture had been, how thrilled he was with America but how certainly she'd bring him back for Christmas. Doubts could creep in later.

He glanced over the letters. Most were for Hermione. From the Sinclairs, the Wallingfords, the vicar, and a business letter from Holt & Sons, Builders and Decorators.

He stood in the lounge, people brushing by him. He opened the letters with his thumb, reading here and there, smiling. They all seemed very confident he would be back for Christmas. They relied on Hermione. "That's where they make their big mistake," said the Doctor, who had taken to American phrases. The builders' letter he kept to the last. Some bill, probably. It was:

Dear Madam,
We are in receipt of your kind acceptance of estimate as below and also of key.

We beg to repeat you may have every confidence in same being ready in ample time for Christmas present as stated. We are setting men to work this week.

We are, Madam,
Yours faithfully,
PAUL HOLT & SONS

To excavating, building up, suitably lining one sunken wine bin in cellar as indicated, using best materials, making good, etc.....£1800

Roots

by
AUDREY THOMAS
(1935–)

*It's funny, but there are certain stories that I just know I
couldn't bring off reading aloud. One of the biggest blocks is
gender. There are many women writers whose work I very
much admire, but when I begin to read aloud from a woman's
point of view it somehow comes out wrong. There is the
famous example of Joyce Marshall, who I think is one of the
overlooked gems of Canadian literature. I tried recording several of her stories, over and over. Nothing worked. The harder
I tried, the sillier it sounded. This is not always the case, thank
goodness, and Janette Turner Hospital's "Morgan Morgan" is a
story that works, I think, extremely well. "Roots" is a story
that starts from a specific point—the breaking of a teapot—
and spreads out in unexpected directions. For a moment you
don't think it's going to make sense, and then the story folds
together in all sorts of wonderful and intricate ways.*

ow I understand about smithereens," Louise said. The teapot lay in pieces on the kitchen floor. "There's an interesting word," her husband said, getting up from the table. "Irish, I'll bet. I'll just go look it up." His ears stood out from his head, as did the ears of his sons. Because of who he was (a radio sound technician and a lover of words) she always saw his ears as some sort of catcher's mitt, plucking out of the air whatever new and exciting word was hurled his way. Nine years ago she had thought it was charming; now it drove her nuts.

"And poor Earl Grey," he said, "a soggy mess. Never mind, there's more of him in the cupboard." But she did mind. There he was, off to his dictionaries while she got paper towels and the dustpan. The teapot, a Brown Betty, was the first present he had ever given her. It had survived several moves and a trip across the ocean. She hadn't been paying attention—it was her own fault the teapot broke, but that didn't make it any better. She'd been thinking about the new neighbour and how she always, always, always had to deal with the real world while Michael went around with his head in the clouds.

Yesterday the neighbour, a short, fat, fussy man in his sixties, had come over to complain about the dandelions. If they weren't mowed down soon, they would turn white and the dandelion seeds would travel next door and along the street. Kevin and Alexander had stopped riding their tricycle and junior bike and come to listen. Now Kevin interrupted. "Did you know they're called dandelions because their leaves look like lion's teeth? Did you know that? Here, I'll show you." He picked one (one of dozens that dotted the lawn) and brought it over. Alexander, who copied what he could of everything his older brother said and did, grabbed some yellow heads. "Lion," he said to the neighbour, "grrr, grrr." The neighbour was not amused.

Louise was about to remind Michael about the lawn, which had remained half-mowed for weeks, when her elbow knocked the teapot off the counter. And here he was now, coming down the stairs all smiles, with a dictionary in his hand.

"Just as I thought," he said, "Anglo-Irish, from smithers, 'small pieces or fragments, ultimately from smith.' But dictionaries don't always tell the truth. Maybe, like the Hooligans, they were an Irish family, small people (from years of inter-marriage and god knows what kind of incestuous slap and tickle going on)—sort of a cross between leprechauns and munchkins. They lived on a farm in Kerry and begat nothing but daughters. Three daughters—as in all the best tales it had to be three—named Eileen, Maureen and Kathleen. Three lovely colleens from Kerry. They were highly emotional girls, as was their mother. They keened a lot, at weddings, at funerals, at births, the phases of the moon, the price of two yards of ribbon for their petticoats. When they appeared in the nearest village the villagers would shout, 'Here come the wailing women,' and lock their doors. For when they got really worked up they threw things, smashed them into small pieces which came to be call smithereens. It was because of this smashing habit that the girls, in spite of their great beauty, remained unmarried until their dying day."

"Oh," he said, "oh don't!" He took the last two steps in a leap, the dictionary tumbling to the floor. She was standing there holding the yellow dustpan and sobbing. There was a bright spot of blood on the tip of her nose where she had pricked herself while bent down and searching for the last fragments. "Oh love, don't," he said, holding her tight, "I'll buy you another." He tilted her head back and licked her nose with his tongue. "You've pricked your nose." "Have I?" she said bitterly, drawing away. "Have I pricked myself and no prince came? Just not my lucky day." She knew she had wounded him but was beyond caring.

His voice shook a little. "No, no prince. Whoever heard of a prince with a bald spot on the top of his head? Princes have luxuriant heads of hair, always, which they wear in an attractive pageboy bob." "I'm sorry," she said, and she was. "But you drove me to it. Whoever heard of a princess with stretch marks?"

He had been right there when the boys were born, rubbing her back, encouraging her. She'd hated him then as well. "Why are there men!" she yelled, when Kevin's head broke through the ring of fire that was her vagina, her "birth canal" as the nurse had called it during pre-natal classes. Canal had sounded cool and green, but there had been nothing cool or orderly about that birth or the next one. Afterwards, she felt as though she were straddling a barbed-wire fence. Both children were born face up.

"I think his ears got caught," he said that first night. "Next time choose a man with a pinhead and ears like cockleshells, and you'll do better. Mothers should tell their daughters that; never mind income or colour of his eyes. Measure his head before you make any commitments."

But the pain was soon forgotten and the love remained. "Listen," she said now, leading him over to the table and sitting down. "Maybe I'm just getting old or something, but I can't take it any more. And I'm ashamed of that fact: I feel I've failed because these days your silliness drives me crazy. Oh, I know, as an article in one of those women's magazines we'd go over big. 'Cheerful disorder,' they'd say. 'Comfortably shabby,' they'd call this place—or I'd say it, so they'd know I like it the way it is. And you'd be the loving, playful, imaginative father

who reads poetry to his sons every night and teaches them
that the word 'salary' comes from salt, and why, and the word
'tulip' comes from an Eastern turban. Who enriches their
childhood world with his love of words." He opened his
mouth to speak, but she held up her hand. "Let me finish.
Meanwhile, meanwhile, while all this enrichment is going on
the lawn remains half-mowed and the lawn-mower rusts
because you and the boys are off on some adventure. And the
neighbour complains to me, not to you, about the dandelions.
As though I were responsible."

"You could have finished the lawn."

"You said you'd do it, therefore it's your job."

He stood up shouting, "Oh job blob gob slob fob/ oh *fuck*
the new neighbour. What is the matter with you?" Louise
looked down at the placemat and not at him. It was a copy of
an old nineteenth-century label. Her sister had sent them a set
for Christmas last year. This one was of an enormous red
tomato. Wayne County Preserving Co. was printed below. The
tomato mocked her with its healthy red perfection.

"I don't know, Michael. But I just don't find it enchanting
any more, that you treat life as a game."

"I take life very seriously." He sat down again.

"No you don't."

"Indeed I do. It's far more important to take the boys to see
the dinosaur exhibit than it is to finish the lawn. I want to
awaken all their senses. I want to teach them to think. You
used to come on our 'adventures' as well, remember?"

"You know what I think? I think you want to be the perfect
father, that's what I think. Some kind of over-compensation
maybe, who knows." Oh how could she have said such a terrible thing! She reached for him but he stood up again. His face
was white.

"Forgive me for ending this interesting conversation, but
duty calls. I must arise now and go to mow the lawn. Honour
thy neighbour or something like that." He left the house calling for the boys to get the rake.

The kitchen window was open. "Dad, why was Mum cryin',
Dad?" "She broke something special. Remember when you

broke your new kite. You cried really hard?" "But why are you cryin', Dad?" Louise put her hands over her ears.

Louise met Michael in a pub in London, England. He had come up to her and her girlfriend and while waiting for his pint (the place was very crowded) he asked, in a broad Texas drawl, if London was always so dark and rainy. When they answered with North American accents he seemed taken aback for a minute and then grinned and continued. You didn't notice his ears at first; you noticed the grin and the dark curly hair. "Ah guess ah read too much Wordsworth at school," he said, accepting his drink from the barmaid and squeezing onto the banquette where they were sitting. "Ah thought spring would be full of daffodils and sunshine. That fellow Browning misled me as well. Perhaps it was all part of an early public-relations plot, like Greenland or the Cape of Good Hope. Where you-all from?"

He relaxed when they said they were Canadians on holiday from their au pair jobs in Toulouse. Maybe he just didn't want to meet fellow Americans. "London's really very nice," Louise said, "even in the rain. Galleries and movies and bookshops and plays. Or maybe you don't like any of those things?" There was definitely something strange about him, the intent look as well as the ears, which she now noticed, sitting as she was, only inches away from him. He was attractive nevertheless. She'd never met a Texan before; maybe that was it.

"Ah've been spendin' a lot of my time [mah tie-um] in the British Museum Readin' Room," he said. "Ah'm doin' a dissertation on Dickens. He lived right around here for a while, on Doughty Street. This here is supposed to have been his favourite pub. That's why Ah came in." He paused. "And because Ah was so darned bored and lonely and tired of walkin' around in the rain." His curly hair was just beginning to dry out. Stuck to his head like that, it reminded Louise of the chiselled hair on Greek and Roman statues. However, it made his ears even more noticeable than they might otherwise have been. "Ah see you-all are fascinated by mah ears." "Oh no, no. Really." Was her face as red as Deborah's? "Oh yes, yes, really. Well mah mother did her best. She stuck them back against mah head every night with stickin' plaster; she turned me to one side and then the other every night of my infant life, but it didn't do any good." He smiled at her anxiously. "Do you think my children would be affected? I mean, mah Daddy and Granddaddy had ears like this. Do you think it would be fair to bring more of us into the world? Ah mean, would you marry a man whose ears stood out like this?" "Of course." He grabbed her hand. "Good, then we're engaged. How long will you be in town?"

The bartender called time and the stranger let go of her hand. He stood up as they gathered their coats and bags. "I've got a confession to make," he said in a very English voice. "I'm not a Texan at all. I was so relieved when you two said you were Canadians. Tell me, did I fool you?" "Not for a minute," Louise said and headed for the door. "Come on Deborah. It's been nice meeting you, whoever you are. I hope you won your bet." She was furious. To have been taken in like that! No doubt he and his buddies would have a big laugh about it later. He followed them out of the pub. "Good-night Michael," the barmaid called. "Look," he said, "don't be angry. It wasn't a bet, except with myself maybe. I'm an actor and at 10 A.M. tomorrow I have to audition for a part in a Sam Shepard play. I'd been practising all day, and seeing you two in the pub, hearing you when you ordered, well I thought you were Americans. So I took the plunge." He said all this to their backs, following them to the end of the street.

"Right!" he suddenly shouted, "look right!" He yanked them back on the curb. "Oh Lord," he said as they stood there in the rain. "Think how I'd feel if you two got knocked down because you were mad at me. Please, forgive me. May I take you both to dinner tomorrow night? If I get the part we might even have a bottle of wine. If I don't we can have beer."

"Did I really fool you?" he asked, as he left them at the door of their Bed and Breakfast. They assured him he had, but they were only Canadians after all. "I've never even met a Texan," Louise said. "You sounded like a television Texan at any rate," Deborah said. "My French family watches 'Dallas.'" He disappeared into the rain and mist. *Merde!* They called after him, "Break a leg!"

He—Michael—didn't get the part and Louise bought the wine. He took her to a pizza parlour where a string quartet played Mozart. Deborah decided not to come along. "It's you he's after." "Don't be silly. Anyway, we're leaving tomorrow." "We're only going across the Channel." "Don't be such a romantic!" "Tell me one thing," Deborah said, "would you really marry a man whose ears stuck out like that?" "I can't see what ears have to do with it?" "Good. Well then, honeychile Ah'm goin' ta that new art movie in Brunswick Square. You can tell me all about your evening when you come in."

The dictionary was still sprawled on the bottom step. Mare to Z and Addenda. All sort of things had fallen out because he marked places in books with whatever was to hand! Popsicle sticks, shoelaces, envelopes, colour strips for paint, dollar bills. It occurred to her now that he must care deeply to throw down one of his beloved dictionaries. She picked it up, intending to put it back upstairs but the book fell open to a page where a red rose had been carefully taped in. Louise sat on the bottom step and began to read.

"It doesn't really matter all that much about the part," he said that night in the pizza parlour, "except for money—the lack of it, or course. My ego isn't shattered is what I mean. My real love is radio. Why on radio a blind man can play a World War II flying ace. If he should care to do so, a one-legged man can tap dance, a fellow with jug-ears and the right voice can play the romantic lead. It's the most democratic place imaginable. I love it. I'd far rather work in radio than on the stage. But I'll always be grateful to Sam Shepard—I might even sit down tonight and pen him a thank-you letter." "Why's that?" "Because he led me to you. Gave me both an excuse and the courage to talk to you. Now I wonder if you'll let me write to you, maybe even come to Toulouse for a visit?" Which he did, after several letters. Charming Louise's "family" with his terrible French and bearing flowers for Maman. A brown teapot for

Louise. In the kitchen that night, the children in bed and Maman and Papa gone to their country house for the weekend, Michael insisted on making a pot of good English tea. "I can do it." "No, no. You've put the little monsters to bed, I'll do it. Besides, you're a Canadian, it isn't the same if a Canadian makes it. I mean, do you always take the pot to the kettle? Do you?" From one of his pockets he produced a tea-ball already filled with tea. "I was a Scout," he said, "you know our motto."

As they sat at the kitchen table, waiting for the tea to steep, he said, "Canada or Australia, what do you think? I'd say Canada myself, Australians always seem to be somewhere else sending postcards home. The girls I meet—the Australian girls [her heart gave a little lurch]—don't just go away on holiday for a month or two, they go for years. Doesn't that tell you something about Australia? Their slang might be fun to study however." Here he did an imitation of a jackaroo. "Have you already had enough of Canada or would you be interested in returning there?" "I am returning there. In exactly two months and seven days. I'm travelling for a month with Deborah and then we have to go home and get ready to go back to school." Louise was intent on getting a degree in early-childhood education.

He poured out the tea, frowned at the teapot and held it up to his ear. "I think there's something funny about this teapot." "What?" "I'm not sure." From another pocket he produced a bag of sweet biscuits. "Is that a fixed ticket. I mean, can you change it?" "Why would I do that?" They looked at one another. "These biscuits," she said "are called '*les langues de chat.*' Cat's tongues. Or did you already know that?" "I just pointed." "Liar." He drank all his tea in three swallows.

"God I'm thirsty. It must be all that garlic in the soup. You know, when somebody takes a leave without permission we say in England that they take 'French leave.' The French say, 'To take English leave.' There's a lot of animosity between the French and English. Funny, I like the French. Especially their language. Hey, think about that word, language. And these biscuits, these '*langues.*' I'd never really thought of that before, about language and tongue. Of course, we say our 'mother tongue' is such and such, but we say it without thinking." He was talking faster and faster, holding the teapot up to his ear and shaking it. Finally, he went and poured the rest of the tea into the sink. Then he pulled out the tea-caddy and presented it to her. "I think this is the problem," he said, setting it before her on a tea-towel. "What d'you mean?" "Open it," he said. "Don't burn your fingers." In the midst of the wet tea-leaves was an old-fashioned Victorian ring with a tiny garnet in its centre. "You're an idiot," Louise said, blinking away the tears, "you hardly know me." "You don't know me at all," he said, suddenly really serious. "Remember all that palaver about my daddy and granddaddy's ears in the Lamb that night? Well, I have no idea what my granddaddy's ears looked like, or my daddy's, or any other part of him for that matter. I'm an orphan, Louise. Were I a word, the *Oxford English Dictionary* would put o.o.o. after me!" "Of obscure origin." "Other dictionaries might put etym. dub. I am eternally grateful to my adoptive parents, who live just outside Liverpool. I hope you will come with me to meet them. Can you imagine anyone choosing a jug-eared baby and taking him home? I am eternally grateful to them for that, but they aren't exactly affectionate people, my mother and father. They made sure I had good health and a good education and that I didn't end up talking with a Merseyside accent. I teased them about that later on, after the Beatles. Just think, I could have had every girl in England hanging on my words!" "How would they feel about your leaving England?" "They might be a bit sad, but they would feel I was doing the right thing. I would come back and visit, of course. And they could come out. They aren't rich, but they aren't poor either. My dad's retired now but he used to be Chief Accountant with the Midland Bank. But that's not important. What is important, Louise, is that there may be stranger things in my genetic background than big ears. Would that worry you?" "No," she said. "I don't think so. But don't your adopted parents know anything at all?" "Nothing. I was found screaming my head off in the ladies' cloakroom of a department store. Very early one morning. I had probably been there overnight." He smiled painfully. "Liverpool is—

was—a big port. No doubt, my father was a sailor. Or one of the Irish who came over to find work on the docks. I keep thinking I'll see him someday—I have a feeling I'd hardly fail to recognize him." He smiled painfully. "Did you know that 'to abandon' means 'to set free'?" he asked. (Louise could hear her parents . . . "But his background darling? What are his roots?")

"Michael," Louise said, "will you marry me? I should tell you right now that I want children. More than one, anyway. Two or three."

The lawn was mowed and the mower put away, but Michael and the boys were nowhere around. They had probably gone downtown to buy her a new teapot. Or maybe not. What she had said was unforgiveable. She decided to have him paged at all the department stores she could think of but he wasn't there—not at any of them. She tried the Provincial Museum. Not there either. Words were such powerful things. Sometimes they were like dangerous animals—once let out there was no telling the damage they could do. She grabbed her jacket and decided to go in search of her family.

And she found them in the park, at the petting zoo. Michael was taking a picture of a young Japanese couple. The girl was very pretty. Kevin took his mother's hand, just as if it were the most natural thing in the world that she should rush up at that moment, wild-haired and red in the face from running. "They're on their animal," Kevin said, "that's why Dad's taking their picture."

"Animoo," said Alexander. The girl giggled and called to Louise, "Yes, yes, on our animoo." "Honeymoon," Michael said, "you're on your honeymoon." "Yes, yes," the girl said, laughing, "hanimoo."

After the picture had been taken and introductions made, the Japanese girl explained that she taught "baby school." She knelt in the grass in her beautiful red wool suit, and sang them a nursery song in Japanese. "I was wondering," Michael said, "if you'd like to invite the Tanabes back for tea?" He held up a square box with a Union Jack on the side. "What did the song say?" Kevin asked. Louise looked at him. "Does it matter?"

The Japanese girl was rummaging through her shopping bags. "We too!" she said. And held up a square box with a Union Jack on the side. "Genuine alicah," her husband said.

They stood there, holding their teapots, smiling at one another. What will my sons remember, Louise thinks, years from now? The new black lamb, the pretty Japanese woman in her red suit, the dandelions? Or their father and mother shouting about a teapot broken on the kitchen floor.

The Tranter's Party

by
THOMAS HARDY
(1840–1928)

*"The Tranter's Party" gives us a charming glimpse of rural life
in the England of the last century. There is a real sense of old
festivity here: the fiddles, the reels, the cider and smoked
hams. A more entertaining group of crusty old characters is
hard to imagine. Christmas night is the setting for the party,
and there are many peculiar traditions to be observed, old
superstitions to be discussed, and such a general round of
feasting and drinking and dancing to be done that you would
almost wish you were there.*

During the afternoon unusual activity was seen to prevail about the precincts of tranter Dewy's house. The flagstone floor was swept of dust, and a sprinkling of the finest yellow sand from the innermost stratum of the adjoining sand-pit lightly scattered thereupon. Then were produced large knives and forks, which had been shrouded in darkness and grease since the last occasion of the kind, and bearing upon their sides, 'Shear-steel, warranted,' in such emphatic letters of assurance, that the warranter's name was not required as further proof, and not given. The key was left in the tap of the cider-barrel instead of being carried in a pocket. And finally the tranter had to stand up in the room and let his wife wheel him round like a turnstile, to see if anything discreditable was visible in his appearance.

"Stand still till I've been for the scissors," said Mrs. Dewy.

The tranter stood as still as a sentinel at the challenge.

The only repairs necessary were a trimming of one or two whiskers that had extended beyond the general contour of the mass; a like trimming of a slightly-frayed edge visible on his shirt-collar; and a final tug at a grey hair—to all of which operations he submitted in resigned silence, except the last, which produced a mild "Come, come Ann," by way of expostulation.

"Really, Reuben, 'tis quite a disgrace to see such a man," said Mrs. Dewy, with the severity justifiable in a long-tried companion, giving him another turn round, and picking several of Smiler's hairs from the shoulder of his coat. Reuben's thoughts seemed engaged elsewhere, and he yawned. "And the collar of your coat is a shame to behold—so plastered with dirt, or dust, or grease, or something. Why, wherever could you have got it?"

"'Tis my warm nater in summer-time, I suppose. I always did get in such a heat when I bustle about."

"Ay, the Dewys always were such a coarse-skinned family. There's your brother Bob just as bad—as fat as a porpoise—wi' his low, mean, 'How'st do, Ann?' whenever he meets me. I'd 'How'st do' him indeed! If the sun only shines out a minute, there be you all streaming in the face—I never see!"

"If I be hot week-days, I must be hot Sundays."

"If any of the girls should turn after their father 'twill be a bad look-out for 'em, poor things! None of my family was sich vulgar sweaters, not one of 'em. But, Lord-a-mercy, the Dewys! I don't know how ever I cam' into such a family!"

"Your woman's weakness when I asked ye to jine us. That's how it was, I suppose." But the tranter appeared to have heard some such words from his wife before, and hence his answer had not the energy it might have shown if the inquiry had possessed the charm of novelty.

"You never did look so well in a pair o' trousers as in them," she continued in the same unimpassioned voice, so that the unfriendly criticism of the Dewy family seemed to have been more normal than spontaneous. "Such a cheap pair as 'twas too. As big as any man could wish to have, and lined inside, and double-lined in the lower parts, and an extra piece of stiffening at the bottom. And 'tis a nice high cut that comes up right under your armpits, and there's enough turned down inside the seams to make half a pair more, besides a piece of cloth left that will make an honest waistcoat—all by my contriving in buying the stuff at a bargain, and having it made up under my eye. It only shows what may be done by taking a little trouble, and not going straight to the rascally tailors."

The discourse was cut short by the sudden appearance of Charley on the scene, with a face and hands of hideous blackness, and a nose like a guttering candle. Why, on that particularly cleanly afternoon, he should have discovered that the chimney-crook and chain from which the hams were suspended should have possessed more merits and general interest as playthings than any other articles in the house, is a question for nursing mothers to decide. However, the humour seemed to lie in the result being, as has been seen, that any given player with these articles was in the long-run daubed with soot. The last that was seen of Charley by daylight after this piece of ingenuity was when in the act of vanishing from his father's presence round the corner of the house—looking back over his shoulder with an expression of great sin on his face, like Cain as the Outcast in Bible pictures.

The guests had all assembled, and the tranter's party had reached that degree of development which accords with ten o'clock p.m. in rural assemblies. At that hour the sound of a fiddle in process of tuning was heard from the inner pantry.

"That's Dick," said the tranter. "That lad's crazy for a jig."

"Dick! Now I cannot—really, I cannot have any dancing at all till Christmas-day is out," said old William emphatically. "When the clock ha' done striking twelve, dance as much as ye like."

"Well, I must say there's reason in that, William," said Mrs. Penny. "If you do have a party on Christmas-night, 'tis only fair and honourable to the sky-folk to have it a sit-still party. Jigging parties be all very well on the Devil's holidays; but a jigging party looks suspicious now. O yes; stop till the clock strikes, young folk—so say I."

It happened that some warm mead accidentally got into Mr Spinks's head about this time.

"Dancing," he said, "is a most strengthening, livening, and courting movement, 'specially with a little beverage added! And dancing is good. But why disturb what is ordained,

Richard and Reuben, and the company zhinerally? Why, I ask, as far as that do go?"

"Then nothing till after twelve," said William.

Though Reuben and his wife ruled on social points, religious questions were mostly disposed of by the old man, whose firmness on this head quite counterbalanced a certain weakness in his handling of domestic matters. The hopes of the younger members of the household were therefore relegated to a distance of one hour and three-quarters—a result that took visible shape in them by a remote and listless look about the eyes—the singing of songs being permitted in the interim.

At five minutes to twelve the soft tuning was again heard in the back quarters; and when at length the clock had whizzed forth the last stroke, Dick appeared ready primed, and the instruments were boldly handled; old William very readily taking the bass-viol from its accustomed nail, and touching the strings as irreligiously as could be desired.

The country-dance called the "Triumph, or Follow my Lover," was the figure with which they opened. The tranter took for his partner Mrs. Penny, and Mrs. Dewy was chosen by Mr. Penny, who made so much of his limited height by a judicious carriage of the head, straightening of the back, and important flashes of his spectacle-glasses, that he seemed almost as tall as the tranter. Mr. Shiner, age about thirty-five, farmer and church-warden, a character principally composed of a crimson stare, vigorous breath, and a watch-chain, with a mouth hanging on a dark smile but never smiling, had come quite willingly to the party, and showed a wondrous obliviousness of all his antics on the previous night. But the comely, slender, prettily-dressed prize Fancy Day fell to Dick's lot, in spite of some private machinations of the farmer, for the reason that Mr. Shiner, as a richer man, had shown too much assurance in asking the favour, whilst Dick had been duly courteous.

We gain a good view of our heroine as she advances to her place in the ladies' line. She belonged to the taller division of middle height. Flexibility was her first characteristic, by which she appeared to enjoy the most easeful rest when she was in gliding motion. Her dark eyes—arched by brows of so keen, slender, and soft a curve that they resembled nothing so much as two slurs in music—showed primarily a bright sparkle each. This was softened by a frequent thoughtfulness, yet not so frequent as to do away, for more than a few minutes at a time, with a certain coquettishness; which in its turn was never so decided as to banish honesty. Her lips imitated her brows in their clearly-cut outline and softness of bend; and her nose was well shaped—which is saying a great deal, when it is remembered that there are a hundred pretty mouths and eyes for one pretty nose. Add to this, plentiful knots of dark-brown hair, a gauzy dress of white with blue facings; and the slightest idea may be gained of the young maiden who showed, amidst the rest of the dancing-ladies, like a flower among vegetables. And so the dance proceeded. Mr. Shiner, according to the interesting rule laid down, deserted his own partner and made off down the middle with this fair one of Dick's—the pair appearing from the top of the room like two persons tripping down a lane to be married. Dick trotted behind with what was intended to be a look of composure, but which was, in fact, a rather silly expression of feature—implying, with too much earnestness, that such an elopement could not be tolerated. Then they turned and came back, when Dick grew more rigid around his mouth, and blushed with ingenuous ardour as he joined hands with the rival and formed an arch over his lady's head, which presumably gave the figure its name; relinquishing her again at setting to partners, when Mr. Shiner's new chain quivered in every link, and all the loose flesh upon the tranter—who here came into action again—shook like jelly. Mrs. Penny, being always rather concerned for her personal safety when she danced with the tranter, fixed her face to a chronic smile of timidity the whole time it lasted—a peculiarity which filled her features with wrinkles, and reduced her eyes to little straight lines like hyphens, as she jigged up and down opposite him; repeating in her own person not only his proper movements, but also the minor flourishes which the richness of the tranter's imagination led him to introduce from time to time—an imitation which had about it something of slavish obedience, not unmixed with fear.

The ear-rings of the ladies now flung themselves wildly about, turning violent summersaults, banging this way and that, and then swinging quietly against the ears sustaining them. Mrs. Crumpler—a heavy woman, who, for some reason which nobody ever thought worth inquiry, danced in a clean apron—moved so smoothly through the figure that her feet were never seen; conveying to imaginative minds the idea that she rolled on castors.

Minute after minute glided by, and the party reached the period when ladies' back-hair begins to look forgotten and dissipated; when a perceptible dampness makes itself apparent upon the faces of even delicate girls—a ghastly dew having for some time rained from the features of their masculine partners; when skirts begin to be torn out of their gathers; when elderly people, who have stood up to please their juniors, begin to feel sundry small tremblings in the region of the knees, and to wish the interminable dance was at Jericho; when (at country parties of the thorough sort) waistcoats begin to be unbuttoned, and when the fiddlers' chairs have been wriggled, by the frantic bowing of their occupiers, to a distance of about two feet from where they originally stood.

Fancy was dancing with Mr. Shiner. Dick knew that Fancy, by the law of good manners, was bound to dance as pleasantly with one partner as with another; yet he could not help suggesting to himself that she need not have put quite so much spirit into her steps, nor smiled quite so frequently whilst in the farmer's hands.

"I'm afraid you didn't cast off," said Dick mildly to Mr. Shiner, before the latter man's watch-chain had done vibrating from a recent whirl.

Fancy made a motion of accepting the correction; but her partner took no notice, and proceeded with the next movement with an affectionate bend towards her.

"That Shiner's too fond of her," the young man said to himself as he watched them. They came to the top again, Fancy smiling warmly towards her partner, and went to their places.

"Mr. Shiner, you didn't cast off," said Dick, for want of something else to demolish him with; casting off himself, and being put out at the farmer's irregularity.

"Perhaps I shan't cast off for any man," said Mr. Shiner.

"I think you ought to, sir."

Dick's partner, a young lady of the name of Lizzy—called Lizz for short—tried to mollify.

"I can't say that I myself have much feeling for casting off," she said.

"Nor I," said Mrs. Penny, following up the argument; "especially if a friend and neighbour is set against it. Not but that 'tis a terrible tasty thing in good hands and well done; yes, indeed, so say I."

"All I meant was," said Dick, rather sorry that he had spoken correctingly to a guest, "that 'tis in the dance; and a man has hardly any right to hack and mangle what was ordained by the regular dance-maker, who, I daresay, got his living by making 'em, and thought of nothing else all his life."

"I don't like the casting off; then very well; I cast off for no dance-maker that ever lived."

Dick now appeared to be doing mental arithmetic, the act being really an effort to present to himself, in an abstract form, how far an argument with a formidable rival ought to be carried when the rival was his mother's guest. The dead-lock was put an end to by the stamping arrival up the middle of the tranter, who, despising minutia on principle, started a theme of his own.

"I assure you, neighbours," he said, "the heat of my frame no tongue can tell!" He looked around and endeavoured to give, by a forcible gaze of self-sympathy, some faint idea of the truth.

Mrs. Dewy formed one of the next couple.

"Yes," she said in an auxiliary tone, "Reuben always was such a hot man."

Mrs. Penny implied the species of sympathy that such a class of affliction required by trying to smile and to look grieved at the same time.

"If he only walk round the garden of a Sunday morning his

shirt-collar is as limp as no starch at all," continued Mrs. Dewy, her countenance lapsing parenthetically into a housewifely expression of concern at the reminiscence.

"Come, come, you women-folk; 'tis hands-across—come, come!" said the tranter; and the conversation ceased for the present.

Dick had at length secured Fancy for that most delightful of country-dances, opening with six-hands-round.

"Before we begin," said the tranter, "my proposal is, that 'twould be a right and proper plan for every mortal man in the dance to pull off his jacket, considering the heat."

"Such low notions as you have, Reuben! Nothing but strip will go down with you when you are a-dancing. Such a hot man as he is!"

"Well, now, look here, my sonnies," he argued to his wife, whom he often addressed in the plural masculine for economy of epithet merely: "I don't see that. You dance and get hot as fire; therefore you lighten your clothes. Isn't that nature and reason gentle and simple? If I strip by myself and not neces-sary, 'tis rather pot-housey I own; but if we stout chaps strip one and all, why, 'tis the native manners of the country, which no man can gainsay? Hey—what did you say, my sonnies?"

"Strip we will!" said the three other heavy men who were in the dance; and their coats were accordingly taken off and hung in the passage, whence the four sufferers from heat soon reap-peared marching in close column, with flapping shirt-sleeves, and having as common to them all a general glance of being now a match for any man or dancer in England or Ireland. Dick, fearing to lose ground in Fancy's good opinion, retained his coat like the rest of the thinner men; and Mr. Shiner did the same from superior knowledge.

And now a further phase of revelry had disclosed itself. It was the time of night when a guest may write his name in the dust upon the tables and chairs, and a bluish mist pervades the atmosphere, becoming a distinct halo round the candles; when people's nostrils, wrinkles, and crevices in general seem to be getting gradually plastered up; when the very fiddlers as well as the dancers get red in the face, the dancers having advanced further still towards incandescence, and entered the cadaverous phase; the fiddlers no longer sit down, but kick back their chairs and saw madly at the strings with legs firmly spread and eyes closed, regardless of the visible world. Again and again did Dick share his Love's hand with another man, and wheel round; then, more delightfully, promenade in a circle with her all to himself, his arm holding her waist more firmly each time, and his elbow getting further and further behind her back, till the distance reached was rather noticeable; and, most blissful, swinging to places shoulder to shoulder, her breath curling round her neck like a summer zephyr that had strayed from its proper date. Threading the couples one by one they reached the bottom, when there arose in Dick's mind a minor misery lest the tune should end before they could work their way to the top again, and have anew the same exciting run down through. Dick's feelings on actually reaching the top in spite of his doubts were supplemented by a mortal fear that the fiddling might even stop at this supreme moment; which prompted him to convey a stealthy whisper to the far-gone musicians to the effect that they were not to leave off till he and his partner had reached the bottom of the dance once more, which remark was replied to by the nearest of those convulsed and quivering men by a private nod to the anxious young man between two semiquavers of the tune, and a simultaneous "all right, ay, ay," without opening the eyes. Fancy was now held so closely that Dick and she were practically one person. The room became to Dick like a picture in a dream; all that he could remember of it afterwards being the look of the fiddlers going to sleep as humming-tops sleep, by increasing their motion and hum, together with the figures of grandfather James and old Simon Crumpler sitting by the chimney-corner talking and nodding in dumb-show, and beating the air to their emphatic sentences like people near a threshing machine.

The dance ended. "Piph-h-h-h!" said tranter Dewy, blowing out his breath in the very finest stream of vapour that a man's lips could form. "A regular tightener, that one, sonnies!" He wiped his forehead, and went to the cider and ale mugs on the table.

"Well!" said Mrs. Penny, flopping into a chair, "my heart haven't been in such a thumping state of uproar since I used to sit up on old Midsummer-eves to see who my husband was going to be."

"And that's getting on for a good few years now, from what I've heard you tell," said the tranter without lifting his eyes from the cup he was filling. Being now engaged in the business of handing round refreshments he was warranted in keeping his coat off still, though the other heavy men had resumed theirs.

"And a thing I never expected would come to pass, if you'll believe me, came to pass then," continued Mrs. Penny. "Ah, the first spirit ever I see on a Midsummer-eve was a puzzle to me when he appeared, a hard puzzle, so say I!"

"So I should have fancied," said Elias Spinks.

"Yes," said Mrs. Penny, throwing her glance into past times and talking on in a running tone of complacent abstraction, as if a listener were not a necessity. "Yes; never was I in such a taking as on that Midsummer-eve! I sat up, quite determined to see if John Wildway was going to marry me or no. I put the bread-and-cheese and beer quite ready, as the witch's book ordered, and I opened the door, and I waited till the clock struck twelve, my nerves all alive and so strained that I could feel every one of 'em twitching like bell-wires. Yes, sure! and when the clock had struck, lo and behold I could see through the door a little small man in the lane wi' a shoemaker's apron on."

Here Mr. Penny stealthily enlarged himself half an inch.

"Now, John Wildway," Mrs. Penny continued, "who courted me at the time, was a shoemaker, you see, but he was a very fair-sized man, and I couldn't believe that any such a little small man had anything to do wi' me, as anybody might. But on he came, and crossed the threshold—not John, but actually the same little man in the shoemaker's apron—"

"You needn't be so mighty particular about little and small!" said her husband.

"In he walks, and down he sits, and O my goodness me, didn't I flee upstairs, body and soul hardly hanging together! Well, to cut a long story short, by-long and by-late John Wildway and I had a miff and parted; and lo and behold, the coming man came! Penny asked me if I'd go snacks with him, and afore I knew what I was about a'most, the thing was done."

"I've fancied you never knew better in your life; but I mid be mistaken," said Mr. Penny in a murmur.

After Mrs. Penny had spoken, there being no new occupation for her eyes she still let them stay idling on the past scenes just related, which were apparently visible to her in the centre of the room. Mr. Penny's remark received no reply.

During this discourse the tranter and his wife might have been observed standing in an unobtrusive corner in mysterious closeness to each other, a just perceptible current of intelligence passing from each to each, which had apparently no relation whatever to the conversation of their guests, but much to their sustenance. A conclusion of some kind having at length been drawn, the palpable confederacy of man and wife was once more obliterated, the tranter marching off into the pantry humming a tune that he couldn't quite recollect, and then breaking into the words of a song of which he could remember about one line and a quarter. Mrs. Dewy spoke a few words about preparations for a bit of supper.

The elder portion of the company which loved eating and drinking put on a look to signify that till this moment they had quite forgotten that it was customary to expect suppers on these occasions; going even further than this politeness of feature, and starting irrelevant subjects, the exceeding flatness and forced tone of which rather betrayed their object. The younger members said they were quite hungry, and that supper would be delightful that it was so late.

Good luck attended Dick's love-passes during the meal. He sat next Fancy, and had the thrilling pleasure of using permanently a glass which had been taken by Fancy in mistake; of letting the outer edge of the sole of his boot touch the lower verge of her skirt; and to add to these delights the cat, which had lain unobserved in her lap for several minutes, crept across into his own, touching him with fur that had touched her hand a moment before. There were, besides, some little pleasures in the shape of helping her to vegetable she didn't want, and when it had nearly alighted on her plate taking it across for his own use, on the plea of waste not, want not. He also, from time to time, sipped sweet sly glances at her profile; noticing the set of her head, the curve of her throat, and other artistic properties of the lively goddess, who the while kept up a rather free, not to say too free, conversation with Mr. Shiner sitting opposite; which, after some uneasy criticism, and much shifting of argument backwards and forwards in Dick's mind, he decided not to consider of alarming significance.

"A new music greets our ears now," said Miss Fancy, alluding with the sharpness that her position as village sharpener demanded, to the contrast between the rattle of knives and forks and the late notes of the fiddlers.

"Ay; and I don't know but what 'tis sweeter in tone when you get above forty," said the tranter; "except, in faith, as regards father there. Never such a mortal man as he for tunes. They do move his soul; don't 'em, father?"

The eldest Dewy smiled across from his distant chair an assent to Reuben's remark.

"Spaking of being moved in soul," said Mr. Penny, "I shall never forget the first time I heard the 'Dead March.' 'Twas at poor Corp'l Nineman's funeral at Casterbridge. It fairly made my hair creep and fidget about like a vlock of sheep—ah, it did, souls! And when they had done, and the last trump had sounded, and the guns was fired over the dead hero's grave, a' icy-cold drop o' moist sweat hung upon my forehead, and another upon my jawbone. Ah, 'tis a very solemn thing!"

"Well, as to father in the corner there," the tranter said, pointing to old William, who was in the act of filling his mouth; "he'd starve to death for music's sake now, as much as when he was a boy-chap of fifteen."

"Truly, now," said Michael Mail, clearing the corner of his throat in the manner of a man who meant to be convincing; "there's a friendly tie of some sort between music and eating."

He lifted his cup to his mouth, and drank himself gradually backwards from a perpendicular position to a slanting one, during which time his looks performed a circuit from the wall opposite him to the ceiling overhead. Then clearing the other corner of his throat: "Once I was a-setting in the little kitchen of the Dree Mariners at Casterbridge, having a bit of dinner, and a brass band struck up in the street. Such a beautiful band as that were! I was setting eating fried liver and lights, I well can mind—ah, I was! and to save my life, I couldn't help chawing to the tune. Band played six-eight time; six-eight chaws I, willynilly. Band plays common; common time went my teeth among the liver and lights as true as a hair. Beautiful 'twere! Ah, I shall never forget that there band!"

"That's as tuneful a thing as ever I heard of," said grandfather James, with the absent gaze which accompanies profound criticism.

"I don't like Michael's tuneful stories then," said Mrs. Dewy. "They are quite coarse to a person o' decent taste."

Old Michael's mouth twitched here and there, as if he wanted to smile but didn't know where to begin, which gradually settled to an expression that it was not displeasing for a nice woman like the tranter's wife to correct him.

"Well, now," said Reuben, with decisive earnestness, "that sort o' coarse touch that's so upsetting to Ann's feelings is to my mind a recommendation; for it do always prove a story to be true. And for the same reason, I like a story with a bad moral. My sonnies, all true stories have a coarse touch or a bad moral, depend upon't. If the story-tellers could ha' got decency and good morals from true stories, who'd have troubled to invent parables?" Saying this the tranter arose to fetch a new stock of cider, ale, mead, and home-made wines.

Mrs. Dewy sighed and appended a remark (ostensibly behind her husband's back, though that the words should reach his ears distinctly was understood by both): "Such a man as Dewy is! Nobody do know the trouble I have to keep that man barely respectable. And did you ever hear too—just now at suppertime—talking about 'taties' with Michael in such a work-folk way. Well, 'tis what I was never brought up to!

With our family 'twas never less than 'taters,' and very often
'pertatoes' outright; mother was so particular and nice with us
girls; there was no family in the parish that kept themselves up
more than we."

The hour of parting came. Fancy could not remain for the
night because she had engaged a woman to wait up for her. She
disappeared temporarily from the flagging party of dancers,
and then came downstairs wrapped up and looking altogether
a different person from whom she had been hitherto, in fact (to
Dick's sadness and disappointment), a woman somewhat
reserved and of a phlegmatic temperament—nothing left in her
of the romping girl that she had seemed but a short quarter-
hour before, who had not minded the weight of Dick's hand
upon her waist, nor shirked the purlieus of the mistletoe.

"What a difference!" thought the young man—hoary cynic
pro tem. "What a miserable deceiving difference between the
manners of a maid's life at dancing times and at others! Look
at this lovely Fancy! Through the whole past evening touch-
able, squeezable—even kissable! For whole half-hours I held
her so close to me that not a sheet of paper could have been
slipped between us; and I could feel her heart only just outside my own, her life beating on so close to mine, that I was
aware of every breath in it. A flit is made upstairs—a hat and a
cloak put on—and I no more dare to touch her than—"
Thought failed him, and he returned to realities.

But this was an endurable misery in comparison with what
followed. Mr. Shiner and his watch-chain, taking the intrusive
advantage that ardent bachelors who are going homeward
along the same road as a pretty young woman always do take
of that circumstance, came forward to assure Fancy—with a
total disregard of Dick's emotions, and in tones which were
certainly not frigid—that he (Shiner) was not the man to go to
bed before seeing his Lady Fair safe within her own door—not
he, nobody should say he was that;—and that he would not
leave her side an inch till the thing was done—drown him if
he would. The proposal was assented to by Miss Day, in Dick's
foreboding judgement, with one degree—or at any rate, an
appreciable fraction of a degree—of warmth beyond that

required by a disinterested desire for protection from the dangers of the night.

All was over; and Dick surveyed the chair she had last occupied, looking now like a setting from which the gem has been torn. There stood her glass, and the romantic teaspoonful of elder wine at the bottom that she couldn't drink by trying ever so hard, in obedience to the mighty arguments of the tranter (his hand coming down upon her shoulder the while like a Nasmyth hammer), but the drinker was there no longer. There were the nine or ten pretty little crumbs she had left on her plate; but the eater was no more seen.

There seemed a disagreeable closeness of relationship between himself and the members of his family now that they were left alone again face to face. His father seemed quite offensive for appearing to be in just as high spirits as when the guests were there; and as for grandfather James (who had not yet left), he was quite fiendish in being rather glad they were gone.

"Really," said the tranter, in a tone of placid satisfaction, "I've had so little time to attend to myself all the evenen that I mean to enjoy a quiet meal now! A slice of this here ham—neither too fat nor too lean—so; and then a drop of this vinegar and pickles—there, that's it—and I shall be as fresh as a lark again! And to tell the truth, my sonny, my inside has been as dry as a lime-basket all night."

"I like a party very well once in a while," said Mrs. Dewy, leaving off the adorned tones she had been bound to use throughout the evening and returning to the natural marriage voice; "but, Lord, 'tis such a sight of heavy work next day! What with the dirty plates, and knives and forks, and dust and smother, and bits kicked off your furniture, and I don't know what all, why a body could a'most wish there were no such things as Christmases . . . Ah'h dear!" she yawned, till the clock in the corner had ticked several beats. She cast her eyes round upon the displaced, dust-laden furniture, and sat down overpowered at the sight.

"Well, I be getting all right by degrees, thank the Lord for't!" said the tranter cheerfully through a mangled mass of ham and bread, without lifting his eyes from his plate, and chopping away with his knife and fork as if he were felling trees. "Ann, you may as well go to bed at once, and not bide there making such sleepy faces; you look as long-favoured as a fiddle, upon my life, Ann. There, you must be wearied out, 'tis true. I'll do the doors and draw up the clock; and you go on, or you'll be as white as a sheet tomorrow."

"Ay; I don't know whether I shan't or no." The matron passed her hand across her eyes to brush away the film of sleep till she got upstairs.

Dick wondered how it was that when people were married they could be so blind to romance; and was quite certain that if he ever took to wife that dear impossible Fancy, he and she would never be so dreadfully practical and undemonstrative of the Passion as his father and mother were. The most extraordinary thing was that all the fathers and mothers he knew were just as undemonstrative as his own.

The *Lady* or the *Tiger?*

by
FRANK STOCKTON
(1834–1912)

*I ended up doing a fair bit of research in putting together this
collection—checking names and dates, that sort of thing. One
thing that frequently amazed me was how much some people
actually managed to write in a lifetime. I guess you sort of just
get on a roll and keep going. Anyway, Frank Stockton wrote,
at a rough count, some twenty books for children and another
thirty books for adults. Yet, so far as I know, the only thing
that he is remembered for is "The Lady or the Tiger?" It's a bit
of a trick story, so I can't really say too much, but, for my
part, I'm betting on the tiger.*

I n the very old time, there lived a semi-barbaric king, whose ideas, though somewhat polished and sharpened by the progressiveness of distant Latin neighbors, were still large, florid, and untrammelled, as became the half of him which was barbaric. He was a man of exuberant fancy, and, withal, of an authority so irresistible that, at his will, he turned his varied fancies into facts. He was greatly given to self-communing, and when he and himself agreed upon anything, the thing was done. When every member of his domestic and political systems moved smoothly in its appointed course, his nature was bland and genial; but whenever there was a little hitch, and some of his orbs got out of their orbits, he was blander and more genial still, for nothing pleased him so much as to make the crooked straight, and crush down uneven places.

Among the borrowed notions by which his barbarism had become semified was that of the public arena, in which, by exhibitions of manly and beastly valor, the minds of his subjects were refined and cultured.

But even here the exuberant and barbaric fancy asserted itself. The arena of the king was built, not to give the people an opportunity of hearing the rhapsodies of dying gladiators, nor to enable them to view the inevitable conclusion of a conflict between religious opinions and hungry jaws, but for purposes far better adapted to widen and develop the mental energies of the people. This vast amphitheatre, with its encircling galleries, its mysterious vaults, and its unseen passages, was an agent of poetic justice, in which crime was punished, or virtue rewarded, by the decrees of an impartial and incorruptible chance.

When a subject was accused of a crime of sufficient importance to interest the king, public notice was given that on an appointed day the fate of the accused person would be decided in the king's arena—a structure which well deserved its name; for, although its form and plan were borrowed from afar, its purpose emanated solely from the brain of this man, who, every barleycorn a king, knew no tradition to which he owed more allegiance than pleased his fancy, and who ingrafted on every adopted form of human thought and action the rich growth of his barbaric idealism.

When all the people had assembled in the galleries, and the king, surrounded by his court, sat high up on his throne of royal state on one side of the arena, he gave a signal, a door beneath him opened, and the accused subject stepped out into the amphitheatre. Directly opposite him, on the other side of the enclosed space, were two doors, exactly alike and side by side. It was the duty and the privilege of the person on trial to walk directly to these doors and open one of them. He could open either door he pleased. He was subject to no guidance or influence but that of the aforementioned impartial and incorruptible chance. If he opened the one, there came out of it a hungry tiger, the fiercest and most cruel that could be procured, which immediately sprang upon him, and tore him to pieces, as a punishment for his guilt. The moment that the case of the criminal was thus decided, doleful iron bells were clanged, great wails went up from the hired mourners posted on the outer rim of the arena, and the vast audience, with bowed heads and downcast hearts, wended slowly their homeward way, mourning greatly that one so young and fair, or so old and respected, should have merited so dire a fate.

But if the accused person opened the other door, there came forth from it a lady, the most suitable to his years and station that his Majesty could select among his fair subjects; and to this lady he was immediately married, as a reward of his innocence. It mattered not that he might already possess a wife and family, or that his affections might be engaged upon an object of his own selection. The king allowed no such subordinate arrangements to interfere with his great scheme of retribution and reward. The exercises, as in the other instance, took place immediately, and in the arena. Another door opened beneath the king, and a priest, followed by a band of choristers, and dancing maidens blowing joyous airs on golden horns and treading an epithalamic measure, advanced to where the pair stood side by side, and the wedding was promptly and cheerily solemnized. Then the gay brass bells rang forth their merry peals, the people shouted glad hurrahs, and the innocent man, preceded by children strewing flowers on his path, led his bride to his home.

This was the king's semi-barbaric method of administering justice. Its perfect fairness is obvious. The criminal could not know out of which door would come the lady. He opened either he pleased, without having the slightest idea whether, in the next instant, he was to be devoured or married. On some occasions the tiger came out of one door, and on some out of the other. The decisions of this tribunal were not only fair— they were positively determinate. The accused person was instantly punished if he found himself guilty, and if innocent he was rewarded on the spot, whether he liked it or not. There was no escape from the judgements of the king's arena.

The institution was a very popular one. When the people gathered together on one of the great trial days, they never knew whether they were to witness a bloody slaughter or a hilarious wedding. This element of uncertainty lent an interest to the occasion which it could not otherwise have attained. Thus the masses were entertained and pleased, and the thinking part of the community could bring no charge of unfairness against this plan; for did not the accused person have the whole matter in his own hands?

This semi-barbaric king had a daughter as blooming as his most florid fancies, and with a soul as fervent and imperious as his own. As is usual in such cases, she was the apple of his eye, and was loved by him above all humanity. Among his courtiers was a young man of that fineness of blood and lowness of station common to the conventional heroes of romance who love royal maidens. This royal maiden was well satisfied with her lover, for he was handsome and brave to a degree unsurpassed in all this kingdom, and she loved him with an ardor that had enough of barbarism in it to make it exceedingly warm and strong. This love affair moved on happily for many months, until, one day, the king happened to discover its existence. He did not hesitate nor waver in regard to his duty in the premises. The youth was immediately cast into prison, and a day was appointed for his trial in the king's arena. This, of course, was an especially important occasion, and his Majesty, as well as all the people, was greatly interested in the workings and development of this trial. Never before had such a case occurred—never before had a subject dared to love the daughter of a king. In after years such things became commonplace enough, but then they were, in no slight degree, novel and startling.

The tiger cages of the kingdom were searched for the most savage and relentless beasts, from which the fiercest monster might be selected for the arena, and the ranks of maiden youth and beauty throughout the land were carefully surveyed by competent judges, in order that the young man might have a fitting bride in case fate did not determine for him a different destiny. Of course, everybody knew that the deed with which the accused was charged had been done. He had loved the princess, and neither he, she, nor any one else thought of denying the fact. But the king would not think of allowing any fact of this kind to interfere with the workings of the tribunal, in which he took such great delight and satisfaction. No matter how the affair turned out, the youth would be disposed of, and the king would take an aesthetic pleasure in watching the course of events which would determine whether or not the young man had done wrong in allowing himself to love the princess.

The appointed day arrived. From far and near the people gathered, and thronged the great galleries of the arena, while crowds, unable to gain admittance, massed themselves against its outside walls. The king and his court were in their places, opposite the twin doors—those fateful portals, so terrible in their similarity!

All was ready. The signal was given. A door beneath the royal party opened, and the lover of the princess walked into the arena. Tall, beautiful, fair, his appearance was greeted with a low hum of admiration and anxiety. Half the audience had not known so grand a youth had lived among them. No wonder the princess loved him! What a terrible thing for him to be there!

As the youth advanced into the arena, he turned, as the custom was, to bow to the king. But he did not think at all of that royal personage; his eyes were fixed upon the princess, who sat to the right of her father. Had it not been for the moiety of barbarism in her nature, it is probable that lady would not have been there. But her intense and fervid soul would not allow her to be absent on an occasion in which she was so terribly interested. From the moment that the decree had gone forth that her lover should decide his fate in the king's arena, she had thought of nothing, night or day, but this great event and the various subjects connected with it. Possessed of more power, influence, and force of character than any one who had ever before been interested in such a case, she had done what no other person had done—she had possessed herself of the secret of the doors. She knew in which of the two rooms behind those doors stood the cage of the tiger, with its open front, and in which waited the lady. Through these thick doors, heavily curtained with skins on the inside, it was impossible that any noise or suggestion should come from within to the person who should approach to raise the latch of one of them. But gold, and the power of a woman's will, had brought the secret to the princess.

Not only did she know in which room stood the lady, ready

to emerge, all blushing and radiant, should her door be opened, but she knew who the lady was. It was one of the fairest and loveliest of the damsels of the court who had been selected as the reward of the accused youth, should he be proved innocent of the crime of aspiring to one so far above him; and the princess hated her. Often had she seen, or imagined that she had seen, this fair creature throwing glances of admiration upon the person of her lover, and sometimes she thought these glances were perceived and even returned. Now and then she had seen them talking together. It was but for a moment or two, but much can be said in a brief space. It may have been on most unimportant topics, but how could she know that? The girl was lovely, but she had dared to raise her eyes to the loved one of the princess, and, with all the intensity of the savage blood transmitted to her through long lines of wholly barbaric ancestors, she hated the woman who blushed and trembled behind that silent door.

When her lover turned and looked at her, and his eye met hers as she sat there paler and whiter than any one in the vast ocean of anxious faces about her, he saw, by that power of quick perception which is given to those whose souls are one, that she knew behind which door crouched the tiger, and behind which stood the lady. He had expected her to know it. He understood her nature, and his soul was assured that she would never rest until she had made plain to herself this thing, hidden to all other lookers-on, even to the king. The only hope for the youth in which there was any element of certainty was based upon the success of the princess in discovering this mystery, and the moment he looked upon her, he saw she had succeeded.

Then it was that his quick and anxious glance asked the question, "Which?" It was as plain to her as if he shouted it from where he stood. There was not an instant to be lost. The question was asked in a flash; it must be answered in another.

Her right arm lay on the cushioned parapet before her. She raised her hand, and made a slight, quick movement toward the right. No one but her lover saw her. Every eye but his was fixed on the man in the arena.

He turned, and with a firm and rapid step he walked across the empty space. Every heart stopped beating, every breath was held, every eye was fixed immovably upon that man. Without the slightest hesitation, he went to the door on the right, and opened it.

Now, the point of the story is this: Did the tiger come out of that door, or did the lady?

The more we reflect upon this question, the harder it is to answer. It involves a study of the human heart which leads us through devious mazes of passion, out of which it is difficult to find our way. Think of it, fair reader, not as if the decision of the question depended upon yourself, but upon that hot-blooded, semi-barbaric princess, her soul at a white heat beneath the combined fires of despair and jealousy. She had lost him, but who should have him?

How often, in her waking hours and in her dreams, had she started in wild horror and covered her face with her hands as she thought of her lover opening the door on the other side of which waited the cruel fangs of the tiger!

But how much oftener had she seen him at the other door! How in her grievous reveries had she gnashed her teeth and torn her hair when she saw his start of rapturous delight as he opened the door of the lady! How her soul had burned in agony when she had seen him rush to meet that woman, with her flushing cheek and sparkling eye of triumph; when she had seen him lead her forth, his whole frame kindled with the joy of recovered life; when she had heard the glad shouts from the multitude, and the wild ringing of the happy bells; when she had seen the priest, with his joyous followers, advance to the couple, and make them man and wife before her very eyes; and when she had seen them walk away together upon their path of flowers, followed by the tremendous shouts of the hilarious multitude, in which her one despairing shriek was lost and drowned!

Would it not be better for him to die at once, and go to wait for her in the blessed regions of semi-barbaric futurity?

And yet, that awful tiger, those shrieks, that blood!

Her decision had been indicated in an instant, but it had been made after days and nights of anguished deliberation. She had known she would be asked, she had decided what she would answer, and, without the slightest hesitation, she had moved her hand to the right.

The question of her decision is one not to be lightly considered, and it is not for me to presume to set up myself as the one person able to answer it. So I leave it with all of you: Which came out of the opened door—the lady or the tiger?

Morgan Morgan

by

JANETTE TURNER HOSPITAL

(1942–   )

As I think I was saying earlier, one of the main things in choosing a story to read aloud is finding a voice that you're comfortable with. Not simply your voice, but the voice of the story. Morgan Morgan's voice when he yodels is like a silk ribbon unfurling itself. You've got to love a yodeller. To me it is the voice of Morgan Morgan that first drew me to the story— you can almost hear him in your ear as you're reading to yourself. It is one of those voices you remember: it's full and rich and clear, but has its funny little halts and stops. It is the voice of the storyteller—of the old man who plants dahlias and yodels and tells tall tales.

My grandfather, Morgan Morgan, was a yodeller and a breeder of dahlias. On Collins Street and Bourke Street, I could tug at his hand and implore, "Please, Grandpa, please!" and he would throw back his head and do something mysterious in his throat and his yodel would unfurl itself like a silk ribbon. All the trams in Melbourne would come to a standstill, entangled. Bewitched pedestrians stopped and stared. But this was nothing compared with former powers: when he was a young man on the goldfields, handsome and down on his luck, the girls for miles around would come running. Yodel-o-o-o, my grandfather would sing, snaring them, winding them in. The girls would sigh and sway like cobras in the strands of his voice. He was a charmer.

"Get along with you, Morg. You're bad for business," Mrs. Blackburn would say. Flowers bloomed by the bucketful around her. She would lean across roses and carnations, she would catch at his sleeve. "Here's a daisy for the nipper," and she'd tuck it behind my ear. She didn't want him to move on at all, even I knew that. "Your grandpa," she had said to me often enough, "is a fine figure of a man, they don't make men like him anymore." She'd pull one of her carnations from a bucket and swing the stem in her fingers. "A gentleman is a gentleman," she'd sigh. "Even if he is poor as a church mouse and never found a thimbleful of gold."

It was not entirely true, Grandpa told me, that he never struck it rich on the goldfields—the *Kalgoorlie* goldfields, he'd say, with a loving hesitation on the *o*'s and *l*'s, a rallentando which intimated that music had gone from the language since The Rush petered out.

In those exotic and demented times, men were obsessed with the calibration of luck. Not Morgan Morgan. While other men mapped out their fevers with calipers, measuring the likely run of a seam from existing strikes, Grandpa Morgan simply watched for the aura. Wherever the aura settled, he panned or dug.

"Crazy as a bandicoot," the publican told him. "You've got to have a *system*, mate!"

But Morgan Morgan knew that gold was a gift, it never came to men of system, never had. "King David danced before the Lord," he pointed out, "which goes to show; and his gold mines were the richest in the world, I read it somewhere, some archaeologist bloke has proved it." Grandpa had his own methods of fossicking, in scripture or creek bed, it was all the same to him. He found what he wanted, or at any rate learned to want what he found.

He laboured at strings of waterholes that were known to be panned out. He was after the Morgan Nugget. This was how it appeared to him in a vision: as big as a man's fist, blackened, gnarled like a prune, cobwebby with the roots of creek ferns. He expected its presence to be announced by an echo of Welsh choirs in the tea-tree and eucalypt scrub. And it was, it was. One day, with the strains of *Cwm Rhondda* all around him, he scratched at a piece of rock with a broken fingernail and the sun caught the gash and almost blinded him.

"Solid gold," he told me. "And big as a man's fist." Not for the first time, he knew himself to be a man of destiny.

"What did you do with it, Grandpa?" I was full of awe. When he spoke of the past, I heard the surf of the delectable world of turbulence that raged beyond our garden wall. We were still at the old place in Ringwood then, across from the railway station. If I buried my face in the box-hedge of golden privet, I could hear the rush of Grandpa's life, the trains careering past to Mitcham and Box Hill and Richmond. He would listen too, leaning into the sound, and I would see his eyes travel on beyond Richmond, beyond Footscray even, out towards the unfenceable Nullarbor Plain and Kalgoorlie.

"What did you do with it, Grandpa?"

"With what?" he would ask from far away.

"With the Morgan Nugget?"

"I put it down again," he said, "right back down where I found it, inside the vision. It's still waiting just where I put it. Listen," he said, "if you put your ear to the Morgan Dahlia, you can hear it waiting."

I buried my ear in those soft salmon ruchings of petals and heard the deep hush of the past. And then *pop, pop*: he pinched the calix with his fingers. "That's the sound of the Morgan Nugget," he said, "when it gets impatient. It's waiting for one of us to find it again."

"Dad!" Grandma Morgan, with a basket of eggs on her arm, came down the path from the hen house. "Don't confuse the child with your nonsense." She lifted her eyebrows at me. "Always could talk the leg off an iron pot, your Grandpa."

"Pot calling the kettle black, I'd say," he grumbled. He hated to be listened in on; I hated it too. I didn't like the way the Morgan history drooped at the edges when other people were around.

Grandma Morgan was picking mint and tossing the sprigs into her basket. The leaves lay green and vivid against the eggs. "Came to tell you the pension cheques have arrived," she said.

"Well, praise be," said Grandpa, mollified. "Praise be. There's corn in Egypt yet. And on top of that," he whispered, as she moved off towards the house, "the Morgan Nugget's still waiting."

"Dad! No more nonsense. That child is never going to know the difference between truth and lies, you mark my words."

"Got eyes in the back of her head," Grandpa grumbled. "And ears in the wind. No flies on her, no siree."

It was one of his favourite sayings: *No flies on so-and-so, no siree*. To me it implied an opposite state, an unsavory kind of person, stupid, sticky, smelling overly sweet in the manner of plums left on the ground beneath our tree for too long. I imagined this person—the person on whom there *were* flies—to be pale and bloated, and to have bad breath and unwashed socks.

There was a man who delivered bonemeal for the dahlia garden on whom I thought there might be flies—if only one could see him at an unguarded moment. His clothes gave off a rich rancid smell. When he laughed it was like looking into the squishy dark mush of fruit I had to collect from the lawn before mowing. Those few teeth which the bonemeal man still had—they announced themselves like unvanquished sentinels on a crumbling rampart—were given over to a delicate vegetation. I recognised it: it was the same silky green fur that coated the fallen plums over which floated little black parasols of flies.

Yet one day, when I came out to the dahlia garden just as the bonemeal man was leaving, Grandpa Morgan was tossing his fine head of hair in the wind and laughing his fine Welsh laugh. The bonemeal man was laughing too, trundling his barrow down our path, doubled up with mirth between its shafts, his green teeth waving about like banners.

"Grandpa, what is it, what is it? Why are you laughing, Grandpa?"

"Oh," Grandpa gasped, patting me on the head in the way that meant a subject was not for discussing. "No flies on *him,* no siree."

This was the best thing: I could always count on Grandpa Morgan to be outrageous. That was the word people used: the neighbours, my grandmother, my mother, my uncles. "He's *outrageous*," they would say, shaking their heads and throwing up their hands and smiling.

If I asked him to, he would yodel in the schoolyard when he came to fetch me, and abracadabra, we two were in the hub of a circle of awed envy. When I passed the Teacher's Room at morning tea time, I'd hear the older ones whisper and smile: "That's Morgie's granddaughter."

On our walks he would stop and talk to everyone we met, "to *anyone,* anyone at all," Uncle Cyril would groan. He spoke to the butcher, the baker, the lady in the cake shop, to men who did shady undiscussable things, even men who smelled of horses and *took bets,* whatever that was.

"What can you be thinking of?" Grandma would say, "with the child hearing every word? A man *known* to be mixed up with off-course betting."

I knew bets to be deeply evil. I imagined them to be huge and ravenous and almost hidden behind fearful masks. Once upon a time, in Kalgoorlie, Grandpa himself had made bets, but that was before the Lord saved him and showed him the light. Now, he said, he only bet on the Day of Judgement. Still, he couldn't see any harm in talking to people who "knew horses." He would introduce me. "This is Paddy," he would say; "a man who knows horses if ever anyone did." I myself had no interest in knowing horses on account of their large and alarming teeth, but I rather liked those brave horse-know-ing men.

Sometimes Grandma, shocked, would call out: "Dad! I want to have a word with you, Dad." From the front window, she would have watched us coming over the bridge from the Ringwood Station. The most *interesting* people came off the trains and walked over that bridge. Grandma would have seen us stop and talk to some gentleman who wore string, perhaps, for suspenders, and whose shoes were stuffed in an intricate way with newspapers, and who gave off the rank smell of pubs. "Dad!" she would say. "What are you *thinking* of, to introduce the child to such strangers?"

"Strangers?" Grandpa would raise his eyebrows in surprise. "That wasn't a stranger. That was Bluey McTavish from back of Geelong. We don't know any strangers."

This was certainly true, though we'd only just met Mr. Bluey McTavish of Geelong, whose life history we would dis-cuss over the sorting of dahlia bulbs. I don't know what it was about Grandpa Morgan, but people told him a great deal about themselves very quickly. "There aren't any such people as strangers," he told me. "Or if there are, I've never met them."

"I don't know what's going to come of that child," Grandma Morgan said, throwing up her hands and trying not to smile. "But one thing's certain: she'll never know the difference between truth and lies."

Grandpa said with ruffled dignity: "One thing she'll know about is dahlias."

The dahlias, the dahlias. They stretched to the edge of the world. When I stood between the rows, I saw nothing but jungle, with great suns of flowers above me, so heavy they nodded on their stalks and shone down through the forests of their own leaves. Such a rainbow of suns: from the creamy white to a purple that was almost black. The dahlias believed in excess: they could never have too many petals. The dahlia which could crowd the most pleatings of pure light about its centre won a blue ribbon at the Melbourne Show. It was an article of faith with us that some year the Morgan Dahlia would win that ribbon.

Grandpa Morgan did things to the bulbs and the soil. He married broad-petalled pinks to pin-tucked yellows; he introduced sassy purples to smocked whites with puffed sleeves and lacy hems. He watched over his nurslings, he crooned to them, he prayed. To birds and snails, he issued strong Welsh warnings (the Lord having taken away a certain range of Australian vocabulary). As his flowerlings grew, he murmured endearments; and they gathered themselves up into a delirium of pleats, rank upon rank of petals, tier upon tier, frilled prima donnas. The colour of the Morgan dahlia was a salmon that could make judges weep, the salmon of a baby's cheek, the colour of a lover's whisper. And it did win yellow ribbons, and red, at the Melbourne Show, but never the coveted blue.

"Is it waiting till we find the Morgan Nugget again?" I asked.

"Very likely," Grandpa said. "Very likely."

The day Grandma came out with the news of Uncle Charlie, we were deep in dahlias.

"Dad," she said. "Charlie's gone."

Grandpa paused in mid-weeding. A clump of clover and crabgrass dangled from between his fingers. He sank down on the ground between the dahlias and rested his head in his hands. "Well," he said, sadly and slowly. "Charlie. So Charlie went first."

"Where's he gone?" I wanted to know.

"Uncle Charlie's gone to heaven," Grandma told me, and Grandpa said: "He's dead." He pushed his trowel into the soil and lifted up a handful of earth. It was alive with ants and worms, we watched it move in the palm of his hand. "I'm next," he sighed, and he smelled the earth and held it for me to smell, and he rubbed it against his cheek as though it were a kitten. "I'm next, I suppose."

"Next for what?"

"Next for dying," he said.

"What happens when you die, Grandpa?"

"They put you in a box and they bury you under the ground with the dahlia bulbs."

I stared at him in horror. "Uncle Charlie should run away and hide."

"You can't run away when you're dead," he said.

"Grandpa," I whispered, beginning to shiver, "will they do it to you?"

"Yes," he said.

"And to me?"

I crept between his earth-covered arms and he held me tightly and rocked me back and forth between the dahlias. "Yes," he sighed, "one day, yes. That's the way it is. But then we'll be with the Lord."

I didn't want to be with the Lord. I had a brilliant idea. "Grandpa," I said, "we'll run away *before* we die. I know a very good place in the woodshed, they'd never find us."

"Dad!" Grandma's voice steamed over with exasperation. "Now just what have you been telling her this time? How will that child ever know the difference between truth and a lie?

Uncle Charlie," she said to me, "has gone straight to heaven, and that is the simple truth."

Mr. Peabody knew the truth. Every Sunday it spoke in his bones, it shook him from head to foot.

There must have been some obscure and ancient rule at church. It must have been this rule which forced Mr. Peabody, week after week, to sit directly in front of Grandpa Morgan. Mr. Peabody was a tiny man, elderly, and seemingly frail as a sparrow, though he must have had enormous reserves of stamina on which to draw.

Behind him, sheltering in the leeside of the Spirit of the Lord as it blustered and rushed through Grandpa, my little brother and I kept score. When the spirit moved, Grandpa shouted *hallelujah* in his fine Welsh voice. The shock waves hit Mr. Peabody sharply in the nape of his neck and travelled down his spine with such force that he would rise an inch or two from the pew. Most of his body would go rigid, but his head and his hands would quiver for seconds at a time. *Glory, glory,* he would murmur in a terror-stricken prayerful voice.

These seismic interludes infused Sundays with extraordinary interest. And there was also this: from monitoring the passions of Mr. Peabody, my brother and I learned self-control, the ability to tamp down an explosion of mirth and turn it into a mere telegraphed signal of gleaming eyes and a coded numerology of fingers.

But then came the day that a shaft of sunlight fell from a high amber-glass window in the church and place a crown of gold on Mr. Peabody's head. "Oh!" I gasped aloud. "*Look!*" And Grandpa shouted *Hallelujah!* and Mr. Peabody rose up into his corona like a skyrocket and I saw a million golden doves and the gilded petals of all the dahlias in the world rising up into the pointed arch above, where God lived.

"It was the Holy Spirit you saw," the pastor told me. "The Holy Spirit descending as a dove."

"Going *up*," I corrected. "Lots and lots of them, and dahlias too."

"The Holy Spirit," he said again, less certainly. "In the form of a dove."

"I'm not so sure," my Sunday School teacher said. "She makes things up."

"Out of the mouths of babes," the pastor reminded her.

"She makes things up," my Sunday School teacher insisted. "She handles the truth very carelessly. She believes her own lies."

"Grandpa," I asked, "how can you tell the difference between truth and a lie?"

He was working bonemeal into the soil around his dahlias; over us nodded those heavy salmon suns. He went on kneading the rich black loam, intent on his labour.

Apprehensively I persisted: "Is the Morgan Nugget true?"

He went on sifting the soil.

I thought hopefully; perhaps he made up death.

"The truth," he said at last, "shall make you free. John, chapter 8, verse 32."

"Grandpa," I said, "there were doves with gold wings, and dahlias too. Mr. Peabody made them fly. I saw them."

"I know you did."

I leaned towards him. "And the Morgan Nugget?" I breathed.

"Is true," he said. "Is true."

The Tell-Tale Heart

by
EDGAR ALLAN POE
(1809–1849)

I really had a dilemma over this one: choosing my favourite Poe story. In the end I think I chose "The Tell-Tale Heart" simply for the sheer drama of the thing—the idea of a someone being caught out by a beating heart which nobody else can hear. The momentum builds and builds. You can almost hear the heart beating as you read. Like the beating of a drum. Really, the story has such a rhythm about it that it's hard not to get caught up in the close atmosphere of that room—how Poe does it I don't know, but he really knows how to make a moment stand still.

TRUE!—nervous—very, very dreadfully nervous I had been and am; but why will you say that I am mad? The disease had sharpened my senses—not destroyed—not dulled them. Above all was the sense of hearing acute. I heard all things in the heaven and in the earth. I heard many things in hell. How, then, am I mad? Hearken! and observe how healthily—how calmly I can tell you the whole story.

It is impossible to say how first the idea entered my brain; but once conceived, it haunted me day and night. Object there was none. Passion there was none. I loved the old man. He had never wronged me. He had never given me insult. For his gold I had no desire. I think it was his eye! yes, it was this! He had the eye of a vulture—a pale blue eye, with a film over it. Whenever it fell upon me, my blood ran cold; and so by degrees—very gradually—I made up my mind to take the life of the old man, and thus rid myself of the eye forever.

Now this is the point. You fancy me mad. Madmen know nothing. But you should have seen *me*. You should have seen how wisely I proceeded—with what caution—with what fore-sight—with what dissimulation I went to work! I was never kinder to the old man than during the whole week before I killed him. And every night, about midnight, I turned the latch of his door and opened it—oh so gently! And then, when I had made an opening sufficient for my head, I put in a dark lantern, all closed, closed, so that no light shone out, and then I thrust in my head. Oh, you would have laughed to see how cunningly I thrust it in! I moved it slowly—very, very slowly, so that I might not disturb the old man's sleep. It took me an hour to place my whole head within the opening so far that I could see him as he lay upon his bed. Ha!—would a madman have been so wise as this? And then, when my head was well in the room, I undid the lantern cautiously—oh, so cautiously—cautiously (for the hinges creaked)—I undid it just so much that a single thin ray fell upon the vulture eye. And this I did for seven long nights—every night just at midnight—but I found the eye always closed; and so it was impossible to do the work; for it was not the old man who vexed me, but his Evil Eye. And every morning, when the day broke, I went boldly into the chamber, and spoke courageously to him, calling him by name in a hearty tone, and inquiring how he had passed the night. So you see he would have been a very profound old man, indeed, to suspect that every night, just at twelve, I looked in upon him while he slept.

Upon the eighth night I was more than usually cautious in opening the door. A watch's minute hand moves more quickly than did mine. Never before that night, had I *felt* the extent of my own powers—of my sagacity. I could scarcely contain my feelings of triumph. To think that there I was, opening the door, little by little, and he not even to dream of my secret deeds or thoughts. I fairly chuckled at the idea; and perhaps he heard me; for he moved on the bed suddenly, as if startled. Now you may think that I drew back—but no. His room was as black as pitch with the thick darkness, (for the shutters were close fastened, through fear of robbers) and so I knew that he could not see the opening of the door, and I kept pushing it on steadily, steadily.

I had my head in, and was about to open the lantern, when my thumb slipped upon the tin fastening, and the old man sprang up in bed, crying out—'Who's there?'

I kept quite still and said nothing. For a whole hour I did not move a muscle, and in the meantime I did not hear him lie down. He was still sitting up in the bed listening;—just as I have done, night after night, hearkening to the death watches in the wall.

Presently I heard a slight groan, and I knew it was the groan of mortal terror. It was not a groan of pain or of grief—oh, no!—it was the low stifled sound that arises from the bottom of the soul when overcharged with awe. I knew the sound well. Many a night, just at midnight, when all the world slept, it has welled up from my own bosom, deepening, with its dreadful echo, the terrors that distracted me. I say I knew it well. I knew what the old man felt, and pitied him, although I chuckled at heart. I knew that he had been lying awake ever since the first slight noise, when he had turned in the bed. His fears had been ever since growing upon him. He had been trying to fancy them causeless, but could not. He had been saying to himself—'It is nothing but the wind in the chimney—it is only a mouse crossing the floor,' or 'it is merely a cricket which has made a single chirp.' Yes, he had been trying to comfort himself with these suppositions: but he had found all in vain. *All in vain;* because Death, in approaching him had stalked with his black shadow before him, and enveloped the victim. And it was the mournful influence of the unperceived shadow that caused him to feel—although he neither saw nor heard—to *feel* the presence of my head within the room.

When I had waited a long time, very patiently, without hearing him lie down, I resolved to open a little—a very, very little crevice in the lantern. So I opened it—you cannot imagine how stealthily, stealthily—until, at length a simple dim ray, like the thread of the spider, shot from out the crevice and fell full upon the vulture eye.

It was open—wide, wide open—and I grew furious as I gazed upon it. I saw it with perfect distinctness—all a dull blue, with a hideous veil over it that chilled the very marrow in my bones; but I could see nothing else of the old man's face or person: for I had directed the ray as if by instinct, precisely upon the damned spot.

And have I not told you that what you mistake for madness is but over acuteness of the senses?—now, I say, there came to my ears a low, dull, quick sound, such as a watch makes when enveloped in cotton. I knew *that* sound well, too. It was the beating of the old man's heart. It increased my fury, as the beating of a drum stimulates the soldier into courage.

But even yet I refrained and kept still. I scarcely breathed. I held the lantern motionless. I tried how steadily I could maintain the ray upon the eye. Meantime the hellish tattoo of the heart increased. it grew quicker and quicker, and louder and louder every instant. The old man's terror *must* have been extreme! It grew louder, I say, louder every moment!—do you mark me well? I have told you that I am nervous: so I am. And now at the dead hour of the night, amid the dreadful silence of that old house, so strange a noise as this excited me to uncontrollable terror. Yet, for some minutes longer I refrained and stood still. But the beating grew louder, louder! I thought the heart must burst. And now a new anxiety seized me—the sound would be heard by a neighbour! The old man's hour had come! With a loud yell, I threw open the lantern and leaped into the room. He shrieked once—once only. In an instant I dragged him to the floor, and pulled the heavy bed over him. I then smiled gaily, to find the deed so far done. But, for many minutes, the heart beat on with a muffled sound. This, however, did not vex me; it would not be heard through the wall. At length it ceased. The old man was dead. I removed the bed and examined the corpse. Yes, he was stone, stone dead. I placed my hand upon the heart and held it there many minutes. There was no pulsation. He was stone dead. His eye would trouble me no more.

If still you think me mad, you will think so no longer when I describe the wise precautions I took for the concealment of the body. The night waned, and I worked hastily, but in silence. First of all I dismembered the corpse. I cut off the head and the arms and the legs.

I then took up three planks from the flooring of the chamber, and deposited all between the scantlings. I then replaced the boards so cleverly, so cunningly, that no human eye—not even *his*—could have detected any thing wrong. There was nothing to wash out—no stain of any kind—no blood-spot whatever. I had been too wary for that. A tub had caught all—ha! ha!

When I had made an end of these labors, it was four o'clock—still dark as midnight. As the bell sounded the hour, there came a knocking at the street door. I went down to open it with a light heart—for what had I *now* to fear? There entered three men, who introduced themselves, with perfect suavity, as officers of the police. A shriek had been heard by a neighbour during the night; suspicion of foul play had been aroused; information had been lodged at the police office, and they (the officers) had been deputed to search the premises.

I smiled—for *what* had I to fear? I bade the gentlemen welcome. The shriek, I said, was my own in a dream. The old man, I mentioned, was absent in the country. I took my visitors all over the house. I bade them search—search *well*. I led them, at length, to *his* chamber. I showed them his treasures, secure, undisturbed. In the enthusiasm of my confidence, I brought chairs into the room, and desired them *here* to rest from their fatigues, while I myself, in the wild audacity of my perfect triumph, placed my own seat upon the very spot beneath which reposed the corpse of the victim.

The officers were satisfied. My *manner* had convinced them. I was singularly at ease. They sat, and while I answered cheerily, they chatted of familiar things. But, ere long, I felt myself getting pale and wished them gone. My head ached, and I fancied a ringing in my ears: but still they sat and still chatted. The ringing became more distinct—it continued and became more distinct: I talked more freely to get rid of the feeling: but it continued and gained definiteness—until, at length, I found that the noise was *not* within my ears.

No doubt I now grew *very* pale—but I talked more fluently, and with a heightened voice. Yet the sound increased—and what could I do? It was *a low, dull, quick sound—much such a sound as a watch makes when enveloped in cotton.* I gasped for breath—and yet the officer heard it not. I talked more quickly—more vehemently; but the noise steadily increased. I arose and argued about trifles, in a high key and with violent gesticulations; but the noise steadily increased. Why *would* they not be gone? I paced the floor to and fro with heavy strides, as if excited to fury by the observations of the men—but the noise steadily increased. Oh God! what *could* I do? I foamed—I raved—I swore! I swung the chair upon which I had been sitting, and grated it upon the boards, but the noise arose over all and continually increased. It grew louder—louder—*louder!* And still the men chatted pleasantly, and smiled. Was it possible they heard not? Almighty God!—no, no! They heard! they suspected!—they *knew!*—they were making a mockery of my horror!—this I thought, and this I think. But anything was better than this agony! Anything was more tolerable than this derision! I could bear those hypocritical smiles no longer! I felt that I must scream or die! and now—again!—hark! louder! louder! louder! *louder!*

'Villains!' I shrieked, 'dissemble no more! I admit the deed!—tear up the planks! here, here!—it is the beating of his hideous heart!'

Hoof-Beats on a **Bridge**

by
ALEXANDER WOOLLCOTT
(1887–1943)

A friend once said to me that parents are in the business of creating memories and traditions. What shape those memories take is often related to how they were received. For me, Christmas would not be Christmas without the smell of the Christmas tree. The smell of roasting chestnuts might take you to Athens or Rome. The sound of the dentist drill brings back a flurry of childhood fears. I always think that memory is tied to the senses, and "Hoof-Beats on a Bridge" is all about how we remember—how a certain sound takes you back to a certain time and place.

One December my path by chance at Christmas time crossed that of a neighbor of mine who was also far from home. Thus it befell that Katherine Cornell and I, she trouping with a play and I on a lecture-tour, observed the day by dining together in a Seattle hotel. I remember that my present to her was a telephone call whereby she could send her love across the continent to a friend we both cherish—a dear friend endowed with so many more senses than the paltry five allotted to the rest of us that I have no doubt she knew what we were up to before ever the bell rang in that Connecticut cottage of hers and the operator said, "Seattle calling Miss Helen Keller."

I have said that in that Seattle hotel Miss Cornell and I were two travelers far from home. But mine was more than a mere three thousand miles away. It was three thousand miles and a quarter of a century away. And if nowadays I try to fill each Christmas Eve with the hubbub of many manufactured preoccupations, it is probably in the dread of being trapped alone in the twilight by the ghosts of Christmas past. Then sharp but unmistakable and inexpressibly dear to me there would be borne across the years a music that is for me more full of

Christmas than sleigh-bells ever were or all the carols flung
down from all the belfries in the world. It is the ghost of a
sound that must haunt many an old dirt road—the thud of
hoof-beats on a wooden bridge. By them when I was young
we could tell on the darkest night that we were nearing home.

The house where I was born was a vast, ramshackle weath-
erbeaten building which had already seen better days but not
recently. A tangle of vines—trumpet vines and wisteria and
white grape and crimson rambler—curtained the twelve
ground-floor windows looking out toward the high road and
tactfully concealed the fact that the house had not been paint-
ed since before the Civil War. We used to speak grandly of the
ballroom but I cannot remember a time when the musicians'
gallery was not taken up with stacks of old Harpers and other
dusty unbound magazines. In my time at least, we could not
hold a dance without first sweeping the fallen plaster from the
floor. But this dear old house which had belonged to my
grandfather remained the one constant in the problem of a far-
flung tribe and back to it most of us managed to make our
way at Christmas time. Often the railroad fare was hard to
come by but somehow, as long as my mother was alive, from
school or college or work I made my way home every
Christmas for more than twenty years.

What ticking off of the days on the calendar as the time
grew near! Then at last the arrival at the railroad station after
dark on Christmas Eve, with home only five miles away. I
could always find a hack—it would smell of moth-balls and
manure and the driver could usually tell me how many of the
cousins had got there ahead of me. A dozen or so, maybe.
Then the jog-trot in the deepening darkness with one eager
passenger inside—hungry for home and no longer counting
the days or even the minutes. By this time I was counting the
bridges. I knew them by heart. Three more. Two more. At the
next if I sat forward and peered through the window I would
see the house through the leafless trees, every window down
the long front agleam with a welcoming lamp, each light a
token of all the loving-kindness that dwelt under that old,
shingled roof. Then the long slow pull up the drive. Before I

could get out of the hack and pay the driver, the door would be flung open and my mother would be standing on the threshold.

Small wonder I like to be busy at Christmas. Small wonder I feel a twist at my heart whenever at any time anywhere in the world I hear the sound of a hoof-beat on a wooden bridge.

Two Friends

by

GUY DE MAUPASSANT
(1850–1893)

Choosing a Maupassant story was even more difficult than choosing a Poe. There are so many fine stories to choose from. What I like most about Maupassant is that no matter how many of his stories you have read, each new story holds a new surprise. Some new twist. There is always something unexpected.

"Two Friends" is a story that really strikes to the bone. Maupassant has a real genius for the dramatic moment—and "Two Friends" is a story that you will remember, almost unconsciously, long after you have finished reading it.

Two
Friends

Paris was under siege, starving and at her last gasp. The sparrows were disappearing from the roofs, and the city's sewers were being depopulated. People were eating anything they could find.

One bright morning in January Monsieur Morissot, a watchmaker by trade but an idler by necessity, was walking sadly along the outer boulevard with an empty stomach and his hands in the pockets of his uniform trousers when he came face to face with a comrade in arms whom he recognized as an old friend. It was Monsieur Sauvage, a riverside acquaintance.

Every Sunday before the war Morissot used to leave home at dawn with a bamboo rod in his hand and a tin box on his back. He took the Argenteuil train, got out at Colombes, and walked to Marante Island. As soon as he reached this place of his dreams he started fishing and he went on fishing till nightfall.

There, every Sunday, he used to meet another fanatical angler, a stout, jolly little man called Monsieur Sauvage, a haberdasher from the Rue Notre-Dame-de-Lorette. They often spent half the day sitting side by side with their rods in their hands and their feet dangling over the water; and they had become firm friends.

Some days they never said a word; sometimes they chatted. But they understood each other perfectly without any need for words, having similar tastes and identical feelings.

On spring mornings, about ten o'clock, when a faint mist was rising from the smooth surface of the river and drifting along with the current, and the two enthusiastic anglers could feel the pleasant warmth of the spring sun on their backs, Morissot would say to his neighbour: 'This is the life, eh?'

And Monsieur Sauvage would reply: 'This is the life all right.'

That was all that was necessary for them to understand and respect one another.

In the autumn, towards the end of the day, when the setting sun reddened the sky and stained the river crimson, when the horizon was ablaze and the water reflected the shapes of scarlet clouds, and when the trees between the two friends, already russet-coloured and shivering with the foretaste of winter, turned fiery red and gold, Monsieur Sauvage would look at Morissot with a smile and say: 'What a picture!'

And Morissot, struck by the beauty of the scene but keeping his eyes fixed on his float, would reply: 'Better than the boulevard, isn't it?'

They had no sooner recognized each other than they shook hands warmly, struck by the changed circumstances in which they had met. Monsieur Sauvage heaved a sigh and murmured: 'What a mess we're in!'

Morissot answered gloomily: 'And what weather we're having! This is the first fine day we've had this year.'

The sky was indeed a bright unclouded blue.

They walked on together, side by side, sad and thoughtful.

'Remember our fishing?' Morissot went on. 'Those were the days!'

'I wonder when we'll go fishing again,' said Monsieur Sauvage.

They went into a little café and had an absinthe together. Then they resumed their stroll along the pavement.

Suddenly Morissot stopped short.

'What about another?'

'I won't say no,' replied Monsieur Sauvage, and they went into another café.

When they came out they were rather fuddled, as people are when they have been drinking spirits on an empty stomach. It was a mild day and a gentle breeze fanned their faces.

The warm air made Monsieur Sauvage, already intoxicated by the absinthe, quite tipsy. He stopped and said: 'Let's go.'

'Where?'

'Fishing of course.'

'But where?'

'Why, our usual island. The French outposts aren't far from Colombes. I know Colonel Dumoulin: they'll let us through without any trouble.'

Quivering with excitement, Morissot replied: 'Right, I'm with you.'

And they separated to go and get their fishing tackle.

An hour later they were walking side by side along the main road. Eventually they reached the villa which the colonel was using as his headquarters. He smiled at their whimsical request and gave his consent. They set off again, armed with a pass.

Before long they had crossed the line of outposts, passed through the deserted village of Colombes, and found themselves on the edge of the little vineyards which sloped down to the Seine. It was about eleven o'clock.

Across the river, the village of Argenteuil looked dead. The heights of Orgemont and Sannois dominated the whole countryside. The great plain which stretches as far as Nanterre was empty, completely empty, with its bare cherry trees and its grey fields.

Pointing to the high ground, Monsieur Sauvage murmured: 'The Prussians are up there.'

And a paralysing sense of anxiety took hold of the two friends as they looked at this deserted scene.

The Prussians! They had never seen any of them, but for months they had been aware of their presence around Paris, bringing ruin on France, looting, murdering, starving, invisible and irresistible. And a sort of superstitious terror was added to the hatred they felt for that unknown, victorious people.

'Suppose we met some of them,' stammered Morissot, 'what would we do?'

With that mocking Parisian humour which had survived in spite of everything, Monsieur Sauvage replied: 'We'd offer them some fish to fry.'

But they hesitated about venturing into the open country, intimidated by the silence all around them.

At last Monsieur Sauvage made up his mind.

'Come on, let's go,' he said, 'but keep your eyes skinned!'

And they went down into a vineyard, bent double or crawling along, their ears cocked and their eyes darting about nervously.

They still had a strip of open ground to cross to reach the river bank. They broke into a run, and as soon as they got to the bank they crouched down among the dry rushes.

Morissot put his ear to the ground to listen for the sound of footsteps in their vicinity. He heard nothing. They were alone, absolutely alone.

Feeling reassured, they started to fish.

In front of them Marante Island, now deserted, hid them from the opposite bank. The little restaurant was closed and looked as if it had been abandoned for years.

Monsieur Sauvage caught the first gudgeon, Morissot the second, and after that they kept lifting their rods every other moment with little silver creatures wriggling at the end of the lines—a miraculous draught of fishes!

They carefully slipped the fish into a fine-meshed net bag dangling in the water at their feet, and a feeling of joy took hold of them, that delicious joy one feels at rediscovering a pleasure after being deprived of it for months.

The kindly sun warmed their backs; they heard nothing and thought of nothing; the rest of the world no longer existed for them; they simply fished.

But suddenly a dull roar which seemed to come from under the ground made the earth tremble. The big guns were opening up again.

Morissot turned his head, and above the bank, away to the left, he saw the great bulk of Mont-Valérien, its summit sporting a white plume, a puff of smoke it had just spat out.

The next moment a second puff of smoke came from the top of the fort, and a few seconds later the boom of another detonation reached their ears.

Others followed, as in quick succession the hill sent out its deadly breath, emitting clouds of milky vapour which rose slowly into the peaceful sky to form a cloud above the fort.

Monsieur Sauvage shrugged his shoulders.

'There they go, at it again!' he said.

Morissot, who was anxiously watching the feather on his float bobbing up and down, was suddenly filled with a peace-loving man's anger at these madmen who insisted on fighting one another, and he growled: 'They must be fools, killing each other like that.'

'They're worse than wild beasts,' said Monsieur Sauvage.

And Morissot, who had just hooked a bleak, declared: 'To think that it'll always be like that as long as we have governments!'

Monsieur Sauvage corrected him: 'The Republic would never have declared war...'

'With kings,' Morissot broke in, 'you have war abroad; with republics, you have war at home.'

They started a friendly argument, discussing the great political problems with the sweet reasonableness of peaceful men of limited intelligence, and agreeing on one point: that men would never be free. And all the time Mont-Valérien went on thundering, destroying French houses with its shells, pulverizing human lives, crushing bodies, putting an end to countless dreams, countless expectations, countless hopes of happiness, and inflicting wounds that would never heal on the hearts of girls, wives and mothers in other lands.

'Such is life,' said Monsieur Sauvage.

'Or rather, such is death,' retorted Morissot with a laugh.

Then they gave a start of terror as they became aware that somebody was moving behind them. Looking round they saw four armed men standing right behind them—four big, bearded men, dressed like liveried servants with flat caps on their heads, covering them with rifles.

The two rods dropped from their hands and floated away down the river.

In a matter of seconds they were seized, bound, marched off, thrown into a boat, and ferried across to the island.

Behind the house they had thought to be deserted they saw a score of German soldiers.

A hairy giant of a man, sitting astride a chair and smoking a porcelain pipe, asked them in excellent French: 'Well, gentlemen, have you had a good day's fishing?'

Just then one of the soldiers deposited at his feet the net bag full of fish, which he had taken care to bring along.

The Prussian soldier smiled: 'Ah, I see you weren't doing so badly. But that's not what I want to talk to you about. Listen to me and don't get alarmed.

'As far as I'm concerned, you are a couple of spies sent to keep an eye on me. I capture you and shoot you. You pretend to be fishing to conceal your real intentions. You have fallen into my hands: so much the worse for you. War is war.

'But as you came out here through your own lines, I presume you have a password in order to get back. Give me that password and I'll spare your lives.'

The two friends were standing side by side, ashen-faced. Their hands were trembling slightly, but they said nothing.

The officer went on: 'Nobody will be any the wiser. You will go back as if nothing had happened, and the secret will go with you. If you refuse, you die—you die on the spot. Now choose.'

They remained motionless and made no reply.

The Prussian pointed to the water and calmly continued: 'Five minutes from now you will be at the bottom of that river. Five minutes! You've got relatives waiting for you, I presume?'

Mont-Valérien was still firing.

The two anglers stood there silent. The German gave an order in his own language. Then he moved his chair so as not to be too close to the prisoners; and twelve men took up a position at a distance of twenty paces, their rifles at the order.

'I give you one minute,' said the officer, 'not a second more.'

Then he suddenly got to his feet, went over to the two Frenchmen, took Morissot by the arm, and led him to one side.

'Quick, the password,' he whispered. 'Your friend will never know. I'll pretend I've relented.'

Morissot made no reply.

The Prussian then took Monsieur Sauvage aside and made the same suggestion to him.

Monsieur Sauvage said nothing.

They found themselves together again, side by side.

The officer gave an order. The soldiers raised their rifles.

Just then Morissot's eye fell on the net bag full of gudgeon lying on the grass a few feet away. The pile of fish, which were still wriggling, glistened in a ray of sunshine. He felt a momentary weakness. Try as he might to hold them back, tears came into his eyes.

'Good-bye, Monsieur Sauvage,' he stammered.

'Good-bye, Monsieur Morissot,' said his friend.

They shook hands, trembling uncontrollably from head to foot.

'Fire!' shouted the officer.

The twelve shots rang out together.

Monsieur Sauvage fell forward like a log. Morissot, being taller, swayed, spun round, and fell across his friend's body. He lay there with his face to the sky while blood gushed out of the holes in the front of his tunic.

The German gave another order.

His men dispersed and came back with some lengths of rope and some stones which they fastened to the feet of the two dead men; then they carried them to the bank.

Mont-Valérien was firing all the time, capped now by a huge cloud of smoke.

Two soldiers took Morissot by the head and feet. Two others picked up Monsieur Sauvage in the same way. They swung them backwards and forwards and threw them as far as they could. The bodies described a curve in the air, then, weighted by the stones, plunged feet-first into the river.

The water splashed, bubbled and quivered, then became calm again. A few tiny waves spread to each bank.

A little blood was floating on the surface.

Still perfectly calm, the officer murmured to himself: 'Now it's the fishes' turn.'

And he set off back to the house.

Suddenly he noticed the bag of gudgeon on the grass. He picked it up, examined it, smiled, and shouted: 'Wilhelm!'

A soldier in a white apron came running up. Throwing him the two dead men's haul, the officer said: 'Fry these little things for me straight away while they are still alive. They'll be delicious.'

Then he lit his pipe again.

An Evening
with Dickens
in Manitou
Town Hall

by
NELLIE MCCLUNG
(1873–1951)

Nellie McClung has achieved an almost mythic stature in the history of Canadian women: writer, teacher, politician, suffragette, temperance reformer, member of the Alberta provincial assembly, first woman member of the board of governors of the CBC, Canadian delegate to the League of Nations. As a writer it is perhaps for the two volumes of her autobiography, Clearing in the West *(1935) and* The Stream Runs Fast *(1945), that McClung will continue to be known, though she also wrote some fifteen volumes of fiction. For my part, "An Evening with Dickens," extracted from* The Stream Runs Fast, *has a warmth and vigour about it that makes me want to read further. The story also, incidentally, serves nicely as a preface to the Dickens piece to follow.*

Mr. Vander was 'a meek little man with a Byronic face who spoke beautiful English and read from the classics.' His wife 'went out working by the day, a tired draggled woman, who accepted her lot in life without complaint.'

He tried teaching in a country school, but soon gave up because he could not 'reach' people in the district. His neighbors remonstrated with him:

'Mr. Vander,' I went on, 'you should try to grow up and assume some responsibility. You left that school because you wanted to come back to that easy chair where food and lodging are provided by your wife's efforts. Have you no pride?'

'Pride!' He caught at the word eagerly. 'Yes, madam, I have pride. I have pride of ancestry, nationality and tradition. I am proud of my heritage of English literature and if you and my wife will refrain from interrupting me I will take you into my confidence. I have a plan to help my fellow men, an infinitely better plan than this teaching scheme, one into which I can put my whole heart.'

He was off on his magic carpet, leaving the cares of the world behind him, and strangely enough he was able to make us listen.

His plan was, in brief, to give readings from Dickens' *Christmas Carol* two days before Christmas. He would make his own tickets and send the children out to sell them:

AN EVENING WITH DICKENS—THE CHRISTMAS CAROL
Interpreted by Frederick T. Vander,
late of Drury Lane, London
Manitou Town Hall
Admission by Ticket Only

That cold December night came down in the best Manitoba tradition, a windy night, with stars hanging low in a sky of cold steel. A cold night never held any of us in if we wanted to go out so the McClung family was represented by three members—Jack, Florence and myself.

The hall was a draughty place, heated by one stove in the middle of the room. A straggling audience occupied the zone around the stove and a fair pile of firewood promised a continuance of heat. (The newspaper said in its account of the gathering that 'the intelligence of the audience made up for the smallness of its numbers.')

Promptly at eight o'clock the Interpreter, Mr. Frederick T. Vander, in evening dress, came out from the back room with a copy of the *Christmas Carol* in his hand. He was in good voice and looked like a perfect Bob Cratchit. He even had the white scarf inside his coat with its fluttering white ends. I resolutely put aside the opinion I had of him as a husband and father and settled down to enjoy the performance.

'Marley was dead,' he began, and we were off. Let the wind blow, let the tin roof crackle and buckle, we were listening to an immortal tale. The little man knew how to present his story. He played all parts with equal facility; he was Scrooge, tight-fisted and wizened, harsh of voice and hard of heart; he was the timid little clerk trying to warm himself at the candle. He was the fog that came pouring into every chink, 'making the houses across the street into mere phantoms.' And how well he did the nephew all in a glow of good fellowship who came in to wish old Scrooge a merry Christmas!—which he defined as—'A kind forgiving charitable time...when men and women open their shut-up hearts freely and think of the people below them as fellow passengers to the grave, and not another race bound on other journeys!'

So intent were we on the story that no one noticed that the fire was burning low and it was not until the knocker on the door changed to Marley's face that someone on the outer fringe of the audience came forward and mended the fire noisily. The Interpreter glared at the interruption but resumed the story. The caretaker of the hall, Mr. Miller, roused to his duty by this alien hand laid on his stove, reasserted his authority by piling in more wood and more wood, and soon the crackling of the stove joined the rumbling of the tin roof. The audience stretched their chilly hands to the warmth and went adventuring on the high seas where grizzled men raised their voices in praise of Christmas.

It was not until the Second Spirit entered that we began to feel sudden draughts across the floor as certain members of the audience drifted out. Each time the door opened a blast from the Arctic Circle smote us. Then, by sign language, we urged Mr. Miller to greater efforts.

About ten o'clock when Scrooge and the Spirit of Christmas Present went through the streets and saw 'The brightness of the roaring fires in kitchens where preparations for the Christmas dinner were going on and tantalizing smells of turkey and sage came through the doors as happy children ran out to meet their cousins arriving'—it was then I missed my firstborn who had noiselessly departed, but Florence stayed on. She was drawn as far into her coat as she could get and had gathered her feet under her for warmth.

We lost another detachment when the Cratchits sat down to the goose, and the young Cratchits crammed spoons into their mouths lest they should shriek for goose before their turn came to be helped.

By the time the last Spirit had taken Scrooge to see his grisly ending, the wind had risen to new heights, and not only the tin roof, but the timbers of the hall creaked and groaned, and made strange and threatening noises. The audience were all around the stove now and the Speaker was with us too. He had put on his overcoat and mittens.

We looked in vain for Mr. Miller, but it appeared that he had gone, and evidently had taken the last of the firewood with him, so there we were at the end of our resources, but not the end of the story.

We saw it out; we stayed until the end, which came about eleven; and in spite of the cold and the burned out fire, the crackling roof and the bitter wind that found out every crack in the old Orange Hall, in spite of everything, we felt the thrill of the awakened soul of Ebenezer Scrooge, as the magic of Christmas ran in our veins, setting at naught the discomfort of the hour.

Since then, many many times we have heard the story told in the golden voices of John and Lionel Barrymore, heard it in warm rooms brightened by wood fires, with plates of apples waiting for us, and the fragrance of coffee on the air. But it was on that cold night in the old Orange Hall in Manitou that Florence and I, numb to the knees, really entered into the magic circle of the Dickens' Fellowship, and we felt ever since that we have the right to gather with the faithful wherever they are.

The Queer Chair, or The Bagman's Story

by
CHARLES DICKENS
(1812–1870)

I've saved my very favourite for last. "The Queer Chair" is one of those stories in which the characters (and the chairs) simply seem to leap right off the page. Tom Smart, the buxom widow, the vixenish mare—the printed page seems almost too small to contain them. The story, itself, is of the most engaging sort. A roadside inn with a roaring fire on a winter's night, and Tom Smart, with his hot punch, his hearty appetite and his keen sense of things—what better companion with whom to while away a winter's night?

One winter's evening, about five o'clock, just as it began to grow dusk, a man in a gig might have been seen urging his tired horse along the road which leads across Marlborough Downs, in the direction of Bristol. I say he might have been seen, and I have no doubt he would have been, if anybody but a blind man had happened to pass that way; but the weather was so bad, and the night so cold and wet, that nothing was out but the water, and so the traveller jogged along in the middle of the road, lonesome and dreary enough. If any bagman of that day could have caught sight of the little neck-or-nothing sort of gig, with a clay-coloured body and red wheels, and the vixenish ill-tempered, fast-going bay mare, that looked like a cross between a butcher's horse and a two-penny post-office pony, he would have known at once, that this traveller could have been no other than Tom Smart, of the great house of Bilson and Slum, Cateaton Street, City. However, as there was no bagman to look on, nobody knew anything at all about the matter; and so Tom Smart and his clay-coloured gig with the red wheels, and the vixenish mare with the fast pace, went on together, keeping the secret among them: and nobody was a bit the wiser.

There are many pleasanter places even in this dreary world, than Marlborough Downs when it blows hard; and if you throw in beside, a gloomy winter's evening, a miry and sloppy road, and a pelting fall of heavy rain, and try the effect, by way of experiment, in your own proper person, you will experience the full force of this observation.

The wind blew—not up the road or down it, though that's bad enough, but sheer across it, sending the rain slanting down the lines they used to rule in the copy-books at school, to make the boys slope well. For a moment it would die away, and the traveller would begin to delude himself into the belief that, exhausted with its previous fury, it had quietly lain itself down to rest, when, whoo! he would hear it growling and whistling in the distance, and on it would come rushing over the hill-tops, and sweeping along the plain, gathering sound and strength as it drew nearer, until it dashed with a heavy gust against horse and man, driving the sharp rain into their ears, and its cold damp breath into their very bones; and past them it would scour, far, far away, with a stunning roar, as if in ridicule of their weakness, and triumphant in the consciousness of its own strength and power.

The bay mare splashed away, through the mud and water, with drooping ears; now and then tossing her head as if to express her disgust at this very ungentlemanly behaviour of the elements, but keeping a good pace notwithstanding, until a gust of wind, more furious than any that had yet assailed them, caused her to stop suddenly and plant her four feet firmly against the ground, to prevent her being blown over. It's a special mercy that she did this, for if she had been blown over, the vixenish mare was so light, and the gig was so light, and Tom Smart such a light weight into the bargain, that they must infallibly have all gone rolling over and over together, until they reached the confines of earth, or until the wind fell; and in either case the probability is, that neither the vixenish mare, nor the clay-coloured gig with the red wheels, nor Tom Smart, would ever have been fit for service again.

'Well, damn my straps and whiskers,' say Tom Smart, (Tom sometimes had an unpleasant knack of swearing), 'Damn my straps and whiskers,' says Tom, 'if this ain't pleasant, blow me!'

You'll very likely ask me why, as Tom Smart had been pretty well blown already, he expressed this wish to be submitted to the same process again. I can't say—all I know is, that Tom Smart said so—or at least he always told my uncle he said so, and it's just the same thing.

'Blow me,' says Tom Smart; and the mare neighed as if she were precisely of the same opinion.

'Cheer up, old girl,' said Tom, patting the bay mare on the neck with the end of his whip. 'It won't do pushing on, such a night as this; the first house we come to we'll put up at, so the faster you go the sooner it's over. Soho, old girl—gently—gently.'

Whether the vixenish mare was sufficiently well acquainted with the tones of Tom's voice to comprehend his meaning, or whether she found it colder standing still than moving on, of course I can't say. But I can say that Tom had no sooner finished speaking, than she pricked up her ears, and started forward at a speed which made the clay-coloured gig rattle till you would have supposed every one of the red spokes were going to fly out on the turf of Marlborough Downs; and even Tom, whip as he was, couldn't stop or check her pace, until she drew up, of her own accord, before a road-side inn on the right-hand side of the way, about half a quarter of a mile from the end of the Downs.

Tom cast a hasty glance at the upper part of the house as he threw the reins to the hostler, and stuck the whip in the box. It was a strange old place, built of a kind of shingle, inlaid, as it were, with cross-beams, with gabled-topped windows projecting completely over the pathway, and a low door with a dark porch, and a couple of steep steps leading down into the house, instead of the modern fashion of half a dozen shallow ones leading up to it. It was a comfortable-looking place though, for there was a strong cheerful light in the bar-window, which shed a bright ray across the road, and even lighted up the hedge on the other side; and there was a red flickering light in the opposite window, one moment but faintly discernible, and the next gleaming strongly through the drawn

curtains, which intimated that a rousing fire was blazing within. Marking these little evidences with the eye of an experienced traveller, Tom dismounted with as much agility as his
half-frozen limbs would permit, and entered the house.

In less than five minutes' time, Tom was ensconced in the
room opposite the bar—the very room where he had imagined
the fire blazing—before a substantial matter-of-fact roaring
fire, composed of something short of a bushel of coals, and
wood enough to make half a dozen decent gooseberry bushes,
piled half way up the chimney, and roaring and crackling with
a sound that of itself would have warmed the heart of any rea-
sonable man. This was comfortable, but this was not all, for a
smartly-dressed girl, with a bright eye and a neat ankle, was
laying a very clean white cloth on the table; and as Tom sat
with his slippered feet on the fender, and his back to the open
door, he saw a charming prospect of the bar reflected in the
glass over the chimney-piece, with delightful rows of green
bottles and gold labels, together with jars of pickles and pre-
serves, and cheeses and boiled hams, and rounds of beef,
arranged on shelves in the most tempting and delicious array.
Well, this was comfortable too; but even this was not all—for
in the bar, seated at tea at the nicest possible little table, drawn
close up before the brightest possible little fire, was a buxom
widow of somewhere about eight-and-forty or thereabouts,
with a face as comfortable as the bar, who was evidently the
landlady of the house, and the supreme ruler over all these
agreeable possessions. There was only one drawback to the
beauty of the whole picture, and that was a tall man—a very
tall man—in a brown coat and bright basket buttons, and
black whiskers, and wavy black hair, who was seated at tea
with the widow, and who it required no great penetration to
discover was in a fair way of persuading her to be a widow no
longer, but to confer upon him the privilege of sitting down in
that bar, for and during the whole remainder of the term of his
natural life.

Tom Smart was by no means of an irritable or envious disposition, but somehow or other the tall man with the brown
coat and the bright basket buttons did rouse what little gall he

had in his composition, and did make him feel extremely indignant: the more especially as he could now and then observe, from his seat before the glass, certain little affection-ate familiarities passing between the tall man and the widow, which sufficiently denoted that the tall man was as high in favour as he was in size. Tom was fond of hot punch—I may venture to say he was very fond of hot punch—and after he had seen the vixenish mare well fed and well littered down, and had eaten every bit of the nice little hot dinner which the widow tossed up for him with her own hands, he just ordered a tumbler of it, by way of experiment. Now, if there was one thing in the whole range of domestic art, which the widow could manufacture better than another, it was this identical article; and the first tumbler was adapted to Tom Smart's taste with such peculiar nicety, that he ordered a second with the least possible delay. Hot punch is a pleasant thing, gentle-men—an extremely pleasant thing under any circumstances—but in that snug old parlour, before the roaring fire, with the wind blowing outside till every timber in the old house creaked again, Tom Smart found it perfectly delightful. He ordered another tumbler, and then another—I am not quite certain whether he didn't order another after that—but the more he drank of the hot punch, the more he thought of the tall man.

'Confound his impudence!' said Tom to himself, 'what busi-ness has he in that snug bar? Such an ugly villain too!' said Tom. 'If the widow had any taste, she might surely pick up some better fellow than that.' Here Tom's eye wandered from the glass on the chimney-piece, to the glass on the table; and as he felt himself become gradually sentimental, he emptied the fourth tumbler of punch and ordered a fifth.

Tom Smart, gentlemen, had always been very much attached to the public line. It had long been his ambition to stand in a bar of his own, in a green coat, knee-cords, and tops. He had a great notion of taking the chair at convivial dinners, and he had often thought how well he could preside in a room of his own in the talking way, and what a capital example he could set to his customers in the drinking compartment. All these things passed rapidly through Tom's mind as he sat drinking the hot punch by the roaring fire, and he felt very justly and properly indignant that the tall man should be in a fair way of keeping such an excellent house, while he, Tom Smart, was as far from it as ever. So, after deliberating over the last two tumblers, whether he hadn't a perfect right to pick a quarrel with the tall man for having contrived to get into the good graces of the buxom widow, Tom Smart at last arrived at a satisfactory conclusion that he was a very ill-used and persecuted individual, and had better go to bed.

Up a wide and ancient staircase the smart girl preceded Tom, shading the chamber candle with her hand, to protect it from the currents of air which in such a rambling old place might have found plenty of room to disport themselves in, without blowing the candle out, but which did blow it out nevertheless; thus affording Tom's enemies an opportunity of asserting that it was he, and not the wind, who extinguished the candle, and that while he pretended to be blowing it alight again, he was in fact kissing the girl. Be this as it may, another light was obtained, and Tom was conducted through a maze of rooms, and a labyrinth of passages, to the apartment which had been prepared for his reception, where the girl bade him good night, and left him alone.

It was a good large room with big closets, and a bed which might have served for a whole boarding-school, to say nothing of a couple of oaken presses that would have held the baggage of a small army; but what struck Tom's fancy most was a strange, grim-looking high-backed chair, carved in the most fantastic manner, with a flowered damask cushion, and the round knobs at the bottom of the legs carefully tied up in red cloth, as if it had got the gout in its toes. Of any other queer chair, Tom would only have thought it was a queer chair, and there would have been an end of the matter; but there was something about this particular chair, and yet he couldn't tell what it was, so odd and so unlike any other piece of furniture he had ever seen, that it seemed to fascinate him. He sat down before the fire, and stared at the old chair for half an hour;— Deuce take the chair, it was such a strange old thing, he couldn't take his eyes off it.

'Well,' said Tom, slowly undressing himself, and staring at the old chair all the while, which stood with a mysterious aspect by the bedside, 'I never saw such a rum concern as that in my days. Very odd,' said Tom, who had got rather sage with the hot punch, 'Very odd.' Tom shook his head with an air of profound wisdom, and looked at the chair again. He couldn't make anything of it though, so he got into bed, covered himself up warm, and fell asleep.

In about half an hour, Tom woke up, with a start, from a confused dream of tall men and tumblers of punch: and the first object that presented itself to his waking imagination was the queer chair.

'I won't look at it any more,' said Tom to himself, and he squeezed his eyelids together, and tried to persuade himself he was going to sleep again. No use; nothing but queer chairs danced before his eyes, kicking up their legs, jumping over each other's backs, and playing all kinds of antics.

'I may as well see one real chair, as two or three complete sets of false ones,' said Tom, bringing out his head from under the bed-clothes. There it was, plainly discernible by the light of the fire, looking as provoking as ever.

Tom gazed at the chair, and, suddenly as he looked at it, a most extraordinary change seemed to come over it. The carving of the back gradually assumed the lineaments and expression of an old shrivelled human face; the damask cushion became an antique, flapped waistcoat; the round knobs grew into a couple of feet, encased in red cloth slippers; and the old chair looked like a very ugly old man of the previous century, with his arms a-kimbo. Tom sat up in bed, and rubbed his eyes to dispel the illusion. No. The chair was an ugly old gentleman; and what was more, he was winking at Tom Smart.

Tom was naturally a headlong, careless sort of dog, and he had had five tumblers of hot punch into the bargain; so, although he was a little startled at first, he began to grow rather indignant when he saw the old gentleman winking and leering at him with such an impudent air. At length he resolved he wouldn't stand it; and as the old face still kept winking away as fast as ever, Tom said, in a very angry tone: 'What the devil are you winking at me for?'

'Because I like it, Tom Smart,' said the chair; or the old gentleman, whichever you like to call him. He stopped winking though, when Tom spoke, and began grinning like a superannuated monkey.

'How do you know my name, old nut-cracker face!' inquired Tom Smart, rather staggered—though he pretended to carry it off so well.

'Come, come, Tom,' said the old gentleman, 'that's not the way to address solid Spanish Mahogany. Dam' me, you couldn't treat me with less respect if I was veneered.' When the old gentleman said this, he looked so fierce that Tom began to be frightened.

'I didn't mean to treat you with any disrespect, sir,' said Tom; in a much humbler tone than he had spoken in at first.

'Well, well,' said the old fellow, 'perhaps not—perhaps not. Tom—'

'Sir—'

'I know everything about you, Tom; everything. You're very poor, Tom.'

'I certainly am,' said Tom Smart. 'But how came you to know that?'

'Never mind that,' said the old gentleman; 'you're much too fond of punch, Tom.'

Tom Smart was just on the point of protesting that he hadn't tasted a drop since his last birthday, but when his eye encountered that of the old gentleman, he looked so knowing that Tom blushed, and was silent.

'Tom,' said the old gentleman, 'the widow's a fine woman—remarkably fine woman—eh, Tom?' Here the old fellow screwed up his eyes, cocked up one of his wasted little legs, and looked altogether so unpleasantly amorous, that Tom was quite disgusted with the levity of his behaviour—at his time of life, too!

'I am her guardian, Tom,' said the old gentleman.

'Are you?' inquired Tom Smart.

'I knew her mother, Tom,' said the old fellow; 'and her

grandmother. She was very fond of me—made me this waist-coat, Tom.'

'Did she?' said Tom Smart.

'And these shoes,' said the old fellow, lifting up one of the red-cloth mufflers; 'but, don't mention it, Tom. I shouldn't like to have it known that she was so much attached to me. It might occasion some unpleasantness in the family.' When the old rascal said this, he looked so extremely impertinent, that, as Tom Smart afterwards declared, he could have sat upon him without remorse.

'I have been a great favourite among the women in my time, Tom,' said the profligate old debauchee; 'hundreds of fine women have sat in my lap for hours together. What do you think of that, you dog, eh!' The old gentleman was proceeding to recount some other exploits of his youth, when he was seized with such a violent fit of creaking that he was unable to proceed.

'Just serves you right, old boy,' thought Tom Smart; but he didn't say anything.

'Ah!' said the old fellow, 'I am a good deal troubled with this now. I am getting old, Tom, and have lost nearly all my rails. I have had an operation performed, too—a small piece let into my back—and I found it a severe trial, Tom.'

'I dare say you did, sir,' said Tom Smart.

'However,' said the old gentleman, 'that's not the point. Tom! I want you to marry the widow.'

'Me, sir!' said Tom.

'You,' said the old gentleman.

'Bless your reverend locks,' said Tom (he had a few scattered horse-hairs left), 'bless your reverend locks, she wouldn't have me.' And Tom sighed involuntarily, as he thought of the bar.

'Wouldn't she?' said the old gentleman, firmly.

'No, no,' said Tom; 'there's somebody else in the wind. A tall man—a confoundedly tall man—with black whiskers.'

'Tom,' said the old gentleman; 'she will never have him.'

'Won't she?' said Tom. 'If you stood in the bar, old gentle-man, you'd tell another story.'

'Pooh, pooh,' said the old gentleman. 'I know all about that.'

'About what?' said Tom.

'The kissing behind the door, and all that sort of thing, Tom,' said the old gentleman. And here he gave another impudent look, which made Tom very wroth, because as you all know, gentlemen, to hear an old fellow, who ought to know better, talking about these things, is very unpleasant—nothing more so.

'I know all about that, Tom,' said the old gentleman. 'I have seen it done very often in my time, Tom, between more people than I should like to mention to you; but it never came to anything after all.'

'You must have seen some queer things,' said Tom, with an inquisitive look.

'You may say that, now,' replied the old fellow, with a very complicated wink. 'I am the last of my family, Tom,' said the old gentleman, with a melancholy sigh.

'Was it a large one?' inquired Tom Smart.

'There were twelve of us, Tom,' said the old gentleman; 'fine straight-backed, handsome fellows as you'd wish to see. None of your modern abortions—all with arms, and with a degree of polish, though I say it that should not, which would have done your heart good to behold.'

'And what's become of the others, sir?' asked Tom Smart.

The old gentleman applied his elbow to his eye as he replied, 'Gone, Tom, gone. We had hard service, Tom, and they hadn't all my constitution. They got rheumatic about the legs and arms, and went into kitchens and other hospitals; and one of 'em, with long service and hard usage, positively lost his senses: he got so crazy that he was obliged to be burnt. Shocking thing that, Tom.'

'Dreadful!' said Tom Smart.

The old fellow paused for a few minutes, apparently struggling with his feelings of emotion, and then said: 'However, Tom, I am wandering from the point. This tall man, Tom, is a rascally adventurer. The moment he married the widow, he would sell off all the furniture, and run away. What would be the consequence? She would be deserted and reduced to ruin, and I should catch my death of cold in some broker's shop.'

'Yes, but—'

'Don't interrupt me,' said the old gentleman. 'Of you, Tom, I entertain a very different opinion; for I know well that if you once settled yourself in a public-house, you would never leave it, as long as there was anything to drink within its walls.'

'I am very much obliged to you for your good opinion, sir,' said Tom Smart.

'Therefore,' resumed the old gentleman, in a dictatorial tone; 'you shall have her, and he shall not.'

'What is to prevent it?' said Tom Smart, eagerly.

'This disclosure,' replied the old gentleman; 'he is already married.'

'How can I prove it?' said Tom, starting half out of bed.

The old gentleman untucked his arm from his side, and having pointed to one of the oaken presses, immediately replaced it in its old position.

'He little thinks,' said the old gentleman, 'that in the right-hand pocket of a pair of trousers in that press, he has left a letter, entreating him to return to his disconsolate wife, with six—mark me, Tom—six babes, and all of them small ones.'

As the old gentleman solemnly uttered these words, his features grew less and less distinct, and his figure more shadowy. A film came over Tom Smart's eyes. The old man seemed gradually blending into the chair, the damask waistcoat to resolve into a cushion, the red slippers to shrink into little red cloth bags. The light faded away, and Tom Smart fell back on his pillow, and dropped asleep.

Morning roused Tom from the lethargic slumber, into which he had fallen on the disappearance of the old man. He sat up in bed, and for some minutes vainly endeavoured to recall the events of the preceding night. Suddenly they rushed upon him. He looked at the chair; it was a fantastic grim-looking piece of furniture, certainly, but it must have been a remarkably ingenious and lively imagination, that could have discovered any resemblance between it and an old man.

'How are you, old boy?' said Tom. He was bolder in the daylight—most men are.

The chair remained motionless, and spoke not a word.

'Miserable morning,' said Tom. No. The chair would not be drawn into conversation.

'Which press did you point to?—can you tell me that,' said Tom. Devil a word, gentlemen, the chair would say.

'It's not much trouble to open it anyhow,' said Tom, getting out of bed very deliberately. He walked up to one of the presses. The key was in the lock; he turned it, and opened the door. There was a pair of trousers there. He put his hand in the pocket, and drew forth the identical letter the old gentleman had described!

'Queer sort of thing, this,' said Tom Smart; looking first at the chair and then at the press, and then at the letter, and then at the chair again. 'Very queer,' said Tom. But, as there was nothing in either, to lessen the queerness, he thought he might as well dress himself, and settle the tall man's business at once—just to put him out of his misery.

Tom surveyed the rooms he passed through, on his way downstairs, with the scrutinising eye of a landlord; thinking it not impossible, that before long, they and their contents would be his property. The tall man was standing in the snug little bar, with his hands behind him, quite at home. He grinned vacantly at Tom. A casual observer might have supposed he did it, only to show his white teeth; but Tom Smart thought that a consciousness of triumph was passing through the place where the tall man's mind would have been, if he had had any. Tom laughed in his face; and summoned the landlady.

'Good morning, ma'am,' said Tom Smart, closing the door of the little parlour as the widow entered.

'Good morning, sir,' said the widow. 'What will you take for breakfast, sir?'

Tom was thinking how he should open the case, so he made no answer.

'There's a very nice ham,' said the widow, 'and a beautiful cold larded fowl. Shall I send 'em in, sir?'

These words roused Tom from his reflections. His admiration of the widow increased as she spoke. Thoughtful creature! Comfortable provider!

'Who is the gentleman in the bar, ma'am?' inquired Tom.

'His name in Jinkins, sir,' said the widow, slightly blushing.

'He's a tall man,' said Tom.

'He is a very fine man,' replied the widow, 'and a very nice gentleman.'

'Ah!' said Tom.

'Is there anything more you want, sir?' inquired the widow, rather puzzled by Tom's manner.

'Why, yes,' said Tom. 'My dear ma'am, will you have the kindness to sit down for one moment?'

The widow looked much amazed but she sat down, and Tom sat down too, close beside her. I don't know how it happened, gentlemen—indeed my uncle used to tell me that Tom Smart said he didn't know how it happened either—but somehow or other the palm of Tom's hand fell upon the back of the widow's hand, and remained there while he spoke.

'My dear ma'am,' said Tom Smart—he had always a great notion of committing the amiable—'My dear ma'am, you deserve a very excellent husband; you do indeed.'

'Lor, sir!' said the widow—as well she might: Tom's mode of commencing the conversation being rather unusual, not to say startling; the fact of his never having set eyes upon her before the previous night, being taken into consideration. 'Lor, sir!'

'I scorn to flatter, my dear ma'am,' said Tom Smart. 'You deserve a very admirable husband, and whoever he is, he'll be a very lucky man.' As Tom said this his eye involuntarily wandered from the widow's face, to the comforts around him.

The widow looked more puzzled than ever, and made an effort to rise. Tom gently pressed her hand, as if to detain her, and she kept her seat. Widows, gentlemen, are not usually timorous, as my uncle used to say.

'I am sure I am very much obliged to you, sir, for your good opinion,' said the buxom landlady, half laughing; 'and if ever I marry again'—

'*If*,' said Tom Smart, looking very shrewdly out of the right-hand corner of his eye. '*If*—'

'Well,' said the widow, laughing outright this time. '*When* I do, I hope I shall have as good a husband as you describe.'

'Jinkins to wit,' said Tom.

'Lor, sir!' exclaimed the widow.

'Oh, don't tell me,' said Tom, 'I know him.'

'I am sure nobody who knows him, knows anything bad of him,' said the widow, bridling up at the mysterious air with which Tom had spoken.

'Hem!' said Tom Smart.

The widow began to think it was high time to cry, so she took out her handkerchief, and inquired whether Tom wished to insult her: whether he thought it like a gentleman to take away the character of another gentleman behind his back: why, if he had got anything to say, he didn't say it to the man, like a man, instead of terrifying a poor weak woman in that way; and so forth.

'I'll say it to him fast enough,' said Tom, 'only I want you to hear it first.'

'What is it?' inquired the widow, looking intently in Tom's countenance.

'I'll astonish you,' said Tom, putting his hand in his pocket.

'If it is that he wants money,' said the widow, 'I know that already, and you needn't trouble yourself.'

'Pooh, nonsense, that's nothing,' said Tom Smart. '*I* want money. 'Tan't that.'

'Oh, dear, what can it be?' exclaimed the poor widow.

'Don't be frightened,' said Tom Smart. He slowly drew forth the letter, and unfolded it. 'You won't scream?' said Tom, doubtfully.

'No, no,' replied the widow; 'let me see it.'

'You won't go fainting away, or any of that nonsense?' said Tom.

'No, no,' returned the widow, hastily.

'And don't run out, and blow him up,' said Tom, 'because I'll do all that for you; you had better not exert yourself.'

'Well, well,' said the widow, 'let me see it.'

'I will,' replied Tom Smart; and, with these words, he placed the letter in the widow's hand.

Gentlemen, I have heard my uncle say, that Tom Smart said the widow's lamentations when she heard the disclosure would have pierced a heart of stone. Tom was certainly very tender-hearted, but they pierced his, to the very core. The widow rocked herself to and fro, and wrung her hands.

'Oh, the deception and villainy of man!' said the widow.

'Frightful, my dear ma'am; but compose yourself,' said Tom Smart.

'Oh, I can't compose myself,' shrieked the widow. 'I shall never find any one else I can love so much!'

'Oh yes, you will, my dear soul,' said Tom Smart, letting fall a shower of the largest sized tears, in pity for the widow's misfortunes. Tom Smart, in the energy of his compassion, had put his arm round the widow's waist; and the widow, in a passion of grief, had clasped Tom's hand. She looked up in Tom's face, and smiled through her tears. Tom looked down in hers, and smiled through his.

I never could find out, gentlemen, whether Tom did or did not kiss the widow at that particular moment. He used to tell my uncle he didn't, but I have my doubts about it. Between ourselves, gentlemen, I rather think he did.

At all events, Tom kicked the very tall man out at the front door half an hour after, and married the widow a month after. And he used to drive about the country, with the clay-coloured gig with red wheels, and the vixenish mare with the fast pace, till he gave up business many years afterwards, and went to France with his wife; and then the old house was pulled down.

PERMISSIONS

John Collier. "Back for Christmas," copyright © 1940, © renewal 1968 by John Collier. Reprinted by permission of Harold Matson Company, Inc.

Alphonse Daudet. "The Fable of the Man with the Golden Brain" from *Letters From My Windmill* by Alphonse Daudet, translated by Frederick Davies (Harmondsworth, Middlesex: Penguin Books Ltd., 1978), pp. 145-149. Copyright © Frederick Davies, 1978. Reproduced by permission of Penguin Books Ltd.

Janette Turner Hospital. "Morgan Morgan" from *Isobars* by Janette Turner Hospital. Used by permission of the Canadian Publishers, McClelland & Stewart, Toronto.

Thomas King. "Trap Lines" by Thomas King, from *One Good Story, That One*, copyright © 1993 by Thomas King. Published in Canada by HarperCollins Publishers Ltd.

Margaret Laurence. "The Loons" from *A Bird in the House* by Margaret Laurence. Used by permission of the Canadian Publishers, McClelland & Stewart, Toronto.

Hugh MacLennan. "An Orange from Portugal" from *Cross Country* by Hugh MacLennan. Used by permission of McGill-Queen's University Press.